AGAINST THE UNDERTOW

A San Juan Islands Murder Mystery

by

BETHANY MAINES

Blue Zephyr Press
2661 N. Pearl, #360
Tacoma WA 98407

Cover art by **LILT**.

ISBN-10: 1-7320863-4-6
ISBN-13: 978-1-7320863-4-0

DEDICATION

This book is dedicated to the many, many people
who offered their opinions on how to spell
"wacky tabacky / tabaccy."
I aplogize that I can only make half of you happy.

TABLE OF CONTENTS

BETHANY MAINES

CHAPTER 1

MONDAY - THE MV TILLIKUM

I could have stayed in L.A. and transitioned to playing the mom of someone five years younger than me.

The rain was blowing sideways, dousing the ferry deck with a slick sheet of sea spray and freezing rain as twenty-seven-year-old Tish Yearly stepped out of her Toyota. The ferry hit a hard wave and Tish pitched back against her car. Shivering, she pulled her jacket out from under her now annotated copy of *Business Planning for Dummies* and yanked it on.

But nooooo, I just had to come home looking for a stable career. Fat lot of good that did me.

Standing on the metal deck, feeling the deep hum of the ferry's engines, she knew that upstairs the passenger decks would be warm. She knew there would be hot chocolate and crappy sandwiches and her grandfather would be happy to have a gin rummy partner. And Tobias probably wouldn't even say anything snarky about her lack of progress toward her goals. She knew all of that and she didn't move. She wasn't in the mood for other people. She also wasn't in the mood to have her legs crammed into the car.

"Tish!"

Tish frowned and looked around, trying to find the source of the voice.

She was parked in an outside lane behind a truck hauling a fishing boat. Behind her was a minivan that had disgorged a clown car's worth of children. They had all disappeared to the upper deck. She stepped closer to the railing and a hand reached out and pulled her outside the skin of the ship to the four-foot walk-way that circumscribed the ferry. The boat lurched, and Tish found herself pressed up against the shell of the ferry and staring into the blue eyes of Orcas Island Sheriff's Deputy Emmett Nash.

"Nash!" she gasped. He was dressed only in soaking wet jeans, a Henley, and a leather motorcycle jacket that wasn't doing much to keep the rain out. He shivered involuntarily in the November wind.

"Tish, I need your help," he said, through clenched teeth.

"Yeah, you need to get upstairs and dry off." Tish reached out, trying to pull him back to the center of the ferry.

"No," he said, "I can't. There are security cameras."

She stared up at him. He was one of the few people that she actually had to look up to. At five foot eight-ish, she generally looked everyone in the eye or in the bald spot if she was wearing heels.

"Nash, what's going on?"

"They want to arrest me for murder," said Nash. "If I'm arrested, no matter what happens next I'll lose my job."

Things like this did not happen until I quit acting and started living with Granddad. Does that say more about me? Or Granddad?

Tish knew she should focus on the *murder* portion of that statement, but she knew immediately that what Nash cared about was that if he didn't have a job, his chances of retaining even joint custody of his daughter were next to nothing.

"If I can get back to the island without anyone seeing me, I've got a chance to stop this before it gets started. Will you help me?"

In the back of her head, Tish recognized that this would be a moment that someone, probably her grandfather, would ask her about later and she would be forced to admit that she never for a moment considered turning Nash in or away. Nash, for all of her other issues with him, was a straight arrow. There was no way he'd killed anyone. And Claire needed her father.

"What do you need?"

"When the ferry gets close to the dock, I'm going to jump and swim for it. I'm going to need you to pick me up at the beach."

Well, that's just the dumbest idea ever.

"Mmm, maybe we should try the next plan?" suggested Tish. "Or the next nine plans? Pretty much anything but that plan."

Plan 9 From Outer Space, 1959, directed and written by Ed Wood.

"I don't have a plan *B*, and we're nearly to the dock," he said, his teeth chattering.

"You're going to get hypothermia and die," said Tish.

"I don't have a lot of time here, Tish. We'll just go with my plan."

"Give me a minute!" snapped Tish. She stepped into the car section and looked around. She spotted a security camera at the entry of the ferry loading area and another on the other end. But she judged that the exit ramp security camera had an obstructed view of her car because of the truck and boat in front of her. That just left one camera.

"OK," said Tish stepping back outside and shivering in the fresh onslaught of rain. "Here's the plan: I've got a blanket in my car. I'm going to hold it up like I'm shaking it out and you're going to duck down behind it and I'll walk you over to the car and you're going to get in the trunk."

He stared at her, his arms clamped around himself, frozen fingers in his armpits. He looked like a semi-drowned puppy.

"That makes you accessory," he said.

"I'm good at accessorizing," said Tish with a shrug. "Plus, dragging your corpse off the beach was also going to make me an accessory."

He looked out at the white capped water. "The trunk does sound warmer," he said, which was probably an indication of how desperate he was. Taking her advice was never something he would do willingly.

"All right, give me a minute to get everything set up. Try not to fall overboard."

"At the moment, I'm so cold, I can't promise anything."

Tish shook her head and went back to the car. She popped the trunk and began to redistribute her junk to the back seat to make room for Nash's tall, well-muscled body. It was a body she'd spent a lot of time trying not to think about.

The previous summer, she'd arrived on Orcas Island after being evicted and losing her job in the same day. She'd come to stay with her paternal grandfather, Tobias Yearly, and ended up involved in a murder investigation, in the hospital, and almost in a relationship with Sheriff's Deputy Emmett Charles Nash. Reginald Stokley's death was resolved, but the relationship had stumbled before it was even out of the starting gate because of a tramp named Lulu, and the fact that Nash was involved in a bitter custody dispute over his daughter Claire. Tish had dated a man with a kid before and they had all ended up heartbroken. Tish had sworn she'd never do that to another kid.

And it wasn't as if Tish didn't have other things to concentrate on. After Reginald's murderer had been caught she had agreed to stay with Tobias while they pursued their dreams of opening a wedding venue on Reginald's property and becoming the first octogenarian Private Investigator in the state.

Tobias was whipping through an online course and was weeks away from being the proud owner of a PI license. But Tish's plans had slammed into the brick wall of San Juan County's permitting processes. And the obstacles between her and opening a business had piled up faster than she could imagine. The county required that she comply with commercial kitchen regulations, then the bathroom facilities had to be ADA compliant, and then, and then, and then.

Meanwhile, Nash had slid into the friend zone without any complaints. And aside for the occasional day dream about his abs…

And arms, and chest, and everything else.

…that was just fine with her.

Except that now she was helping Nash evade the law. Except that he was the law. Except that there wasn't anyone more straight and narrow than Nash. She'd once seen him chase a plastic bag down the street to keep it from blowing out to sea. She'd seen him carting escaped goats back to their owner in the back of a patrol car. She had seen Nash quote Shakespeare.

That probably doesn't have anything to do with him being a good person, but I still feel like it should count.

She picked up the blanket and walked over to where Nash was waiting.

"Lord, what fools these mortals be," said Tish, shaking out the blanket and holding it up.

"Am I ill met by moonlight?" he asked, immediately pegging *A Midsummer Night's Dream.*

Tish looked outside. "More like by Washington winter where the sun never makes an appearance and everything is white and gray forever and ever until we all mold."

"Poetic, but not quite Shakespeare," he said.

"Shut up and get in the trunk," she replied.

He ducked behind the blanket and she walked over to the car with him crouched behind her. He crawled inside the trunk, she tossed the blanket over him, and slammed the lid.

It took another thirty minutes for Tobias to get in the car and for the ferry to dock. Her grandfather was seventy-eight and had a biography that read like an adventure novel. One-time test pilot, ex-CIA agent and still banned from Yugoslavia, Tobias Yearly had retired to Orcas Island several decades ago. He and Tish had barely exchanged Christmas cards the last few years, but she was learning that despite his age, Tobias was still willing to cause more than a little bit of trouble. She supposed that was why when she had tried to subtly suggest that he might be too old to be a hardboiled gumshoe, he had firmly ignored her.

Hardboiled, directed by John Woo, starring Chow Yun Fat, 1993.

Tish also had to admit that she was a little bit worried that he would be too good at it.

Tobias chattered on about having bumped into George Fujiyama as the car bounced over the ramp grating and how George had a plan to bring back salting fish as a preservative method.

"Sounds good," said Tish, staring straight ahead.

"Also, possibly some pickling," said Tobias, looking at her strangely. "We were hoping you'd be the first to test it."

"OK," agreed Tish.

"Tish," began Tobias, but the car was waved to a stop by Sheriff's Deputy Ray Pearson who was standing next to a rigid looking State Trooper. They were both wrapped in plastic parkas and Ray looked miserable as Tish rolled down her window.

"Hey Tish. Hey Tobias," said Ray.

"Hey Ray, what's doin'?" asked Tobias, leaning across Tish to see Ray's face more clearly.

"Have either of you seen Nash?" Ray asked. "On the ferry, I mean."

"Nope," said Tobias. "I saw him on Thursday though. He said he was staying on island this weekend to work on house projects."

Ray nodded. "We were up at his house and he wasn't there." The state trooper cleared his throat and Ray shifted nervously. "Anyway, thanks. Um, if you see him, can you tell him to call in?"

"Sure thing, Ray," said Tish, smiling.

Ray nodded and waved them through.

"That was weird," said Tobias, turning in his seat through the back window. "They're talking to the cars behind us too. Why don't you pull in at the Orcas Hotel and we'll see if we can pick up any gossip about what's going on. I could use a Bloody Mary anyway."

"No, I don't think that's a good idea," said Tish.

"Why not?" demanded Tobias.

She cleared her throat and checked the traffic before pulling out into the street. "Because I have Nash in the trunk of the car."

Tobias twisted to look in the backseat. "Um. He wasn't in the trunk at Anacortes, was he?"

"No," said Tish.

"So, we're smuggling him off the ferry?"

"Yes," said Tish.

"Well," he said, "then you'd better keep driving. But not too fast. We don't want to attract attention."

CHAPTER 2
THE YEARLY RESIDENCE

Tish and Tobias sat on the Chesterfield and stared at Nash who was dripping a little on the carpet. He had a blanket wrapped around his shoulders and if he stood any closer to the fireplace he risked becoming enflamed. Or at least he might have if he weren't still soaking wet. Coats, her grandfather's chocolate Lab snuffled around Nash's feet with interest.

"So, let me get this straight," said Tobias. "You went over to Anacortes to have a few words with your wife's new boyfriend?"

"Ex-wife," said Nash.

"Uh-huh. So, you had an appointment with the boyfriend at a bar and you kept it."

"Yes," said Nash, wrapping the blanket around himself more firmly. "And he was alive when I left."

"But he ain't alive this morning," said Tobias.

"It would appear not," said Nash. "But I wasn't there, so I don't know."

"I have questions," said Tobias.

"So do the cops," said Tish.

"Their first question is going to be the same as mine: if you weren't killing the dead guy, where were you?"

"His name is, was, Tyler Reich. And I'd rather not say."

"Married, is she?" asked Tobias.

"It wasn't a she!"

"That seems unexpected," said Tobias, looking at Tish. "Tish-kins, you weren't expecting that, were you?"

"I mean, I wasn't with anyone!" snapped Nash.

"Then why don't you want to say where you were?"

"I'm never letting either of you direct," said Tish. "You two have no sense of narrative."

"You think you can do better?" demanded Tobias. Tish shrugged, and Tobias gestured to the room. "Well, take it away DeMille."

"You're lucky I actually get that reference," said Tish. "Although, I think, with you in my life, any movie of mine would probably be more like Wes Anderson."

"Not David Lynch?" asked Nash, a smile quirking up one side of his mouth.

"You had better hope not. There's usually a higher body count in Lynch movies." He flinched a little and Tish felt guilty. "All right," she paused, trying to formulate her line of attack. Where was the start of the story?

What was Nash's motivation for going to meet Tyler—a man he hated? And if he had wanted to meet Tyler, why go to Anacortes? Why not just make Tyler come to the island or meet at the ferry dock? The San Juan Islands were an archipelago of islands off the coast of Washington State, four of which were accessible by ferry. Getting off the islands was free but getting back on was expensive unless you were a walk-on passenger. Getting off the ferry on the mainland at Anacortes with a vehicle—even for a few hours—meant paying full fare and waiting in the ferry line to get back home. If he was meeting with Tyler long enough to warrant paying that amount of money, it would have to be a pretty important conversation.

But he had seemed convinced that getting back to Orcas Island would enable him to stave off questions. That meant that he thought he could pull off a convincing alibi. That meant he thought no one knew he had gone off island. How would he accomplish that?

Tish frowned. She was getting ahead of herself. The how was important, but not as important as the why.

"Why did Tyler want to meet?" asked Tish.

Nash blinked like a deer in the headlights. "Nailed it," said Tobias, recognizing Nash's guilty expression. "Whatever it is Nash, you might as well just spill it."

"I didn't want to involve either of you in this," said Nash. "I thought I could get back to the island and my house, I could say I'd been in all night."

What isn't he telling us?

"No dice," said Tobias. "They already checked out your place."

"I heard," said Nash gloomily.

"That isn't a problem," said Tish. They both stared at her in surprise. "You were working on home repairs. A fuse blew and the heat went out late last night. Since you couldn't fix it in the dark, you drove over to Reginald's and stayed there. You called us this morning to let us know. You have a key from this summer when I was babysitting Claire."

"That's not bad," said Tobias with a nod. "It's a bit thin, but I can go out and break your fuse while you go down to the station to answer questions."

"No…" said Nash. "I should just…"

"Tell us what happened," said Tish. "You didn't kill Tyler. But whatever you did do, you're not too anxious to have anyone know about it."

Nash sighed and rubbed his hair. "A week ago, Tyler called, said he wanted to meet about Claire's custody agreement. I told him to—" He glanced up and shifted. "Well, I told him it was none of his business and I wasn't giving up custody."

"He used more four-letter words than that," said Tobias in a stage whisper.

"Agreed," said Tish.

Nash looked annoyed.

He is such a boy scout. An adorable boy scout.

"Anyway, Tyler asked if I would be interested in having sole custody."

"Tyler offered to give you sole custody? How?" asked Tish.

"Nora hasn't said anything about that before, right?"

"Right. And even this summer, you saw him," he gestured to Tish, "he was trying to get Claire to convince me that she wanted to go live with Nora. And it's total bullshit. I know Nora only wants sole custody so that she and Tyler can move to California. And that will happen over my dead body!"

"Might want to tone that part down when you talk to the cops," observed Tobias.

"So, what was his offer?" asked Tish.

"He said that for ten grand he could convince Nora to give up custody," said Nash, ignoring Tobias. "I was supposed to bring the money to that bar last night."

"Did you bring it?" asked Tobias.

"I thought about it. But I don't have that kind of cash. And the only way I could get it... I would have had to borrow it from Matt Jones. I thought about it, but I just couldn't."

"Could have asked me," said Tobias.

"No," said Nash. "If it's not coming out of your retirement, then Tish will probably need it for the kitchen."

Tobias looked surprised and glanced at Tish uncertainly. Tish immediately tried to divert the conversation away from the dreaded kitchen. "Who's Matt Jones?" asked Tish.

"Drug dealer," said Tobias. "Imports serious weight out of Canada. Flies it down the coast. I did not realize that you and he were so close."

"We went to school together," said Nash. "Every once in a while, he calls me with a tip."

"In exchange for what?" asked Tobias, drily.

"In exchange for nothing," said Nash. "It's stuff like the Mark Rose situation."

I swear they talk in Orcas code on purpose to make the rest of us feel like idiots.

"And who was Mark Rose?" she asked, trying not to let annoyance color her tone.

"Pedophile," said Nash. "Owned a vacation home. He had a twelve-year-old locked in his basement. Matt might be a drug dealer, but he does have standards. Anyway, I called Matt. He sent a boat for me last night, took me over to Orcas and he had the cash, but I chickened out. All I could think is that if Claire ever found out that I'd paid for her mom to go away that she'd never speak to me again. So, I went up to the bar and told Tyler to…go away."

"Probably used the *F* word," said Tobias.

"I should think so," agreed Tish.

"I never went into the bar, so I don't think anyone saw me. And then I crashed at Matt's place. And when I got up this morning, I heard on his police scanner that Tyler was dead. Or if it wasn't Tyler than it was another six-foot white male with a tattoo of an eagle on his chest. Then I heard that I was a person of interest. So I ran over to the ferry dock, but the ferry was just leaving. I wasn't thinking very clearly, I guess because I ran and jumped, grabbed the edge and got on. That's when I saw Tish."

"And she popped you in the trunk," finished Tobias.

"Why can't Matt just testify that you were at his place?" asked Tish.

"He's not testifying to sh…anything. Also, he left before I woke up to make what I assume is a run to Canada. I have no idea when he'll be back. And even if I could convince him to do it, associating with Matt would probably still get me fired."

"Got it," said Tish.

"OK," said Tobias. "We'll do it."

"Do what?" asked Tish.

What is he signing us up for now?

"We'll take your case," said Tobias. "I've got my business license already. Getting my PI license is just a matter of time. This will be good practice. Tish and I will find out who really killed Tyler."

"No," said Nash. "The alibi is good enough. The detectives in

Anacortes can figure out who killed Tyler."

"Package deal," said Tobias.

Nash looked desperately at Tish.

Like I could talk him out of it. Besides, the Anacortes detectives didn't do much last time. Granddad had it solved way before they did.

"I'm going to call George," said Tobias. "I'll need him to do a drive by on your place to make sure they're not watching it."

"What about the motorcycle?" asked Tish. "Nash will need some sort of vehicle to plausibly have driven to Reginald's."

"I can take care of that," said Tobias. "I know a guy. Where'd you park it—in the garage?"

"Yes," said Nash, looking somewhat lost.

"I'll need the keys. You go with Tish and she'll get you into Reginald's. I'll break your fuse, bring the bike over and then you'll call the station and say we told you to call in."

Nash looked at them and she could see the mixture of horror and relief on his face.

"I shouldn't do this," he said.

"It'll be easier if you do," said Tish. "He'll make our lives miserable if you don't."

"You make me sound so vindictive," said Tobias. "I'm not. I'm just a grumpy old man and those are miserable to be around. So, keep me happy and do yourself a favor at the same time."

Grumpy Old Men, 1993, starring Walter Matthau and Jack Lemon.

"What he said," said Tish.

Nash's shoulders sagged. "I really shouldn't," he said.

"But you're going to anyway," said Tobias, with a smile.

He is way too happy about this. I should never have let him take that online course. Not that I could have stopped him. Where I went wrong, was getting internet for the house. I could have kept driving into town scamming wi-fi off the ice cream shop.

"I guess I am," said Nash.

CHAPTER 3

REGINALD'S HOUSE

"I can't believe you're doing this," said Nash as they bumped down the long gravel drive to Reginald's house in Tish's Toyota. She'd had the road re-graveled at the end of the summer, but the pine needles were piling up in drifts and the pine cones were little speed bumps.

"What am I supposed to do—let you get arrested?"

"Yeah, but," he began and then stopped. "I'm not going through with it. I'll just go in and tell them the truth."

"I know it's a little bit off, but it's not as crazy as it sounds. You know Granddad solved Reginald's murder before the police did," said Tish.

"I recall that he had some help," said Nash, looking over at her. Tish waved his memory of events away.

"I was just standing there and got conked on the head. Granddad was in the actual CIA. He may be seventy-eight, but he's smarter and has more experience than most of the Anacortes police force put together."

Nash looked reassured, but still not completely convinced.

She parked the car and led the way up to the back door of Reginald's old house. When Reginald had left the house to Tobias it was with the understanding that Tobias would keep it out of the hands of developers and off-islanders. Tish didn't know if she counted as off-island, but she'd recognized the location as a perfect wedding venue. Everyone who saw the beautiful gardens, fairy tale gazebo, and practically hobbit-like bungalow agreed with her. The only people who didn't agree with her were the state inspectors. Turning the ad-hoc much-remodeled kitchen into something that was acceptable for commercial food preparation was turning out to be the kind of money pit nightmare that Tish had been hoping to avoid. She'd spent most of the summer and her remaining savings trying to renovate. Nash looked around the kitchen at the exposed walls and piping and gaping hole where the dishwasher should be.

"It didn't pass inspection?"

"Not the first time," said Tish, evenly. "But it has now. Sadly, this actually looks better. But by the time I'm through I may be qualified as a junior plumber's apprentice."

He nodded.

Without Tobias, Claire, or imminent death, conversation between them was back to being awkward.

"OK," said Tish. "I'm going to go home. Um, the dryer does work. So maybe toss your stuff in before you go into the station. You still look a bit dampish."

"Thanks," he said.

It was her turn to nod, then she headed for the back door.

"Tish," he said, and she reluctantly turned around. "Why didn't you ask me?"

"Ask you what?"

"If I'd done it. If I'd killed Tyler."

"Because you didn't kill Tyler," said Tish.

He closed his eyes for a second. Possibly counting to ten.

I always manage to piss you off. I don't know what I did this time, but sorry. Like you need the aggravation.

"There are going to be people who won't believe that," he said.

"That's their problem," said Tish, with a shrug. "Do you want me to call Claire or anything?"

"No," he said, shaking his head.

"Are you sure? You know what Nora will say about you."

"I'll call her after I see what kind of trouble I'm in," he said.

Tish couldn't help thinking it was a mistake, but she nodded anyway. She didn't have any say over Claire.

I'm just the babysitter.

"OK, well, call when you get done."

"Thanks," he said. "You do know that you don't have to do this, right? Just say the word and I'll walk myself down to the station and pony up. I don't want you to get in trouble."

"Like either of us has a choice. I can tell Granddad is doing this one way or another. It's just easier if we go along." Nash looked like he was going to argue with that statement, so she hurried to the door. "It'll work out. I promise. Let us know how it goes when you do go in."

"OK," he said, and she had to resist the impulse to hug him. He looked like he was swimming against the tide. She knew how he felt. She felt like everything that had happened to her since moving back to Washington was out of her control. It was an unsettling place to be. Especially, for someone like Nash, who seemed to always have things under control.

She drove back to her grandfather's house thinking that her life was pretty much just a larger version of Reginald's kitchen. Everything she did to fix it just seemed to make it worse. It had all been going so well too.

Well, no. Not really. There was the losing my job, getting evicted because of my coke-head cousin, and then the guy that tried to kill me.

It had all been going really well *after* Nash had shot Reginald's killer—Steve Winslow, the insane land developer who desperately wanted Reginald's property. After that, Tobias had agreed to let her turn Reginald's into a wedding venue. Then she'd started dating Greg Swensen, the chiseled dollop of FBI perfection, and spending a couple of weekends a month with him in Seattle, which had given her the hit of big city life she craved.

She had also started babysitting for Claire Nash.

The journey from so-not-dating-you to being Nash's babysitter had been surprisingly short. All it had taken was one accidental encounter at a thrift shop with gangly ten-year-old Claire Nash who had nervously inquired if Tish thought this dress made Claire look *too tall*. Having spent her entire childhood being the tall kid in class Tish's heart had promptly melted to a puddle. And after a bit of arguing and renegotiating the terms of their so-not-a-relationship, Nash had reluctantly agreed to bring Claire over to help Tish water all of Reginald's plants and generally do chores. Which resulted in Tuesday and Thursday's being lunch with Nash and Claire followed by afternoons of giggles, but not much work being done.

Nash always sat across from her at lunch. There were no meaningful glances. No flirting. Just conversation…

Arguments.

…and lunch.

But also, some arguments. Because that's what we do.

Then he had gone back to work and left Tish and Claire to pretend to know about gardening. He had just sort of faded into the background.

Only he didn't really, did he?

And then fall had hit like a freight train and nothing had gone right since. Apparently, it wasn't going that great for Nash either.

We have to get him out of this. Granddad had better have a few tricks up his sleeve because coming up with plausible lies for an alibi may be within my talents as an ex-actress, but I don't think I've got anything else.

Once at home, Tish realized that Tobias wasn't back from his mission to transport Nash's motorcycle out to Reginald's, so she went into the den and pulled out the stack of print outs from his online courses. Tobias refused to read anything on screen and wasted a mountain of trees printing out everything. As a result, Tish had also read through a majority of his course work.

Becoming a private investigator in Washington required educational hours to be completed in a variety of subjects, from legal powers and limitations to evidence, to report writing and courtroom testimony. And while all of it had been useful on the procedures of how to be a Private Investigator in a professional capacity, she wasn't sure it would help her figure out who had killed someone.

She flipped through the class notes and then sat down at the table. Maybe she was looking at it wrong.

If I were going to kill Tyler, how… No, why, would I do it? Motivation is everything.

She was in the middle of making a list of reasons to kill Tyler when Tobias returned.

"How did it go?" she asked, looking up.

"Easy peasy," said Tobias. "We got the bike unloaded and Nash called the station like we agreed. Of course, they just told him that he needed to come in and that it was important." Tobias made derisive air quotes around *important*. "I can't believe those asshole co-workers of his didn't warn him at all."

"He doesn't need warning," pointed out Tish.

"But they don't know that. Could have at least hinted that maybe he should call his union rep and a lawyer."

"I wish we could have gone with him," said Tish. "He's not a natural born liar."

"You mean like us?" asked Tobias, his eyes twinkling.

"Exactly," agreed Tish, as Tobias lowered himself into a chair opposite her. A few too many crashes in his test pilot days had left his right leg practically unbendable. His health and fitness had improved dramatically over the summer after Tish had found him a personal trainer who had given up being a physical therapist to live in a yurt on Lopez Island, but the leg was still a sticking point.

"He'll be OK," said Tobias, reassuringly. "He did good on the phone. Sounded nice and casual. What are you working on?"

"I'm trying to figure out why someone would want to kill Tyler. And, basically, what I've decided is that we don't know enough about Tyler. We need more cast members. I mean, suspects."

"Yes, we do. Come into the den. We'll run some background checks. Then we'll start making a list of people we want to start interviewing. I don't suppose you could ask Greg if he could poke around in the FBI database?"

"I could ask," said Tish, "but ever since he got assigned to that task force, he's only in town about half the time. And even if he is in town, he might decide that illegal use of FBI resources is, you know, bad."

Tobias snorted. "I thought you'd been seeing less of him. You two break up?"

"Not officially, but it's hard to be real official when I've seen him once in the last month. I think we're on the road to an unintentional ghost break-up."

"Ghost break-up?"

"When you just stop responding to calls and texts and sort of fade away."

"What is wrong with your generation? How can you even tell when you're in a relationship, let alone out of one!"

"It is a challenge," agreed Tish with a shrug. "But OK, so we run a background check. What can we expect to learn?"

"How much debt he's in. Where he's lived. If he has a criminal record or arrests. It's not a complete picture, but it'll give us a window into his life. We'll be able to make a better guess of who we should talk to from the results."

"I think we should talk to Nora," said Tish. "But... I'm not sure that's going to go that well. How do we get people to talk to us?"

"People want to talk," said Tobias. "What people don't understand about the CIA is that actual on the ground, James Bond type operatives, are relatively rare. What they have a lot of are analysts and those in the intelligence gathering arena. An operative can only act if he has information to act on and only if he knows what that information means."

"What did you do in the CIA?"

"Stuff," said Tobias with a shrug. "I moved around a bit. I did do a bit of intelligence gathering and what I learned from that was that in general, people want to talk. You don't usually have to pretend to be anybody. There doesn't have to be a cover story. You just show up and ask questions and seven out of ten times you'll get at least some kind of answer."

"I did telephone debt collections as a temp job one time. Other than the fact that it was bad for my soul, karmically speaking, it was mostly about just being ballsy enough to say horrible things to people."

"Exactly," said Tobias.

"I guess for Nash I can probably show up and talk to his ex-wife. Although frankly, from what I hear about her from Claire I'll have to restrain myself from slapping her six different ways from Sunday."

"Nash never told you about her?"

"He never says a *word* about her. I think he's following the *if you can't say anything nice* rule."

Tobias snorted. "He's more of a saint than I am then. That woman cheated on him, left him and then had the gall to demand full custody and child support saying that he was an unfit parent."

"He is a great father," said Tish, icily.

"Anybody who sees him with Claire can see that," said Tobias with another shrug. "But it didn't please Nora to find out that people were blaming her for the divorce. She's a pretty woman and she expects to be treated with a certain amount of sympathy. I think she was surprised to discover that her actions had negative consequences. Anyway, help me with the computer and we'll run the background check. Then we'll make a list of people to interview."

"Granddad," said Tish, following him into the TV room, "You said seven out of ten people answer questions. What about the other three?"

"The other three require creativity, violence, or leverage," said Tobias. "Sometimes all three."

"Do we have any of those things?" asked Tish, skeptically.

"It's been my experience that violence should only be used as a last resort, leverage can be acquired, but what is most important is creativity. And that's where my secret weapon comes into play."

"What's your secret weapon?" asked Tish laughing.

"You. You're nothing but creative." Tobias patted her shoulder in a pleased manner before dropping into his easy chair.

"Oh," said Tish. "Well, good to know we've got a back-up plan."

We are so screwed.

CHAPTER 4

TUESDAY - DETECTIVE SPRING

The next morning, Tish wanted to immediately start down their list of people to interview, but Tobias was not to be rushed. He wanted breakfast, coffee, and his usual episode of *Matlock* from one of the VHS tapes in the den. But when Tish heard a motor in the driveway, she realized that he'd also been waiting for someone. The doorbell rang, and she went to answer it. Tish opened the door and felt her face flatten out into the blank mask that she used for people she didn't like.

Detective Spring was a short man with thinning hair, with sharp hazel eyes that radiated dedication and thoroughness, and a habit of assuming she was the proverbial dumb blonde.

"Detective Spring. Why am I not surprised?" she asked.

Detective Spring stepped across the threshold. "Probably because you're aware of the jurisdictional boundaries and the recent dead body in Anacortes," he replied. "Also, I'm sure your boyfriend told you I'd be stopping by."

"You talked to Greg?" asked Tish, unable to stop confusion from playing out across her face.

"I meant, Deputy Nash," said Detective Spring, feeling in his pocket for his pen and notebook.

"All right, I'll accept that is who you were referring to," said Tish. "What I fail to understand is why? Did he say he was my boyfriend?"

Nash did not say anything about that. Am I supposed to be lying about that? Why would he say that?

"No," said Detective Spring. "I believe that was the inference of Deputy Fullbright."

"Ronny is a putz," said Tobias coming out of the kitchen, carrying a cup of coffee.

"With short arms," said Tish.

Detective Spring's eye sort of twitched.

"Want some coffee?" asked Tobias, when it seemed clear that Detective Spring didn't know what to say. "I've got a cup ready for you."

"You were expecting me."

"I got a few phone calls this morning on the island grapevine," said Tobias. "I was expecting someone. Do you want coffee or not?"

"I wouldn't mind a cup," said Spring cautiously.

"Come along then," said Tobias, turning to go back in the kitchen. The detective followed, keeping a cautious eye on Tish. He looked as if he suspected a trap to snap on him at any moment.

"So, Detective," said Tobias, plunking a mug down in front of their guest. "I'm assuming you're not going to accuse us of murdering Nora Nash's sleazy boyfriend." Tobias slid the creamer and sugar toward the detective as Tish settled into a bar stool at the kitchen island. "Although, I guess that makes about as much sense as the last time you accused us of murder."

"You know what they say about assuming, Granddad," said Tish. "For all we know, we're the go-to suspects for all murders in a hundred-mile radius."

"Good point," said Tobias. "Well, Detective, come to clap us in cuffs?"

"I have to pursue all suspects and follow the evidence," said Spring, looking annoyed. "It wasn't personal."

"Funny how that don't exactly wash the taste out of my mouth," said Tobias.

"Well, you're not going to like this any better," said Detective Spring. "I'm here to ask about the alibi you're providing for Deputy Nash."

"Wouldn't call it an alibi exactly," said Tobias. "He spent the night up at Reginald's when his heat went out."

"According to his account, yes," said the detective. "But we are pursuing all avenues of inquiry."

"You saying his heat wasn't busted?" asked Tobias and Tish had to restrain herself from rolling her eyes. She'd coached him on his *Gossipy Old Fart* look for a week. It was against his usual stoic nature, but now he rolled it out easily.

"No, it was broken when we inspected it," said the detective looking uncomfortable.

"Someone saw him on the ferry then!" Tobias was going for it.

"I'm not here to discuss the case."

"I'll talk to Barry," said Tobias. "He'll know who on the ferry crew would have seen Nash. Let's see, Nash wasn't on our ferry, so he would have had to go on one of the earlier ones. How many were ahead of us, Tish?"

Tish had to admire the way he managed to reiterate that Nash wasn't on their ferry without sounding like he was making a statement.

"We were on the third ferry of the morning," said Tish, and began to peel an orange from the bowl.

"Should be pretty easy to figure out then," said Tobias. "I'll go down tonight and make inquiries."

"Nobody saw him!" snapped Detective Spring. "We've already inquired."

"Oh." Tobias telegraphed disappointment, but behind his eyes there was the barest hint of smugness. "What are you here about then? If Nash didn't leave the island, then he can't have done it."

"The ferry isn't the only way to leave the island," said Detective Spring. "I have come to ask if you actually saw him at Reginald's house."

"Yes," said Tobias nodding. "He called after we got home to say he'd borrowed a bed. And we told him that Ray had been looking for him, but I was worried that I hadn't really expressed Ray's urgency."

"He means, he wanted to know what the dirt was," said Tish, adding to Tobias's gossip theme.

"That too," said Tobias, looking unrepentant. "He was calling the station when I came in. He left shortly afterwards." The detective looked put out. "It was only later that I heard about Nora Nash's boyfriend turning up dead."

"Nora Harlow," corrected Detective Spring.

"Sure," said Tobias, "if you believe in divorce."

Detective Spring looked more annoyed, if that was possible, but didn't comment.

You're divorced, aren't you?

"All right, in that case, Tish, I'd like to ask about the incident with the deceased at the ferry dock on the twenty-first of October."

"What incident?" asked Tobias, looking from the Detective to Tish.

Tish sighed and put a slice of orange in her mouth. She'd known this would come up. She finished chewing the orange and spoke. "That was the day I got in a fight with Tyler—the dead guy."

The detective took out his pen and clicked the top a few times. "Tell me what happened," he said flipping open his notebook.

"I was at the ferry dock. My friend Sarah had come to visit for the weekend. She left her car in Anacortes and walked over. When she left, we stopped for drinks at the Orcas Hotel and I walked her down for the return trip. As I was leaving, I saw Tyler with Claire, Nash's daughter. I'd been babysitting for Claire a couple of days a week over the summer, but I'd never seen her mom's boyfriend before. All I saw was some strange guy yelling at Claire and then he grabbed her by the arm and shook her."

"What happened next?" asked Detective Spring.

Tish tried to decide how to frame the next events. What had happened, if she was perfectly honest, was that she had gone from confused to absolutely enraged in a split second. She'd sprinted over, slapped Tyler in the face, shoved Claire behind her and then used a few four-letter words to tell Tyler what she thought of grown men who grabbed little girls.

I went full mama bear, is what happened.

"I slapped him," said Tish. "And I yelled at him and told him I was going to call the cops."

Tyler had been blindsided by her sudden onslaught and then she found herself facing an angry six-foot-tall, punk rocker with a fist full of bulky rings raised against her.

"I thought he was going to hit me back," she continued. "And then Nash showed up."

"Some reports have Deputy Nash beating up Mr. Reich."

Tish looked surprised. She was quite good at looking naturally surprised. It was all a matter of timing. "Not even close. He grabbed Mr. Reich by the arm and sort of… spun him away. I don't know fighting or anything, so I don't know what that's called, but it looked fancy."

Tobias was eyeing her skeptically.

"Mr. Reich didn't end up on the ground?" Detective Spring also looked skeptical, but for different reasons.

"He tripped over a garbage can and fell over," said Tish.

"And did Deputy Nash threaten to break Mr. Reich's face?"

"As I recall, he said that if Mr. Reich raised a hand against either Claire or me again that he would arrest Mr. Reich."

And also, that Tyler would be eating through a straw for the next six months.

Detective Spring's shoulders had relaxed somewhat. She thought that she had finally figured out the right note with him. "Then what happened?" he asked.

"Nothing," said Tish. "I picked up Claire and Nash took us back to his car."

And Claire hung onto me like she was drowning, and Nash had his arm around my waist and both of those things felt wonderful and I'm not telling either of you any of that.

"We asked Claire what happened, and she said that Tyler wanted her to talk to Nash about the custody agreement. He wanted Claire to tell Nash that she wanted to go live with her mom full time. But when Claire wouldn't agree to do it, Tyler got mad."

"Tyler was pressuring the kid to go live with Nora?" asked Tobias frowning.

Tish shrugged. "That is what Claire said."

"And what was Deputy Nash's reaction?"

"He was pissed," said Tish, feeling that a touch of honesty here would sell what she was going to say next. "He said he was going to call his lawyer and that he wanted me to fill out a complaint against Tyler, so that it would be on record."

"I don't have that complaint," said the detective and Tish looked guilty. She wasn't quite as good at guilty, but she thought it still read.

"I never went in. I was going to. But Claire was kind of freaking out and needed to go home. And I was going to do it the next day, but I got busy and then I had to go to Seattle to look at commercial grade appliances for Reginald's. And by the time I had time, it seemed kind of too late. I wish I had now."

"It would certainly help Deputy Nash's story to have that on record," said the Detective.

"There is no way he killed Tyler," said Tish reasonably. "You know that, right?"

"I go where the evidence leads," said Detective Spring stoically.

"An elephant's faithful one hundred percent," said Tish and Tobias snorted into his coffee. Detective Spring looked from Tobias to Tish and back, clearly uncertain about what to make of Tish's quote.

"It's my experience that most people are capable of some pretty horrible things. And deciding ahead of time who's guilty or innocent only leads to mistakes. If Nash is innocent, the evidence will clear him."

"And if there isn't enough evidence, you'll just leave the case open and ruin his reputation," said Tobias. "I'm sure that works fine for you, but I don't see that working out too well for Nash."

"You have to trust the process," said Detective Spring.

"Uh-huh," said Tobias. "We'll keep that in mind. Thanks for stopping by. You know where the door is."

Detective Spring looked shocked. Apparently, he'd never been thrown out of a house by an seventy-eight-year-old before. He flipped his notebook closed with a sour expression, clicked his pen off, dropped both items in his pocket and showed himself out.

Together they watched as the Detective's car pulled away.

"Nash never said that about calling a lawyer and you filling out a complaint, did he?" Tobias asked, turning back to Tish.

"No," said Tish.

"And Nash knocked Tyler over at the ferry dock?"

"No, Tyler really did trip over the garbage can. It's just that Nash spun him so hard that tripping over the garbage can was inevitable."

"Nash is too honest to lie about those things," said Tobias. "I think it's going to backfire."

"I'll coach him," said Tish. "It'll be fine. And it's not lying. More like adjusting the viewpoint."

"You can cute it up any way you like it, but Nash will think it's lying. You were the one that thought we were pushing him to lie for the alibi. You don't think this might be stretching it?"

"In for a penny, in for a pound" said Tish. "After the alibi, he can't quibble over these."

Tobias snorted. "You have met the man, right? He'll quibble. Mark my words."

CHAPTER 5

NORA HARLOW

"I don't know about this, Granddad," said Tish, eyeing the modern condo unit on the outskirts of Seattle. In the distance, cranes rose like vultures over the skyline adding skeletons of new construction to their nest. "It feels super aggressive. I mean, her boyfriend just died."

The background check from the previous evening had confirmed that Tyler was living up to his rock and roll reputation with a drug possession arrest, and probation that was set to be completed exactly one week from his death. Other than that, it hadn't turned up any smoking guns or desirable suspects. He had minimal family, terrible credit, and had served a mandatory stint in the Nanamuks Rehab Center. That was about it. His social media accounts and webpage were slightly more profitable. He had a rabid core fan base and had done a few solo albums but had clearly made more money from his studio musician gigs. The basic picture was of someone with talent, who had never quite made it to the big time. But at the moment, Tish was less worried about Tyler and more worried about barging in on Nash's ex-wife.

"You forget that I've met the woman," said Tobias. "We're just fellow island residents stopping by to pay our condolences."

"Are you sure she's going to buy that?" asked Tish.

"Doesn't matter if she believes it," said Tobias. "She won't violate social convention to call us out, so we win. Just pretend you're in a play with an audience of one."

"Small audiences are the worst," said Tish. "Crowds keep things at a distance."

"Interesting," said Tobias, levering himself out of the passenger side of the car. He preferred to have her drive when they went off the island. He said his reflexes weren't good enough for modern traffic.

"So, our goals in this conversation are to discover who would have wanted Tyler dead," said Tobias as they approached the unit. "And if she knows about the blackmail."

"I wish I had a script," said Tish. "I'm no good at improv under pressure."

"Just follow my lead," said Tobias. "You'll be fine."

He rang the doorbell and stood waiting. Tish had made him pick a time during school hours. She was not anxious to have Claire pop up while they were interrogating her mom.

The woman who answered the door was not at all what Tish had come to expect from Orcas residents. The San Juans tended to attract a crunchy granola type who lived in Birkenstocks and braids and didn't believe in tampons (bleach) or hair dye (sulfates) but did believe in at least two conspiracy theories and possibly fairies. Tish had supposed that a bachelor with Nash's qualifications of height, hair, and jawline would rate someone attractive, but she wasn't quite prepared for the diminutive wisp of a dream girl that answered the door. Nora was an auburn-haired beauty with big blue eyes and a delicate bone structure. She oozed fragility and a desperate need to be protected. The effect was only enhanced by the fact that her eyes were red as if she had been crying.

"Tobias?" Nora looked from Tobias to Tish in confusion.

"Hello Nora," said Tobias sounding serious. "We've come to pay our condolences."

Tish, feeling like an idiot, held up the pie they had purchased at the Pie Shop on their way off the island.

"Oh," said Nora, stepping aside as Tobias pushed his way in.

"You've met my granddaughter Tish?"

Tish found herself being scrutinized critically by the shorter woman. Tish had carefully selected her outfit to be slightly on the shrubby side. She had thought that non-threatening was probably the way to go, but now she regretted it. Nora was wearing skin-tight dark wash jeans, rolled at the ankle, kicky little flats, and a plaid shirt, that had been tailored to show off her tiny waist. With Nora's bouncy Bettie Page bangs and a little black eyeliner, it was a look that had probably complimented Tyler's harder rock edge to perfection.

What is she, five-foot-two? I bet she never has a problem wearing heels on her dates.

"I believe you've done some babysitting for Claire," said Nora, her eyes narrowing.

"Yes," agreed Tobias. "That's why we thought we should stop by. Living room's through here? My, this place is modern, isn't it?"

"If you mean that it has a non-composting toilet, then, yes," said Nora.

Nora followed Tobias into the living room and Tish brought up the rear. The condo was furnished in an industrial elegance style that had a distinct rock star vibe. But Tish, whose temporary career as a professional organizer in Hollywood had brought her into contact with actual rock stars could see that, however tasteful, it was still done on a shoe string budget. Tobias was sitting in the one chair that looked stable and Tish perched on the edge of an antique wicker chair that had been painted a glossy magenta, while Nora flopped onto what looked like the bench seat from a fifties Chevy.

"So, babysitter, did you come to check out the competition?" asked Nora.

"Competition?" repeated Tish, clutching the pie. She had the feeling that this interview was not going to go as Tobias predicted.

"You know Nash is always going to have a thing for me, right?"

"I have a boyfriend," said Tish.

"I mean, we were college sweethearts and we have a kid together. You might as well give it up, right now."

"I have pictures on my phone. His name is Greg."

Tobias was watching them as if he'd never seen such alien creatures before in his life.

"Sure, because a grown woman will totally babysit for a guy she's not interested in."

Well, one of us is feeling tied by social convention, but I'm pretty sure it's not her.

"Nora, we just came to talk about Tyler," said Tobias, apparently feeling that some sort of effort should be made.

"Why?" she demanded, sitting up. "I know you're on Nash's side. You're probably just trying to dig up dirt on Tyler to make Nash look good. Tyler didn't do anything wrong!" Nora thumped her fist down on the seat and for the first time Tish saw genuine grief sparkling in the woman's eyes. She also heard the lie in her words. Where other people would have said that Tyler was a good person, Nora denied that actions were taken.

Tobias opened his mouth to speak and then his rarely used cell phone began to ring in his pocket. Tish stared at him in disbelief. In the entire time she'd been living with him, he'd received exactly two phone calls on his cellphone, one of which had been a telemarketer. Tobias patted his pockets while the phone continued to ring.

"Sorry," he said, standing up, "I'm going to have to take this."

Really? You're leaving me? With her?

"I knew I should *not* have come with him," muttered Tish as he let himself back out the front door.

"You have pictures?" asked Nora, turning her gaze to Tish.

"What?"

"You said you had pictures of your boyfriend?"

What are we besties?

Tish found herself pulling her phone out of her pocket and flipping to a recent selfie of herself smooching Greg on the cheek.

"Dreamy," said Nora, in a tone reserved for reporting the weather. "I don't remember seeing him before. Is he new to the island?"

"He lives in Seattle," said Tish.

"Good call," said Nora nodding. "How tall is he?"

"I don't know. Six feet?"

"Mm. Nash is taller."

Of course, he is. Nash is taller than ninety percent of the population. Why do you care?

"Probably?"

"I want a drink. Do you want a drink?" asked Nora, standing up.

"Sure," said Tish.

"Great. Bring the pie."

Nora led the way into the kitchen and pulled a bottle of vodka out of an upper cabinet and a pitcher of orange juice out of the fridge.

Sure, day drinking. Why not? But it seems like a pretty full liquor cabinet for the home of a recovering addict.

The kitchen, like the rest of the condo, had the veneer of elegance on a bare bones frame. Tish thought the cabinets were from IKEA and the duct work over head might say industrial chic, but she thought that it also said couldn't afford drywall.

"I'm driving," said Tish, as Nora began to pour.

"Tobias made you come, didn't he?" asked Nora, adding orange juice to Tish's glass.

"I'm not paying any rent," said Tish. "And he's kind of letting me run with a business idea on Reginald's property."

"I was sorry to hear about Reginald," said Nora, picking up her drink and taking a large swallow. "I always liked him. I was going to get him to give Claire piano lessons. God, that seems like a million years ago."

"Nora, this is none of my business," said Tish, hoping she was hitting the right tone. "But I am really sorry about Tyler."

"It just doesn't make any sense," said Nora, tearing up. "Everything was finally working out. Tyler's probation was up. We were going to go to LA. Tyler had work waiting for him and I was going to start going to auditions. Nash had even agreed to it."

"Nash had agreed to let you take Claire to LA?"

"Well, not right away. He was going to keep her while Tyler did all the moving and then once we were settled he was going to bring her down. Tyler settled it—he got my lawyer to draw papers and everything. Tyler talked to Nash man to man and figured it all out. He said that Nash and I were probably too close to the subject to talk reasonably to each other. And of course, he was right. I should have let him talk to Nash about the divorce agreement too. Tyler could talk anyone into anything. He was always so charming."

Except when he was shaking Claire around like a rag doll.

"That's why I don't understand why Nash would do this," continued Nora with a sad, frustrated sigh, as if Nash had inconveniently borrowed the car.

"You don't really think Nash killed Tyler, do you?" Tish felt shocked. She struggled to keep the emotion out of her face and looked for something to cover her reaction. She grabbed a knife out of the knife block and began to open the pie.

Nora shrugged miserably and took another drink. "He's always had a temper and he didn't really like Tyler."

"Yeah, but there must be other people who didn't like Tyler," said Tish reasonably.

"I guess. I don't know. That stupid woman who was suing him, I guess. But everyone else loved him."

"Someone was suing him?"

"He booked a gig at the Doe Bay Blues Festival," said Nora. "He's a pretty big deal on the blues scene, you know. It was just Doe Bay, and he didn't have anything better to do, so he figured, why not? Only then Jonny Lang's second guitarist got sick right before they were supposed to play here in Seattle. And I mean, Jonny Lang, you know? Is he supposed to say no?"

"He ditched the Doe Bay Blues Festival?"

"Yeah, and that stupid events coordinator woman said it was a breach of contract and that she was suing. She was really pissed off.

She even showed up at one of his gigs, ranting and raving and generally making a scene. She got thrown out, but she did seem pretty crazy."

Nora finished her glass and began to refill. She saw Tish's expression. "What? I need to drink now so I'm sober by the time Claire gets home from school."

Tish shrugged. "None of my business."

"That's right. You're just the babysitter." Nora's eyes narrowed and she scrutinized Tish again. "But you used to be an actress, didn't you?"

"I lived in LA," said Tish with a plastic smile. "In LA isn't everyone an actress?"

"Well, yeah, but Claire said you actually did stuff."

Tish opened cupboards until she found plates. "Yeah, I did a few things."

"How'd you work that?" asked Nora sounding skeptical. "Aren't you too tall? I mean, Tom Cruise is only like five-six."

"Well, no one ever asked me to work with Tom Cruise, so it never really came up. What's your sales pitch going to be?" asked Tish. "You know, when you start doing auditions. You have to have a tagline for yourself."

I remember this. I remember all the measuring and competition. I can't say that I miss it.

"I was thinking MILF. I'm thirty-one and I know the statistics."

A year younger than Nash. That means she had Claire at twenty-one?

"I know I'm too old for any really starring roles, but I think I've got a shot at hot moms. I think if I embrace my age, instead of trying to sell myself as younger, that it might work."

That actually might work.

"You do look younger," agreed Tish. "That means you could claim thirty-one for at least five more years."

"Exactly! I could really target that segment. I would have gone to LA ten years ago, but you know... Claire or whatever. Then once we had her, Nash wouldn't budge off the damn island. He always ruins everything."

Tish handed her a plate with a slice of pie. Nora sniffed it. The pie was still faintly warm from being baked in the early morning hours.

"I don't miss the island, but I do miss the pie," said Nora.

"Your ass won't miss the pie," said Tish. "I don't know how anyone on that island stays thin."

Nora shrugged, and set the pie down without taking a bite. Tish took a bite of her pie, obviously savoring it.

That was a little bit cruel, wasn't it? Somehow, I just don't care. How could Nash be married to her? No wonder he hated me when he met me. I must have pushed all of his shallow actress buttons.

"Hey Tish," said Tobias, coming back in. He eyed the glasses and the pie but said nothing. "That was one of my guys. We have to go. Nora, it's been lovely to see you again."

"Sure," said Nora, raising her glass.

"Sorry for your loss," he said, apparently feeling that it was something that should be said.

"Jump off a cliff and die," said Nora flatly, then she turned to Tish and smiled. "Let me know if you move back to the city. I can always use a reliable babysitter."

Tish returned Nora's fake smile with one of her own and set her pie down.

"So nice to meet you," she said with false cheer and followed Tobias to the door.

"Woo-doggies!" exclaimed Tobias getting into the car. "She did not like us."

"No," agreed Tish. "She didn't."

"What was all that stuff about babysitting and your boyfriend? I felt like I was missing half the conversation. I know I'm going deaf, but it seemed more like a woman thing."

Tish tried not to roll her eyes. Tobias was very liberal minded in some areas, and very narrow in others. *Woman things* was one of the narrow areas.

"You know what they call it when guys try and one up each other? The saying about measuring a particular extremity?"

Tobias barked out a laugh.

"It was like that. She was accusing me of trying to use Claire to get Nash and also staking her claim on Nash. I had to prove that I wasn't on the field of play, so to speak."

"That was why you brought up Greg? That makes sense. Although," he hesitated as if deciding whether or not to continue, and then shrugged, "she's not entirely wrong. I mean, it seemed incredibly tactless of her to bring it up, but the truth is that she and Nash have been together since college. I honestly, think if she'd left Tyler at any point in the last two years, he would have taken her back. Even after the divorce."

"Not surprising. He's a true-blue kind of guy," said Tish. She could feel Tobias watching her carefully.

"Yeah. Anyway, did you get anything out of her while I was on the phone?"

"I learned that Tyler had told Nora that Nash had agreed to keep Claire while they moved to California and was then going to send her when they got settled."

"And she believed that?" asked Tobias.

Tish shrugged. "Apparently, also, Tyler was being sued for being a no-show at the Doe Bay Blues Festival. So, I guess we could talk to the woman who runs that. Seems a bit of a stretch, but we might as well."

"Not exactly a likely suspect," agreed Tobias. "But yes, we'll talk to her. Usually I try not to talk to any of those music freaks. Damn hippies."

"Granddad," said Tish, with a laugh, "you're such a square. Why did you ever move to a hippie island?"

He smiled. "I like to have something to rebel against."

CHAPTER 6

SEATTLE & SARAH BROOK

Tish dropped Tobias at the office of a Seattle lawyer. Most of his business was handled by Sam, Orcas Island's most eligible lesbian and practicing attorney. But if Tish had learned anything about Tobias over the summer it was that he never put all of his eggs in one basket. Everything had a contingency plan, and he always had a *guy* to help out with problems. Tish had not realized until most of the way through the summer that she had become one of the *guys*. She appreciated the nod to equality or at least regional dialect, but she sometimes found his habitual secrecy annoying. She supposed it was hard to get rid of a lifetime of spy habits.

She pulled away from the curb and dialed her friend Sarah. Sarah Brook had been one of the few co-workers from Winthrop Architecture who had bothered to maintain a friendship with Tish after she had been fired and moved to Orcas. Sarah had been promoted to the head of Marketing after their old boss had been laid off. Considering that their boss had been an incompetent idiot and Sarah had been back-channel running the department for years, it was only appropriate.

"Hey," said Sarah, picking up. "I was just thinking about you."

"Were you also thinking about lunch at Doyle's?" asked Tish. "Because I'm going to be there in about twenty minutes." The line of cars lurched forward as three people made it through the light. "I think. Depending on traffic. God, I don't miss this."

"It's a bit late for lunch," said Sarah, ignoring her commentary on Seattle's traffic woes.

"Like you took a lunch. You can knock off early for once and come meet me. Carl used to do it all the time."

"You make excellent points," said Sarah. "I'll meet you there."

"Great," said Tish and realized that she was looking up for a traffic signal instead off to the side of the road and the light was now green. Which explained the honking from behind her. "See ya." She hung up and concentrated on driving.

Tish was already seated and had ordered by the time Sarah arrived. "I've been looking over your marketing plan again," said Sarah, as if she were resuming a conversation from mere moments ago. "I'm concerned."

"You and me both," said Tish, as Sarah slid into the booth. Doyle's was a traditional Irish pub with dark wood, green upholstery and brass accents. It felt a bit dim, but cozy and welcoming.

Sarah was medium height with dark curls, warm brown eyes, a head full of common sense and a closet full of ridiculous shoes. Today Sarah was wearing a pair of two tone, high gloss, high-heel oxfords.

"Because you need to register for the spring wedding shows by December. Early January at the latest. As a new business and without any word of mouth, those are going to be your prime advertising opportunities."

"That's what the market research we did indicated," agreed Tish.

"Yeah, except that your kitchen still hasn't passed inspection and it's November. If you don't think you're going to have it done by December, you may want to pull the plug and move to Plan B: listing it on Air B n' B to generate income over the summer. Commercial kitchens aren't required for rentals."

"So basically, if I haven't got the kitchen ready to go by December, then my wedding venue idea is dead?" asked Tish.

"Or you could ask your grandfather for money and get the renovations done in a hurry," said Sarah. "And it wouldn't be dead. It would just be delayed by a year."

"I can't delay a year," said Tish. "I can't sponge off grandpa for that long. And I'm not asking him for money. This was my idea. If I can't make it work in the time frame, then I need to go get a real job."

"That would suck," said Sarah. "Because I really want to quit my job and come work with you. I can do all the marketing and you can do all the project coordination. We will rule the island wedding venue market with iron fists."

"We're not going to rule anything if I can get the plumbing figured out."

"I can come out next weekend and help," said Sarah with a shrug. "I mean, I don't know how much help I'll be, but I can google stuff."

"Yeah, maybe. Depends on what happens with Nash probably."

"Hot Sheriff guy?" asked Sarah sitting up straight in excitement. "What's happening with him?"

"Getting arrested for murder," said Tish. "Maybe. Hopefully not. We'll see what Granddad and I can come up with."

"Hold on," said Sarah flagging down the waitress. "Right," she said once her drink order was placed, settling back against the upholstered booth. "Continue with the crazy train. We were discussing the hot sheriff's deputy guy you made out with and how he's going to be arrested for murder."

"I didn't make out with him," protested Tish. "We kissed."

"Right. You kissed him once on Mt. Constitution," said Sarah recalling the incident.

"Yeah, once…" said Tish, reaching for her own drink and avoiding Sarah's gaze.

"And where else have we kissed the Deputy?" asked Sarah, her eyes narrowing. Tish shifted awkwardly in her seat. She hadn't told anyone about the second time. "Come on, girl! Spill the beans!"

"OK, so I was babysitting his kid," said Tish sitting down at the table.

"Yeah, so you won't date the guy because he has a kid, but you will babysit the kid. What's with that?"

"I dated a guy with a kid before and I ended up staying six

months longer than I should have because of Royce—the boy. Kids believe in the fairy tale. And that's fine—they're kids, but I don't need to be the one that shatters it for them. I'm not signing up for that again."

"Fair enough, but why babysit at all then?"

"It was summer, so she was out of school and I kept bumping into them. And then Claire would wander off from her daycare group to come hang out. She's really too old to be with them, but he needs childcare, you know? He's got to work. And then Nash would find her with me and then he would be mad at her, and he would be mad at me, and then I would get mad at him for being mad. And I figured it would be easier on everyone if we could all stop being mad and just have her come over and help me weed stuff."

"You didn't have to be the solution," said Claire reasonably.

"No, I didn't. But I like her. She's a great kid. And she really needed someone to tell her how to be tall."

"I have no idea what that means," said Sarah laughing.

Tish sighed. "Nash is like six-foot-four. She hasn't got a chance—she's going to be tall. And I spent most of grade school and junior high being the tallest kid in the room. I would have given anything to have someone, a girl someone, tell me that it was OK to be above average height. And meanwhile, Claire's mom keeps saying things like, *maybe we'll get lucky this summer and you won't grow.*"

"Oh, ugh," said Sarah.

"Yeah. Well, trust me, that's just the least of the reasons to dislike her. Anyway, I babysat her a couple of times a week and got some weeding out of the deal besides. It was no big deal."

"So, what happened?" asked Sarah.

"It was our last day together before she went back to her mom's and back to school, so I thought we'd go do something fun. We went to the bookstore in Eastsound and we were coming out and one of Nash's neighbors walked by and asked how Nash was because he'd just heard the news."

"What news?"

"That's what we asked, and he said he heard Nash had been shot."

"Oh my God! Was he OK?" Sarah looked appropriately horrified.

Sarah's margarita arrived, and Tish paused in her story, remembering what had happened next. They had raced to Nash's house, Tish flooring the gas pedal while at the same time reassuring Claire in a perfectly calm voice that everything was going to be fine. Nash had been in the kitchen with his shirt off and a massive bandage on the back of his shoulder when they burst through the door.

"Dad!" Claire shrieked, diving for a hug.

"Claire-bear! What's going on?"

He looked from Claire to Tish for an explanation.

"We heard you were shot and dying!" Claire clung to his waist, while Tish clutched the back of the kitchen chair and tried to calm her racing heart.

"Well, I'm fine," said Nash, although Tish watched him push a bottle full of pain medication out of view. "See?" He gestured to himself but pivoted slightly so the bandage wasn't in Claire's view. "I'm so fine that I even noticed you didn't clean your toys up in the living room this morning like I asked."

"OK," said Claire, looking over her shoulder at Tish, "you were right. He's fine."

"Yes, I'm fine. Can you go pick up, please?"

"Yeah, yeah," said Claire grabbing her bag and trudging into the living room.

"You are not fine," whispered Tish fiercely, tip-toeing closer.

"I'm OK," he said calmly. "I just got a little buckshot in me from serving a warrant on crazy Roger Burr."

"Not OK, not OK, not OK," she said, whacking at his chest angrily.

He captured her hand, holding it to his chest to prevent more beatings. "Now you know how I feel when you take on psychopathic murderers."

"That was an isolated incident and not at all my fault!" she snapped.

"And this was my fault?" he asked.

Tish found herself suddenly very aware of the heat of his skin and the steady thrum of his heart under her hand. "I—" she began, but he cut her off with a kiss.

If their first kiss was a dramatic debut, the sequel raised the bar. Tish remembered the feeling as though she'd bitten into a highly-spiced curry. Her lips tingled. Her fingers tingled. She tingled.

"What happened next?" asked Sarah, snapping Tish back to the present.

"We rushed home to see if Nash was OK. He had caught some buckshot in the back of his shoulder, but he was mostly fine. But while Claire was in the other room, he kissed me. And I sort of stepped back because… that was definitely not in the babysitting agreement. And I've been dating Greg. I mean, we haven't said anything about being exclusive and it sort of seems to be winding down, but I think he'd be annoyed."

"What did Nash say?"

"He said, *sorry, that was my fault.*" Sarah raised an eyebrow. "Yeah, that's right. Like we'd just bumped shopping carts."

Sarah laughed. "OK, so he's an idiot. But you like the kid and you obviously like him, so seriously, why not date him?"

"Double extra helpings of *no*," said Tish firmly. "I'm not saying we don't have chemistry. We do. But we also piss each other off. And I'm supposed to be Claire's friend. The last thing she needs is to have me popping out of Daddy's bedroom in the morning and then ditching her in a few months."

"You're assuming it's going to go badly," said Sarah.

"I know me," said Tish. "I'm a serial monogamist. I enjoy men right up until the point that they start leaving their stuff everywhere and watching TV on my couch. Six months from now, I'll be bored and wanting out. Greg's only made it this far because he's a ferry ride away and that makes every time we hang out like a little romantic getaway. I don't really think I'm meant to be the permanent type. And kids need permanent types."

"Hm," said Sarah. "OK, but that doesn't explain why he's getting arrested for murder."

"His ex-wife's guitarist boyfriend was killed Sunday night in Anacortes. They think he did it."

"And we're sure he didn't?" asked Sarah.

Tish skewered her with an annoyed look. "Yes, we're sure. Nash isn't like that."

"OK, OK, just saying," said Sarah raising her hands. "You never know with some people. It's always the guys everyone least suspects."

"I get that, but in a way, that's one of the reasons I'm so sure. It's not that he physically couldn't kill Tyler. He could. But he wouldn't. He's a straight arrow, boy scout, goodie-two-shoes, opens doors, saves kittens kind of guy."

"There's the real reason you won't date him," said Sarah, her eyes twinkling.

"It's a contributing factor," said Tish, flashing a smile. "So obviously, we're better off as friends. Anyway, the problem is that even if they don't arrest him, this could still ruin his life. If the case stays open, and we can't find at least another viable suspect, chances are he could lose his job."

"And then, poof, there goes his joint custody," said Sarah.

"And then, poof, there goes his wife and his kid off to California," said Tish.

Sarah wrinkled her nose in dislike. "That sucks. But again, you don't have to be the solution."

"Granddad's on the trail," said Tish shaking her head. "He wants us to solve the case and prove that he can be a PI."

Sarah grinned. "I love your grandpa. I want to adopt him and keep him."

"I'd offer to let you have him, but you'd only bring him back in a week after he's destroyed all your self-delusions and pointed out your annoying habits. Then you'd leave him in a box on my doorstep and we'd never speak again. Probably better if I just hang on to him."

Sarah chuckled. "OK, hog your grandpa, see if I care. But meanwhile, what are you going to do about Nash?"

"We talked to Nora—his ex—earlier and we're making a list of potential suspects—anyone with a grudge against Tyler—and then we'll talk to them. Granddad has dreams of getting the autopsy report, but I think that may be a tad ambitious. We'll see."

"How was his ex-wife?"

"Gorgeous, bitchy, grief-stricken and possibly still into Nash. Or possibly just not wanting anyone else to have him. A little hard to determine. But either way, she definitely wants to move to LA and be an actress."

"Ah!" exclaimed Sarah. "That explains all the friction when you first went up there."

"Yeah, that's what I thought too. Anyway, I'm not sure if we can really solve a mystery Nancy Drew style, but I figure Nash has a better shot with Granddad on the case than if we just let Detective Spring handle it."

"Isn't that the detective that thought your grandpa killed the other guy?"

"Yes. He's methodical, level-headed, and thorough. He also has about as much imagination as a fish."

Sarah took a sip of her drink and eyed Tish thoughtfully. "What do you think Greg will think about you helping Nash?"

"Um."

I hadn't thought about that at all. But why would he care? Nash and I are just friends.

"I don't know. They're both cop sort of people? So he'll probably think it's good?"

Sarah looked amused. "Sure. That's a possibility. Anyway, I think I'll probably try to make a late ferry on Friday. Park my car in Anacortes and walk-over. Should I bring any tools or anything?"

"Do you have tools?" asked Tish, skeptically.

"I think I have a hammer," said Sarah. "And possibly a minus screwdriver."

Tish laughed. "Just bring grubby clothes and I'll put you to work painting the bathroom."

"Done," agreed Sarah.

CHAPTER 7

WEDNESDAY - THE WEST SOUND CAFÉ

"Did you talk to Nash last night?" asked Tish coming downstairs. Tobias was standing in the living room. He leaned on his cane, sipped his coffee, and watched the rain slap against the sliding doors.

Outside, Tobias's property showed a good twenty feet of grass before sloping down toward the trees. A madrona stood near the far edge, the bark curling away from the trunk in rusty swirls. In the summer a peek-a-boo view of the water could be seen through the evergreens, but at the moment everything was gray. Rain came down in gray indecisive drops that wanted to be a downpour but couldn't quite commit. And up from the trees, a soft mist rose as the trees exhaled warm breaths into the chilly air.

"Yes. I think we're going to have to do something about the gutter next time it stops raining. It's not draining properly and we're getting a mud hole."

Tish was aware of the mud hole. Mostly because Coats was a mud hole enthusiast and she'd spent a lot of time wiping his paws recently. But she had been hoping Tobias wouldn't notice.

"When it stops raining? You mean like next June?"

"I was thinking about the two seconds in December when it will freeze," said Tobias, drily.

"Yeah…" said Tish staring at the mud hole with dislike. "Ugh. Yeah, I'll figure out something."

"I'll call one of the Tim's," said Tobias. "Don't worry about it."

"Great," said Tish. The Tim's were a work collective—she wouldn't say business because that would have required licensing—that consisted of four guys and a cat all named Tim. She knew dealing with the Tim's would cost him at least one bottle of the good wine in trade, but she was happy to be out of that home improvement project. She had enough problems up at Reginald's. "What did Nash have to say?"

"They brought him in. They questioned him. They put him on administrative leave. It's what we thought it would be."

"OK, but what did they ask him? What have they got, other than him knocking Tyler over at the ferry dock?"

"Asked about Tyler's phone calls over the last week. Nash told them about the attempted blackmail and that he'd refused to pay. He said they continued to push. So far he's sticking to the story, but I can tell he's starting to sweat."

"That can't be all they've got," said Tish. "That's ridiculous. That's barely circumstantial."

"He thinks they have something else, but he doesn't know what." Tobias continued to stare out the window at the mud hole.

"A witness who saw him in Anacortes?" suggested Tish.

"No way to know," said Tobias. "We'll have to proceed without it."

Tish grunted in frustration. "It's like waiting for the Sword of Damocles to fall."

"Worse for Nash," said Tobias, taking another sip of coffee.

"Yes, I imagine so," said Tish. "All right, what's on the list? Who do I uncomfortably drink with today?"

Tobias snorted in amusement. "The Doe Bay Blues Festival events planner. I asked around. Her name's Clover Augestine. She lives over in West Sound. Used to be an events planner over on the mainland. Moved here a couple of years ago with the understanding that she would grow the festival."

"She's done a good job then," said Tish. "This year was huge."

"Not everyone's happy about that," said Tobias, "but yes. Sadly, I don't have much of a file on her. Mostly just references from others. A bit out of my circle." He exuded an aura of disappointment in himself.

Tish eyed her grandfather in amusement. When he had arrived on Orcas Island, he'd parlayed his intelligence gathering skills into learning all about his fellow island residents. He now had file boxes full of manila folders containing a shocking amount of personal information going back decades. Tish had dreams of being able to get it all into a database that could be cross-referenced, but it was well down on her list of chores.

And who would I trust to build such a database or input the data?

"Well, it's hard to tell sometimes when someone will stick around," said Tish. "Hard to know if they're worth the effort."

"Everyone is worth the effort," said Tobias. "All human beings are full of weird little quirks and secrets. I just don't always have the interest or energy to pursue finding them out."

"Granddad, are we all butterflies in your collection?" asked Tish and Tobias laughed.

"Leave my hobby alone. I don't pick on any of yours."

"I don't have time for any hobbies right now," said Tish.

"Mmm," he said looking at her over the rim of his coffee cup. "You have your pursuits."

"I have kitchen renovations," said Tish. "And crying into my wine over plumbing. What's our plan of attack on Clover?"

"We're going to meet Clover in West Sound for lunch, so that you can pick her brain on event planning. You know, because you're starting your own business."

"How did you arrange that?" asked Tish.

"I made some calls," said Tobias with a shrug.

"Any idea on her basic background?"

"Caucasian, thirty-five, no kids. Lived in a variety of locations. Rumor has it that she moved to Washington for a fiancé who then broke up with her, but that is unsubstantiated."

He glanced over and continued his run-down. "Rumor also has it that she dated Nash a couple of times."

"Great," said Tish. "Maybe he'll have some insight."

"Maybe," agreed Tobias. "As far as lifestyle, she tends toward the Janis Joplin side of the hippie-spectrum."

"Booze and lots of boas?"

"I cannot speak to the boas," said Tobias.

"OK," said Tish, thinking over her wardrobe. It was somewhat limited since she hadn't done much shopping since arriving on the island. Her grubby work clothes collection had expanded, but her work clothes were now obsolete, and she found that her casual dress-up wear was starting to feel lacking. "I'll wear my hair down and maybe jeans and smock top. I really need to do some shopping if we're going to keep doing this kind of thing."

"We could probably go a bit early and stop in at Eleanor's," said Tobias. Eleanor was her grandfather's not-a-girlfriend and she ran a consignment and tailoring shop in Eastsound.

"If we have time," said Tish, feeling a little excited at the prospect.

They entered Eleanor's consignment shop, flapping their jackets to shake off the rain and looked around. Eleanor's Consignment and Tailoring was always cluttered with deals and finds. Disposing of things on Orcas was difficult. There was no dump on the island and part of local culture was a reluctance to part with something that could turn out to be useful... someday.

"Well, hello!" said Eleanor cheerfully, coming out of the back room. She was seventy something, with gray hair that she usually twisted up into some sort of elaborate bun. "I wasn't expecting to see you two today. How're things?"

"Not too good," said Tobias. "You've heard about this mess with Nash?"

Eleanor was also one of the few people that Tobias didn't try to side-step in conversation. Partially, Tish suspected, because Eleanor was not having any nonsense and was too smart not to notice when Tobias sidled up to topics. Tish found her occasionally too blunt, but she thought Tobias liked it.

"Yes," said Eleanor, clucking her tongue. "Nora's lover getting stabbed outside a bar is bad enough but having anyone think Nash had something to do with it is the worst."

Oh, God do we have to use the word lover?

"Anybody seem happy about it?" asked Tobias.

Tish began to flip through the tops, pulling out ones that seemed to match the macramé, embroidered ideal she was searching for.

"Happy? What do you mean?" Eleanor adjusted the massive silver cuff on her arm and looked perturbed.

"We're investigating for Nash," said Tobias, leaning companionably on the counter, as Eleanor settled herself into a chair behind the cash register. "We're looking into people that might have wanted Tyler dead. You hear about anybody being overly happy about the news?"

"You don't think maybe it was just a bar fight gone wrong?"

"Could be, but it feels like the cops are looking at Nash awfully hard for just a simple barfight. Makes me think there's more to it than that."

"No, I don't think there's anybody really happy to hear about Tyler," said Eleanor. "But I do think that there are a few people who are engaging in a bit of *schadenfreude* over Nash's misfortune."

"People always like it when bad things happen to the cops," said Tobias with a nod.

"Too bad we can't somehow figure out how to give Ronny a ticket," said Tish. "The whole island would probably cheer." Eleanor chuckled.

"What are you looking for, dear?" she asked looking over her glasses at Tish's selections.

"We're interviewing Clover Augestine," said Tobias. "She's the event planner or whatever for the Doe Bay Blues Festival. Tish wants to look more hippie-ish to blend in. Have you ever met Clover?"

"I've seen her," said Eleanor. "She's been in to buy a few things.

But no, I can't say that I know her. She struck me as a bit harsh though, from what I overheard of a phone call. But then again, I don't have to deal with musicians all day. Perhaps it's justified."

She came out from behind the counter and pulled a few things from the rack. "Perfect," said Tish, eyeing Eleanor's choices. "You should have been a stylist."

"I always wanted to do costumes for the theater," said Eleanor.

"That seems like a perfect fit," said Tish. "Too bad Orcas doesn't have a theater troop."

"You could start one," offered Tobias.

"No," said Tish. "That sounds like a terrible plan."

She went into the dressing room to try on Eleanor's finds before her grandfather could offer anymore horrible advice.

"You know who you should probably talk to," said Eleanor. "Is Tyler's sister—Sunshine. She lives at the Nanamuks Commune over by Deer Harbor."

"I thought her name was Mary," said Tobias.

"It's a commune," said Eleanor, as though it explained everything. Which it kind of did.

"Nanamuks?" yelled Tish through the dressing room door. "Isn't that the name of the rehab center that Tyler went to?"

"Same place," said Eleanor.

"How can you do rehab at a commune?" asked Tish, peering around the curtain as she pulled on the top Eleanor had picked out.

"Just have to pay to get the right licenses," said Tobias with a shrug. "If whoever's running it managed to wrangle their way onto the preferred vendor list for the courts then the place would be home free. Bit unusual for a commune on Orcas though. They tend to run toward anti-government ranters and kale slash pot growers. They don't usually want a bunch of outsiders running around."

"Wait, back up. The courts have preferred vender lists?" Tish felt disturbed by this.

"Sure," said Tobias. "The state has a lot of paperwork and at some point, it becomes easier for the state to work with businesses who know how to fill out all the forms."

She stepped out of the dressing room to check the first outfit in the long mirror. She sneezed as she turned and Eleanor came over to offer a tissue and to scrutinize the outfit. Like all really good used clothing shops the interior smelled a little like mothballs, BO, and dust. Tish sneezed again and used the tissue. The pants were doing something weird to her butt. She looked at Eleanor who agreed with Tish's silent assessment with a shake of her head.

"I guess that makes sense," Tish said, turning back to her grandfather.

"What?" asked Tobias, reading her face.

"I don't know. It sounds a little wrong. Maybe I've been chatting with Lenny too much."

"Ooh," said Eleanor grimacing over the idea of talking to their conspiracy nut mail man. "You don't want to do that. Next stop is tin foil hat land. Indigo says—" Tobias groaned. He was not a fan of Eleanor's friend, the retired psychologist slash Wiccan practitioner. "Indigo says," repeated Eleanor glaring at him, "that Lenny suffers from paranoia, with proportionality bias and projection."

"I don't know what that means," said Tish.

"Well, people who believe in conspiracies tend to be both authoritarian and individualists."

"Tea Party," coughed Tish into her hand. Tobias glared at her.

"And apparently that means that they are looking for a way to impose their own sense of power on larger world events that may leave them feeling out of control."

"If you say a word about any particular politicians," said Tobias, "I will leave you here with Eleanor."

"Wouldn't dream of it," said Tish with a chuckle and heading back into the dressing room. "But back to the topic at hand," she yelled around the curtain. "Tyler had a sister? She lives on Orcas and now she calls herself Sunshine? I'm going to need to," Tish stopped herself from saying *update Granddad's files*, "make a chart to keep track of who uses aliases on this island."

"They're not aliases," said Eleanor. "Some people just take longer to find their true name."

"Right," said Tobias drily. "Well, Mary or Sunshine or whatever she calls herself is now on our list. We'll have to pay a visit to the commune. Tish, how's it looking in there?"

Tish stepped out of the dressing room in bell bottoms and an embroidered top.

"Spot on," said Eleanor, with a smile.

Orcas Island was shaped like a horseshoe with Eastsound at the inside top edge and West Sound down around the left leg. The distances were not so far, but the speed limit was low. Going anywhere on the island in a hurry was a virtual impossibility and Tish was slowly becoming accustomed to the idea that tasks like going to the grocery store or pharmacy were never going to take less than an hour. They drove the speed limit into the tiny hamlet of West Sound, past the marina filled with boats covered up for the season and parked at the large red barn style building that was the Kingfish Inn.

As they approached the diner, Tish fidgeted with the hood on her jacket. North Face didn't exactly scream hippie. On the other hand, it wasn't a total giveaway. Rain jackets proliferated on the west side of the state like mushrooms. They entered the West Sound Café at the Kingfish Inn and surveyed the glossy natural wood interior. Like most places on Orcas, the West Sound Café specialized in a menu that rotated with the whims of a chef and the seasons, but she knew that her grandfather had probably picked the spot for their wine cellar.

"That's her," said Tobias jerking his head. They both stared at Clover, who was checking her iPhone at one of the booths. Her outfit was similar to Tish's with a loose flowing top and a pair of wide legged capris over boots. But her hair had the gleam and sheen of a salon dye job, her iPhone was the latest model, her watch was a sleek fitness tracker, and her boots were not only completely on trend, but Tish estimated retailed for somewhere north of three hundred dollars. Hippies came in a variety of styles and waves, and today's hippies were allowed to enjoy their consumerism as long as they wrapped their products in a soft blanket of feel good thoughts, carbon off-sets, shoes for children, or vegan leather (whatever that was). This woman was wearing none of those brands. Like Tish, she only looked the part.

"She ain't a hippie, is she?" asked Tobias, frowning. "Her hair it's all…"

"She uses a salon and a crap load of product," said Tish.

"And her shoes are new. And her phone is new. And everything is new. She's a fake."

"Agreed," said Tish, dropping the hood on her jacket. "Do you have somewhere you could be? I think I'm going to get farther without you."

"Not really," said Tobias. "It's not like there's a lot of choices around here. I could probably camp out at the bar though. Give me the high-sign if you need me to go full interfering grandpop and distract her or something."

"Will do," said Tish.

She made her way over to the booth, trying to recall her professional mode from when she'd worked at Seattle, never mind the bellbottoms she was currently sporting.

"Clover Augestine?" Tish smiled down at the woman and held out her hand. "Tish Yearly. Thanks for meeting me today. I know my grandfather pulled some strings to get you to come out to lunch, but I really appreciate it. I'm excited to have an informational interview with you."

Clover shook her hand, her smile growing as Tish talked.

"Nice to meet you," said Clover, gesturing to the opposite seat. "Um, your grandfather said you were opening a wedding business. I wasn't sure how I could help."

"It's a wedding venue," said Tish. "On what was previously private property. I've been working to get the appropriate permits and waivers, but there's a lot I don't know about events. And," Tish leaned in conspiratorially, "this place is weird. Getting a straight answer out of anyone is ridiculous."

"Oh my God! Right?" Clover dropped her phone on the table and waived for the waiter. "You want wine, right?"

"We're talking business, that makes it tax deductible," said Tish. "So, yeah, of course."

Clover laughed. "What were you in before you got here?"

"I was a marketing coordinator," said Tish, honestly. "I handled a lot of the corporate events and did a bunch of project management. Then my job evaporated, and I needed a free place to live, like yesterday, and I had to move in with my grandfather."

Clover nodded understandingly. "I was doing corporate event planning full time and I moved to Seattle for my fiancé."

"How'd you end up here?" asked Tish looking, slightly horrified. "I wouldn't have left Seattle if I didn't have to."

"Trust me, honey, I didn't want to," said Clover. The waiter arrived just then, and Clover ordered an Argentinian red. "We had barely moved into our apartment. I went out on an interview and I came home to find that our doorman was…providing additional services in the downstairs area, if you take my meaning." Clover made significant hand gestures that demonstrated just exactly what kind of services her fiancé had been receiving in his downstairs area.

"So, that got awkward in a hurry." Tish was trying to hold in a laugh.

Clover, you win the Worst Break-up Ever contest.

"The worst part is that all of our friends thought I was being mean to him. They were all, *you should be more supportive now that he's out.*"

"But he cheated on you," said Tish. "With a dude."

"Right! And honestly, I don't think he's even gay. I think he just likes blow jobs."

"I'd be pissed," said Tish. "There would have been some tire slashing for sure."

"Incidences may have occurred," said Clover. "I'm choosing not to comment. Anyway, I needed a job and this one came with a place to live. So here I am. But God, I miss corporate clients. There is too much patchouli on this damn island. And kale. Why the hell does everyone here grow kale?"

"Freezes well," said Tish.

"If you can't smoke it, why would you care?"

Tish chose not to elaborate on the fact that many locals were barely scraping by and having food in the freezer kept families going through the winter from higher food costs.

"Well, you did a fantastic job with the Blues Festival this year," said Tish, changing the topic. "It was so much bigger than when I was a kid. I was impressed."

"Yeah, would have been even better if I'd gotten my bonus," said Clover bitterly.

The waiter returned with their glasses and Tish tried to be patient as he went through the spiel about the specials. Tish hurriedly ordered a scallop dish, while Clover debated between salads.

"I have to have a salad," complained Clover, eyeing Tish's more slender frame. "Not all of us can be as naturally blessed as you."

I worked my ass off for this ass. Bite me.

"Well, not all of us can be so naturally blessed as you," said Tish, subtly nodding toward Clover's eye-catching bosom. Clover laughed.

"So, what happened at the Festival?" asked Tish, putting on her most sympathetic face. "Like I said, I thought it went great."

"Oh my God. It was a flipping disaster. I had booked a headliner for the second stage. A guy named Tyler Reich. Big in the local scene, but not really anywhere else. But we're a local festival, so he was a pretty big draw. And then the bastard was a no show. No call, nothing. Just didn't come. Found out later that he played back up guitar for Jonny Lang that night. And you know what, he probably got paid more. I'm not crazy—I can see why he'd want to skip. But we had a contract."

"What!" exclaimed Tish.

"That wasn't the worst part," said Clover, shaking her head. "My contract is structured so that if I net a certain amount, I get a bonus. The amount of tickets I had to refund because of him took me just under the target."

"That's ridiculous! He can't do that! Did you hunt him down and put two bullets in him, Scorsese style?"

"Someone did," said Clover, looking smug. "I heard he was killed outside a stupid bar in Anacortes last Sunday night. I mean, I don't think he was shot. I heard he was stabbed, but whatever. He's dead and I'm happy."

"Guess you got lucky," said Tish.

"Something like that. But enough about me and my problems. What about you? What's your stumbling block with the venue?"

"Aside from getting my kitchen approved, I'm a little worried about making sure I know what event and alcohol permits to pull. And parking. I'm really worried about parking. I've converted a pasture to a gravel lot, but the neighbors are kind of pissy." Tish shook her head over the imaginary neighbors. "I've been told it's totally legit, but you know…"

"Right. One person says one thing and someone else says something else and none of that matters if Deputy Fullbright gets it into his head that you need a ticket."

"Exactly," said Tish, trying to suppress a chuckle. Ronny's reputation as the ticket king of Orcas was apparently more wide-spread than she had suspected.

"Stick with Deputy Pearson," said Clover. "Chat him up ahead of time, so he knows it's coming and maybe fix a little doggie bag afterwards, and you'll be good to go."

"Good tip," said Tish, nodding fervently.

Clover took a sip of wine and glanced toward the door as it opened. "And whatever you do, don't talk to him," said Clover jerking her head toward the door.

Tish looked up and saw Nash walking through the door. "Deputy Nash?" asked Tish, hoping that Tobias would intercept Nash before he made any moves of recognition.

"He may look like the Mr. November of the island's sexiest man calendar, but trust me, he's a complete a-hole."

"I thought he always seemed OK," said Tish.

"Looks can be deceiving. I tried to date him and well, let's just say, I'm glad I'm not stuck with him. In fact, do you want to go somewhere else. I don't even really want to be in the same room as him."

"Oh, sorry, I have to drive my grandfather home. I can't go," said Tish. "I'll get your wine though, if you want to go."

"The wine's not a problem," said Clover downing the glass. "But thanks! Call me later and I'll actually answer some questions." She slid a business card across the table and got up.

"Thanks," said Tish, taking the card. Clover went past Nash with her nose in the air pretending not to notice him. Tobias and Nash waited until she was well-out of the restaurant and then came over to her table. Nash carried Tobias's meal and glass, setting them down in Clover's vacated spot. Then he sat down next to Tish.

The waiter arrived with the food and a confused expression.

"Right here is fine," said Nash, purloining Tish's appetizer scallop dish, and sliding Clover's salad across the table.

"Yeah, right," said Tish, swapping the dish's back again.

"Oh fine," said Nash grinning. "Mike, can I get a burger?"

"Burgers are not on the menu right now," said the waiter.

"Well, yeah, but you usually can figure one out for me," said Nash.

"Sorry, new rule," said Mike. "No off menu orders. Would you like to order something else?"

Nash stared at Mike and Tish glanced nervously at Tobias. "No, I'm good. Thanks Mike."

"Sure," said Mike with a tight smile and walked off.

"Did my burger privileges just get revoked?" asked Nash, looking around the table.

"Looks that way," said Tobias. "Sorry."

I'd be throwing a fit right now. How is he taking this so calmly?

"Scallop?" offered Tish, sliding her plate his way.

"No," said Nash, taking a deep breath. "It looks like I'd better learn to like salad."

"This is going to be unpleasant," said Tobias.

"Well, I figured," said Nash picking up his fork. "Salad isn't really a food, is it?"

"People don't like cops," said Tobias.

"Well, yeah, but I thought they might actually like me," said Nash sourly.

"They don't like cops," said Tobias said again, "but they all want to be friends with one. You're about to find out which ones like the badge and which ones like you. I'm sorry, but it's not going to be pleasant."

"I didn't think it was going to be," said Nash. "I just didn't think it would be this quick. I guess I underestimated the speed of Orcas gossip."

Tish put a scallop on his plate. He put it back.

"The salad has bacon. I'm OK. So," he said, changing topics, "why are you dressed like Janice from the Muppets and why were you talking to Clover?" His rendition of *Clover* was pricelessly sarcastic.

"She was suing Tyler for breach of contract," said Tish. "I was dressed to ingratiate, but I did not realize that she was a total faker."

Nash grinned broadly. "Spotted it?"

"First thing when we walked in the door," said Tobias.

"Well, then you're smarter than me," said Nash.

"She said you'd dated," said Tish, leaving the floor open for commentary.

"Three dates," said Nash. "And then on our third date, I parked outside the Olga bar and saw that someone was blocking traffic with a crap parking job. I figured I'd run the plate, find out who it belonged to, and then go ask in the bar and give them the opportunity to move it. I called it in and it came back to a Jane Augestine. I'm not an idiot, I recognized the last name, but I thought it might be a relative."

"Jane?" asked Tish, grinning.

"Jane," said Nash. "So, I went in and I yelled for Jane and she flipped out on me. She ran outside, yelled at me some more and drove off."

"I called her the next day, she didn't pick up. At this point, now I'm starting to think it's weird."

"At this point?" asked Tobias. "You already thought it was weird. At this point you just wanted to find out what's going on."

Nash gave an innocent shrug, but his smile said Tobias was right. "Anyway, so then I called her work. More flipping out. She accused me of trying to ruin her. Trying to get her fired. Oppression. Police harassment. Possibly Black Lives Matter, I'm not entirely sure on that one, but there was a host of other things."

"What did you do?" asked Tish.

"I went back to the office and ran her through the computer. Turns out she'd been arrested for assault. The charges had been dropped, but she'd had to go to anger management courses and her ex-boyfriend had a restraining order on her. She couldn't come within two miles of him. Which is why she has to work out here. There's not a lot of places in Seattle that wouldn't bump into that two-mile mark. I figure she's going by Clover and wearing the hippie stuff to get in with the owners out at Doe Bay. I think she was afraid if they found out about her issues with the law that she'd get fired."

"Two miles is a huge restraining order," said Tobias. "What'd she do to the ex?"

"And what about the doorman?" asked Tish.

"Sounds like you heard more gossip than me. What's the doorman got to do with it?"

Tish glanced at Tobias.

I don't think I'm prepared to discuss Clover's ex and the doorman in front of my grandfather.

"Nothing. Moving on. What did she do to the ex?" Both Tobias and Nash looked like they would like to inquire further, but neither did.

"Apparently, she tried to cut bits of him off," said Nash. "Bits that most people find important."

"So she's handy with a knife, has a temper, and hated Tyler," said Tobias. "Excellent."

Nash looked uncomfortable. "I don't know. I mean, yes, based on her history, it seems like she could do it. But would she really plan ahead to get on a ferry, go find Tyler and then stab him? That seems like a lot more planning than she's capable of."

"She plans things for a living," pointed out Tobias. "And she wouldn't have to find him. That gig at the Anacortes bar was listed on Facebook. Tish says it's a thing to stalk people you hate on Facebook. It would hardly take a criminal mastermind to find out where he was."

Tish could tell Nash was holding a laugh in. "All right," he agreed. "But was she even off island last weekend?"

"That's what we'll have to find out," said Tobias.

"And how are you going to do that?" asked Nash.

"I have my ways," said Tobias.

"That we don't want to know about," whispered Tish to Nash.

"Probably true," Nash agreed, with a laugh.

The rest of lunch passed in idle chit-chat, but Tish could spot the dividing line in the restaurant between Nash and non-Nash supporters. Nash supporters all made a point of stopping by to say *hello*.

The rest went straight to their tables. She could tell that, for Nash, the supporters were almost as bad as the haters. Having them make such obvious shows of unity only underscored the fact that he was in trouble.

By the time they were walking out to their cars, Nash looked gloomy.

"Thanks for having lunch with me," he said turning to them both with a smile that seemed a little strained.

"Anytime," said Tobias, nodding and waggling a toothpick around in his mouth.

Nash nodded, pulled his baseball hat on and jogged out to his Bronco.

"He's taking this a lot better than I would," said Tish.

"He's taking it a lot better than I thought *he* would," said Tobias.

"What do you mean?" asked Tish.

"He's got a lot of pride. I'm not saying he's arrogant exactly. But pride, yes. And he's always been proud of the badge too. Not that he shouldn't be. But this hits him right in a soft spot. He's handling it with a lot more… grace, I guess, than I expected."

CHAPTER 8
SUNSHINE & MARS

"Well," said Tish, as they got in the car, "back home for naps?"

"No, I think we should pop into the Nanamuks Commune while we're over here," said Tobias.

"Do you know where to find it?"

He nodded. "Asked up at the bar while you were chatting up Clover. We go toward Deer Harbor and hang a right at the giant fish."

"Which one?" asked Tish.

"The moving one."

"Oh, I love that one. All of the Anthony Howe sculptures are amazing."

"Really? I find them disturbing," said Tobias. "It's like watching an alien eat itself."

Tish laughed. "I can see where you'd get that. But I think they're mesmerizing and meditative."

"Yes, but you do drugs."

"What?" demanded Tish, shocked.

"I know you indulge in the wacky tabaccy."

"Yeah, like once in a blue moon," said Tish laughing. "And I do not smoke and come out and stare at the kinetic sculptures. Although, now that you mention, that does sound like a good idea." Tobias let out a squawk of disapproval. "And I will remind you that it's legal in Washington."

"No, it ain't," said Tobias. "It's not legal anywhere as long as it's illegal at the Federal level."

"And you think that's a good law?"

"Don't matter what I think," said Tobias with a sniff.

"Oh, please," said Tish. "Do you think I don't remember you and Dad arguing over whether or not living by the law absolves a person of individual moral responsibility? You think I don't remember which side you were on."

"Mm," said Tobias, looking at her sidelong. "I suppose it's a bit late for either of us to start living by the letter of the law. Otherwise, I'd have had to turn you in for popping Nash in the trunk."

"You dirty rat," said Tish, feigning outrage in a James Cagney accent.

"You accusing me of being a snitch?" asked Tobias chuckling.

"No snitches in this family," said Tish, turning right at the wind driven kinetic sculpture of a fish.

"And what about Tyler's family? What do you think the odds are of Mary Sunshine talking to us?"

"I have no idea. My experiences with communes and rehab centers is absolute zero."

"Well, we can always turn up and ask about their services for your cousin Sean."

Tish snorted in derision, and then shrugged. "Yeah, why not." Her scumbag cousin Sean had gotten her evicted, stolen her jewelry and then attempted to assault Tobias when he'd been publicly called out. Tish had purposely avoided knowing the state of his legal troubles since then. It was entirely plausible that he would also be in need of some court mandated rehab.

They had gone about a mile inland when they saw a sign for Nanamuks. Tish slowed to a stop in front of the sign. The otter's face leered with a pointed tooth at the roadway and eyes that had no whites, which while technically accurate to the species, left a lot to be desired in a cartoon animal.

"Is it just me or is the otter on that sign incredibly creepy?" asked Tish.

"Not just you," said Tobias, with a sniff.

Tish turned at the sign and the road condition immediately worsened. After nearly six months of island living Tish recognized this as a sign that they had crossed from public to private property. Maintaining private roads and driveways was an expensive proposition and not all property owners held their roads to public standards.

A half-mile later they came out into a clearing with a geodesic dome. It had peeling paint, the perennial water stains of Washington and the silver green tinge of lichen growing up the sides. Around the edge of the clearing a circle of yurts could be seen. Tish had not realized, until moving to Orcas, that anyone could or would actually live in a yurt on purpose. The canvas walls covered a circular wooden frame with a vaguely conical roof. From the top of each yurt a stove pipe extended and breathed out little trickles of smoke. Tish assumed they had wood or pellet stoves. From the quality of the Nanamuks equipment, Tish guessed wood because pellets were probably too expensive. A large fenced garden was next to the dome and a gravel parking area housed a VW micro-bus and much rusted truck. There did not appear to be anyone moving in the compound.

"Why'd you stop the car here?" asked Tobias.

"It's frightened," said Tish quoting *Clue*.

Clue, 1985, starring Tim Curry and Christopher Lloyd.

"What?"

"Oh, come on. Like a summer camp ax-murderer isn't going to pop out at any moment."

I Know What You Did Last Summer, 1997, staring Sarah Michelle Gellar.

"They don't pop out," said Tobias. "They sidle up behind you. Heck, he's probably already in the car."

"Very funny, Granddad," said Tish, trying not to check the backseat in the rearview mirror.

She pulled the car up next to the truck and then reluctantly climbed out, waiting for Tobias to extract himself, his bum leg and his cane. Eventually they were both outside the car, but no one else had appeared. The rain had turned from actual rain drops to an annoying spitting mist that worked its way into sleeves and collars.

"Dome, I guess?" said Tobias, looking around.

"Seems like the best bet," said Tish.

They had almost made it to the dome when they heard a voice call to them from one of the yurts.

"Can I help you?"

Tish turned to see a woman, in a long skirt, rubber boots, and a conical straw Vietnamese hat walking toward them. Behind her, Tish saw other faces peering out of the windows and doors of the yurts. But they withdrew as soon as Tish made eye-contact. As the woman drew closer, Tish saw that she was about thirty-something and had the pinched look that Tish associated with the anorexic models of her acquaintance.

Although, I bet in this case it's just hunger.

"Hi," said Tobias. "Are you Sunshine? We were told that you could answer questions about the rehab process."

Sunshine's face froze momentarily. "I'm Sunshine," she said, her eyebrows drawing together in a nervous frown. "But, like, we're only open for guests in the summer." Her voice had the slow lilt that Tish associated with dude-speak, a California inflection that had gone global. The slow cadence always made the speaker seem younger to Tish, as though only juvenile thoughts could be produced in that voice. It was hard to take from a woman who looked at least five years older than she was.

"I knew Tyler," said Tish. "He recommended this place. I'm really sorry for your loss."

A puzzled frown crossed Sunshine's face. "What do you mean?"

"You're Tyler's sister, right?" Tish was starting to get a bad feeling.

"Well, yes, but what do you mean—*my loss*?" The dude-bro inflection disappeared as her rate of speech picked up.

Tish glanced at Tobias nervously. "No one called you?" asked

Tobias.

"The phone has been out," said Sunshine. "Who would call?"

"Well, Nora?" suggested Tish. "Or the police?"

Sunshine went pale. "What happened to Tyler?" she asked in a tiny voice.

Tish's heart began to pound. Her tongue felt stuck to the roof of her mouth. This was the worst kind of news and she felt like the words were literally stuck in her throat and choking her.

"Mary," said Tobias, reaching out and grasping her hand. Tish thought his voice sounded incredibly kind, carrying none of the usual whiffs of sarcasm that colored most of his dealings with the hippie set. "I'm very sorry to be the one to tell you this, but Tyler was killed last Sunday in Anacortes."

He just said it. He just went ahead and said it. I'm not that brave.

"No," said Sunshine, shaking her head fervently, "that's impossible. I saw him on Sunday. He came to visit us. He brought me vegan burgers. Mars ate half of them already, but it was a nice thought." Tears were filling her eyes and she looked desperately from Tish to Tobias as if willing them to admit that it was a joke.

"What time did you see him?" asked Tish, as gently as possible.

"Time is a meaningless construct," said Sunshine automatically, as if someone had pushed a button. She dropped Tobias's hand and swiped at the tears in her eyes.

"OK," agreed Tish. "Was it during the day or during the night?"

"During the day," said Sunshine. "You're wrong. He can't have…" She looked from Tish to Tobias and back. "I don't understand. He seemed so… He said he was moving back to LA. He said I should come with him. He said Nora was looking forward to spending time with me."

That seems incredibly unlikely.

"You were going to leave the commune?" asked Tish.

Because, dear God, you really should. This place is like an advertisement for tetanus shots and you could use a burger. Or six.

"Mars wouldn't want any of the family to leave." Sunshine looked around nervously. "I told Tyler I didn't have the money to leave, but he said that wasn't a problem. I just…" A tear trickled down her cheek and Tish put a sympathetic hand on her arm. "I can't believe this is real. He was just here!"

The door to the geodesic dome popped open and a man came out. He looked about thirty-five, with long, ash-blonde hair neatly tied back and a well curated beard. He was carrying a beer in one hand and a vegan burger in the other. He saw them and froze awkwardly, half way toward taking a bite.

"Mars!" said Sunshine, jumping slightly, but away from Tish's hand on her arm. "These people say that Tyler's been killed!"

"They don't know what they're talking about," said Mars, instantly. "Death is just the next stage."

"Well, Tyler is playing the main stage on this one," said Tish and then realized it was tasteless. "Sorry," she said to Sunshine. Sunshine simply blinked at her.

She's probably so calorie deficient she didn't get it. Hopefully.

"Who are you people? And what do you want?" demanded Mars, looking around as if he wanted to put down his lunch, but didn't want to put it on the lichen covered fence surrounding the garden. Tish saw Tobias smirk at his predicament, and she knew Mars noticed as well. Mars focused entirely on Tobias and took a drink of the beer as if daring him to comment.

"My name is Tobias Yearly," said Tobias, looking unimpressed by the young man's act of defiance, "of Yearly Investigations. We're looking into anyone who may have wanted to kill Tyler Reich."

Mars stared at him as if weighing his next words. "We're a commune, man. You think, like, because we live an alternative lifestyle that you can just accuse us like common criminals? We will not be harassed by outsiders who judge our every move. You don't have the right to be here." He beckoned peremptorily at Sunshine with his beer and she shuffled toward him, but stopped awkwardly, blocked by Tobias standing like a lump in the path.

We. Us. You. Them. Keeping the dividing lines clear.

"This isn't harassment," said Tobias, leaning on his cane and eyeing Mars critically. "We're simply taking an interest."

"I'm sure they didn't mean—" began Sunshine, but Mars cut her off.

"I know exactly what they mean. You two need to leave. This is private property and you're trespassing."

None of that was hippie-speak.

Tobias handed Tish his cane and reached out to Sunshine. "Mary," he said, taking her hand again and covering it with his, "we're truly sorry for your loss. If you think of anything, please let us know."

"Her name is Sunshine," said Mars, coldly. "We don't need your sympathy. She will not be contacting you. Isn't that right, Sunshine?"

Mary nodded. Tobias ignored him, collected his cane and headed back to the car, but Tish waited until she was certain that Mars wasn't going to charge them from behind like a feral dog before following him back to the car.

I'm probably over-reacting. He only asked us to leave. He didn't offer any sort of violence. He didn't even yell. Somehow that makes me like him even less.

"Well," said Tish, as they jolted back down the long driveway to the main road, "we are just making friends left and right."

"Don't need to make friends," said Tobias.

"I tell you what does need to happen though. Someone needs to punch that Mars jackass in the face. Commune my ass. That place is a cult and Mars is the leader."

Tobias looked surprised. "It might be a cult, I suppose. Mostly that just seemed like hippie crap to me."

"No," said Tish, "he was…" she floundered trying to put her finger on what he was, "not right," she said at last.

Tobias looked at her thoughtfully. "All right," he said at last.

"Let's put him on the list. I'm not entirely sure they're viable suspects, but if nothing else, they ought to be inspected. There is no way that place qualifies as a rehab center."

"And the phone being down? That's a pile of bullpucky. What do you want to bet Mars just didn't want any of his *family* making outside calls? And I am all for people calling themselves whatever they want, but Mars is the damn god of war. Not exactly what you want representing your peace commune."

Tobias looked surprised. "He really got your goat."

"My goat, my sheep and any other type of small herd animal you can think of. I saw plenty of jerks like him in LA. They're users. They use people, tell them it's for their own good and then move on. Always selling some sort of feel good mumbo jumbo that only leaves their flock worse off. It's crap. I hate seeing people get used. Tyler may have been a jerk, but at least he was trying to get his sister out of there."

"Yeah, that point of the story was interesting. Makes me wonder why now and not when he was doing his rehab."

"Maybe he didn't think she'd go earlier."

"Maybe," said Tobias thoughtfully. "Anyway, hopefully she'll call us."

"How would she call us?" asked Tish.

"I slipped her one of our business cards," said Tobias.

"We have business cards?"

Tobias held out a small rectangle of off-white paper. Tish grabbed it, holding it up in front of her as she drove, so she could keep one eye on the road.

"I figured if I just got T. Yearly, we could both use them," said Tobias.

"Granddad! These have my cell number on it!"

"Yeah," said Tobias. "I didn't want people calling my number."

"You are unbelievable!"

"Am I?"

No, not really.

CHAPTER 9
THURSDAY - TOBIAS & TISH

Tish sat on the Chesterfield and listened to Coats snore. Then he began to make a blubbery exhalation that rattled his lips and ended in yip. It was her firm belief that Coats dreamed of the day he caught the chipmunks in the woods.

Tobias came in carrying the mail and sat down in his preferred armchair. Outside, the wind tossed the tree branches like waves and a few crows swooped and dove arguing with some seagulls. Tish considered for a moment the strangeness of color and the fact that the evergreens currently looked as black as crows.

"I'm troubled, Granddad."

"Well, you're young yet," he said. Tish gave him a look. He shrugged. "What particularly is giving you trouble this morning?"

"I feel like we should be further along on solving Tyler's murder. Or have more suspects. Or something."

"It's the suspects that trouble me," said Tobias leaning back. "I'm not saying women can't kill—they're perfectly capable. I just don't particularly see these ones doing it."

"Well, apparently anyone can be a killer," said Tish. "If Detective Spring is to be believed."

"No, not really," said Tobias. "What he means is that evil people can be perfectly normal. You know why the rate of PTSD went up so much in Vietnam?"

"Clearer reporting, destigmatization, and a better understanding of the problem?"

"Thank you, Miss Social Sciences. No. Well, probably those had an effect. But also, there was better training. They trained soldiers to shoot at human shaped targets, made it more instinctual, got better guns and made it easier and easier for kids to shoot people. So, you have a bunch of boys who maybe aren't designed by nature to be killers, who don't want to be there in the first place, and you make them kill someone. Bam. PTSD."

"I'm with you on the theory," said Tish. "What's the point?"

"I'm saying most people don't want to kill anyone. Most people can't even get in a fight. Clover might be insane, and Nora might be a poor excuse for a wife, but neither one of them really feel like killers to me. Most murders come down to love, money, or rage."

"Clover's got plenty of rage," said Tish. "And Nora does love Claire. Maybe she figured out what Tyler was up to and lost her temper."

Tobias shrugged. "I'm also troubled by the money," he said. "He wanted ten thousand from Nash. For what? Nora said he had work waiting for him in LA. Why not just go and leave Nora and Claire here? Why ask for money? His background check didn't turn up a huge amount of debt."

"Granddad," said Tish, "you're supposed to make me feel better. This is not making me feel better."

"It shouldn't make you feel better," said Tobias. "If I'm just looking at the shape of this thing, it feels like it's about money, which is bad because Nash is the only one with a ten-thousand-dollar motive. I mean it would make sense to be annoyed about paying ten grand to get your own kid. Kill Tyler, take the paper work and don't pay the money."

"Nash is not that stupid," said Tish. "Nora would still contest it for one thing and say it was done without her knowledge. And for another, if he didn't break Tyler's nose for shaking Claire, he wouldn't spontaneously kill Tyler in an alley. And also, he didn't do it."

"Agreed," said Tobias. "But I can see what Detective Spring would be thinking."

"What about the custody paperwork that Tyler was supposed to turn over in exchange for the money? Nash didn't take it. It seems like something the police would have asked about if it was on the body."

"Doesn't matter," said Tobias. "Nash told them what Tyler was up to. Spring can confirm with the lawyers to back up Nash's story."

"If they do that, and right now that feels like a strong *if*, Nora will probably find out what Tyler did."

"Probably," said Tobias. "I'm not particularly concerned with Nora."

"What if," said Tish hesitantly, "Nash wasn't the only one Tyler was blackmailing."

"I've been pondering that myself," said Tobias. "Maybe it was Clover, but if it was, what did he have over her? I'll run a background check on Ms. Augestine, but it's my guess that she wouldn't have that kind of money."

"And it still doesn't answer why Tyler needed the money," said Tish. Tobias grunted in agreement.

"OK," said Tish, "let's approach this from the other direction. Assuming that it's about the money. What does that mean? Someone killed him because they didn't want to pay the blackmail? Or did Tyler owe money and someone killed him because he couldn't pay up?"

"Could go either way. If it's someone he owed money to, then chances are it was some sort of illegal gambling. Those people are usually in the system. But if it was someone he was blackmailing who killed him… If I'm guessing, I'd say it's a man. Someone with a job or access to money. And that tells me that it's someone who fits into society."

"That doesn't sound like an Orcas resident," said Tish.

"Ha. Ha. Don't let anyone else hear you making a crack like that," said Tobias.

"I really wasn't making a crack," said Tish. "More of an observation. The permanent residents don't tend to have a lot of money and they also tend to be a little on the alternative side of normal."

Tobias looked annoyed, but she couldn't tell if it was because she was right or because he didn't want her to be right.

Coats woke himself up with a bark and then looked around as if confused about how he ended up in the living room. Shaking himself, his tag clattering against his collar, he stood up and went to the sliding door, looking over his shoulder at them in patient dog telepathy. Tish got up to let him outside. They watched as he immediately plowed into the mud hole and then delicately licked the puddle water as if it were the finest vintage.

"Tell me again why I got a dog?" asked Tobias.

"Reginald said you needed someone to talk to when he wasn't around," said Tish. "Keeps you from looking crazy."

"I think it's a bit late to keep from looking crazy. Pretty sure that reputation is well ingrained at this point."

"Works out for me though," said Tish. "I look sane by comparison."

Tobias laughed. "Your grandmother used to say the same thing."

"She was a very smart lady," said Tish. "Do you need me to call the Tim's about mud pit out there?"

"No," said Tobias. "I'm still considering what I want to do. That spot has always given me trouble—even when the gutter is perfectly clear. I'm wondering if I want to do some sort of rain garden or catch basin that would funnel the water down to a rain barrel. We could use it to water the garden."

"I could see that," said Tish nodding. Reginald had created a similar system over at his garden. She understood it enough to maintain it, but not enough to make a new one.

"I never did it before because when you and your cousins were young I didn't want to interrupt the lawn. But these days there aren't a lot of kids running through and I could use less to mow."

"Good point," said Tish.

"Anyway, once I figure out what I want, I'll get someone in."

Outside, Coats, obeying his genetic instructions, suddenly went into point and then bounded into the woods.

"Hopefully, that will clean off some of the mud," said Tobias, watching him go.

"So, your theory is that Tyler was killed by a socially integrated male who either wanted money or didn't appreciate being blackmailed?" asked Tish, returning to their original topic.

"Yes, basically. And based purely on demographics of the area, I'm going with a white male. Going with the demographics of people most likely to kill and most likely for Tyler to know, I'm going to say somewhere between twenty-five to forty. Did you call your mom back about Thanksgiving?"

"Not yet. Doug banned her from having all of her family over, so they're going to Aunt Cindy's. And I'm not sure I want to go. That's just a lot of…"

"Idiots?" suggested Tobias. His opinion of her mother's sisters and their children had always been low, but she felt like since her cousin Sean had stolen all of her stuff and scammed her out of three months' rent, it had dropped even further. On the other hand, Sean was one of the brighter cousins.

"I'm trying to figure out how to get out of going. If it was just her and Doug at their place, I'd totally go. I actually like Doug."

"He seemed like a decent guy," agreed Tobias.

"I didn't think I was going to," said Tish, sitting back down on the Chesterfield, and pulling the throw blanket onto her lap. "I thought he was going to be a jerk. But he's really smart and helps her not get run over by her sisters. I sometimes forget that she's just a push-over, not a…"

"Idiot, like her sisters?"

"Granddad!"

"What? You can really tell me they're not?"

Tish didn't think that her aunts were stupid necessarily. But by and large they were shallow and self-centered, and generally relied on her mother to fix their problems just as she had when they were kids.

"If I can't make cracks about Orcas, then you can't make cracks about the aunts," said Tish.

"Oh, fine," said Tobias. Which she took to mean that he would stop making cracks for this particular conversation. "But just tell her that you want to stay and keep me company."

"She's only going to say that you're invited too."

"Oh, I'm sure that I am," said Tobias. "But we all know I ain't going. Just tell her you have to stay with me and the problem is solved."

"Except that I did that for the last holiday, whatever that was. She's starting to complain that I never come off the island and I'm going weird."

"Like me, you mean?"

"She does not specify, but I believe that to be heavily implied," said Tish with a grin. "I think I'm probably going to have to pony up and go. But if I play my cards right, maybe I can get them to just do Christmas with just us, or at least skip the big gathering."

"Do what you think best," he said. Which is what he always said when he was trying to keep his opinions on what she should do to himself. "Anyway," he said, changing topics again, "I think I need to figure out who Tyler talked to besides Nora. Someone who might know what he was up to."

"His agent," said Tish. "I don't really know how musicians work, but if he was an actor it would be his agent. I assume musicians have someone who helps them book gigs. Maybe we can check his website and see if there's anyone listed on his contact page."

"That is a good idea," said Tobias nodding. "Here comes Coats."

"I'll get the towel," said Tish with a sigh. "I don't know why I let him out. I'm only going for a run later."

"Might as well leave him out then," said Tobias. "You're both going to end up as wet and muddy as he is right now. I don't know who thought running was a good hobby, but they were wrong."

"It helps me think," said Tish with a laugh.

"Well, maybe that's my problem," said Tobias. "Need to do more jogging and I'd have this thing solved in a jiffy."

CHAPTER 10

GREG & NASH

Tish stretched her legs to make it over a shelf of roots, sliding a little in the mud as she landed. Around her the tall gnarled trunks of pine and evergreen trees rose skyward. The branches blocked what little light there was on the gray day, plunging the trail into a misty gloom. Ahead of her Coats was bounding after a squirrel. It had taken most of the summer to get both of them back into shape. But being only marginally employed and having the use of the home gym in Granddad's shed had helped her return to California levels of fitness. Meanwhile, Coats was benefitting from a newly fenced yard and someone that actually made him walk more than five feet.

Tish knew Sarah and most of her family thought it was odd that she was rooming with her grandfather. Most of their reasons seemed to revolve around the idea that she couldn't have anyone… you know, boys…over. That was probably true. But since she was dating Greg and they mostly confined their romantic moments to his place in Seattle, it never came up. And Tobias never commented about her weekends away. The truth was that he was a pretty good roommate.

He didn't try to make conversation before breakfast. He cleaned up his messes. He generally had interesting things to say. Yes, he did require an extra level of maintenance that a friend roommate wouldn't—driving duties, doctor's appointments, help with the household chores that he could no longer quite manage. But Tish figured that not only were those probably on the list of granddaughter responsibilities, that the free rent and sponsoring of her business venture indebted her.

Besides, it's not forever.

Once her business idea tanked, it was back to the grindstone for her. Tish hadn't admitted to Sarah, but while she had every intention of giving Reginald's kitchen her all, she didn't really expect it to work. She'd never been more than marginally successful at any job she'd ever had. She loved Sarah's dream of crushing the wedding venue market, but she doubted somehow that the universe would ever let her win.

And then this will have been a very nice vacation from real life.

No, the real drawback to rooming with her grandfather, aside from being expected to do the leg work and answer the phone for his detective agency, was getting time alone in her own head. Tobias generally left her alone if she wanted to be alone. But the house was a different story. There was always a list of things that needed to be done. Reginald's was even worse. And even if she ignored those in favor of doing personal projects, her items involved her business plan, working on the business website, and research. Getting away from any of the lists was getting harder. And now she had the added worry of what to do about Nash.

Which is why, even in the middle of a dreary, wet November day, she was out for a run. Running brought on a Zen like OCD state where she could concentrate on the number of steps or trees or minutes. And if she was thinking about breathing it was very difficult to think about all of her impending failures.

And as the winter wore on, she was remembering the joy trail running—an impossibility in LA. Tish felt a thrill as her legs, instead of flattening out like a pair of lead weights, responded to her desire for more speed.

If only she could outrun her problems. Or Nash's problems. It was the fourth day since Tyler's death. She had promised Nash that it would be OK, that they would help, and she didn't think that she or Tobias had made any progress. They'd made a bunch of people angry, but she didn't think that counted.

She reached a flat spot where the trail looped back down to Mountain Lake, and saw another jogger approaching.

Coats barked enthusiastically and bounded toward the runner and Tish realized it was Nash.

"Heading up?" he yelled as they approached the turn off for the steep climb up to Mount Constitution.

On impulse, Tish put on a burst of speed and beat him to the turn.

"Hey!" he barked, half-laughing as she cut him off.

She glanced back over her shoulder, daring him to chase her. She could see that he'd accepted the challenge as he lengthened his stride and began the climb. Realizing that a game of chase was on, Coats scrambled after them, spitting mud behind him like a Duke boy, a look of unbridled joy on his face.

Tish tore her gaze off of Nash's legs and concentrated on not tripping. About half-way up she felt the start of oxygen debt, but pushed forward, scrambling to keep the pace. She could see the medieval outline of the lookout tower through the trees and risked a glance back. Nash was gaining on her. Coats had dropped back and was looking less amused. Chase wasn't supposed to last this long.

She could hear Nash, only footsteps behind her, as she saw the parking lot ahead of her through the narrow opening in the trees. Sprinting, she pushed herself for the final few feet, leaping over a final tree root. Behind her she heard Nash slide in the mud as he leapt over the root and then he crashed into her, grabbing her around the waist and lifting her up, swinging her off to one side as they burst out into the parking lot. Tish gasped for air but started to laugh.

"Put the girl down!" yelled Greg, shoving the gun in Nash's face.

Nash dropped Tish and they both put their hands in the air.

"Greg!" gasped Tish, putting her hands down. "What the hell are you doing?" Greg Swensen was a lean six feet tall, blonde and in certain lights looked like an FBI Ken doll. But at the moment, he simply looked pissed off.

"He grabbed you!"

"I tripped on a root and was trying not to squish her like a bug!" Coats arrived and was now standing in front of Nash, barking at Greg. Coats moved from side to side, uncertainty on his face as he barked. Tish sympathized.

"Greg, put the damn gun away!" snapped Tish. "You're scaring Coats."

"Why were you chasing her?" Greg demanded, not moving.

This was getting out of hand. Greg was refusing to act like a human being. Tish decided that the only way to deal with him was to refuse to match his attitude.

"Because she's faster than me!" Nash at least was being reasonable.

"Ugh," she said, stretching her arms above her head and inhaling. "Not by much. Seriously, Greg, stop. You're really freaking Coats out."

"It's not doing me much good either," said Nash.

"Yes, but you know that Greg is just being weird," said Tish bending over to soothe Coats. "Poor Coats! The last time someone pointed a gun at us we nearly died. Yes, we did, didn't we? Now Coats doesn't like guns. No, he doesn't, does he?" She smooshed the dogs face between her hands and he leaned against her panting. Greg looked uncomfortable with baby dog talk, but reluctantly put his gun away.

"Nash, is the drinking fountain still on?" asked Tish looking around. Above them the World War II era lookout, crafted to look like a castle tower, loomed on the hill.

"No, it won't be back on until at least May."

"I've got water in my car," said Greg, unbending slightly.

"Sweet. Keys?" She held up her hand, setting an expectation of behavior. He tossed them over, his face still unhappy. She jogged over to his car and found two bottles of water in the cup holders. Behind her the two men were making zero conversation. She grabbed both bottles and went back to where they were waiting for her.

"What are you doing here, Greg?" she asked, handing Nash a bottle. "I mean, how did you know I'd be here?"

"I stopped by the house," he said, still glaring suspiciously at Nash. "Tobias said you'd be up here." Nash took a few gulps of water and then knelt down to let Coats drink water out of his hand. "He didn't say you had gone with Deputy Nash."

"Didn't go with me," said Nash, still looking at Coats, who was sucking down most of Nash's water.

"Found him on the trail," said Tish, sucking down most of her water. Then she handed the rest of the bottle down to Nash. "I wish you had called," she said, trying to keep her tone light. "I would have been home."

"I was trying to surprise you," said Greg.

"Well, then, surprise—you get sweaty me," said Tish, kissing him on the cheek. He smiled, but it seemed perfunctory.

Nash finished her bottle of water himself and then stood up.

"I trust you will properly dispose of these," he said, handing her the empty plastic containers.

"No," said Tish, taking them. "I was just going to toss them over the wall." She jerked her head toward the low wall and the drop off to the expansive view of trees.

"I'm not above calling Ronny," said Nash sternly, his eyes twinkling. "You know he'll ticket you for littering."

"Ronny would ticket his mother," said Tish.

"Ronny enjoys ticketing his mother," said Nash and Tish laughed.

"Do you need a ride or anything?" she asked.

"Nah, I'm good. See you later." He turned to jog back down the path.

"Oh! Uh, I forgot," said Tish and he turned back. "You might want to take the slow road home. I saw Elayne this morning in town, and she said she'd be bringing you a casserole later."

Nash snorted. "Thanks for the warning." Then, with a wave, he jogged back into the trees. Coats whined and took a few steps after him.

"No, Coats," said Tish. "Come on." She carried the plastic bottles to the recycling container. Coats looked worried as he followed her. Greg didn't look much happier.

"You shouldn't be spending time with him," he said.

"What?" Tish looked up, startled. She'd expected some sort of commentary on letting herself be manhandled by someone else, but a direct commandment didn't seem to fit with Greg's previous boyfriend behavior.

"He's under investigation for murder. You shouldn't be alone with him. Or with him at all, frankly."

"Well, that didn't take long," said Tish. "I didn't realize you were on the Orcas Island gossip phone tree. Or have they moved to eblasts now? So much for supporting your fellow law enforcement officials."

"He's a Sheriff's Deputy for San Juan County," said Greg. "You'll forgive me if I don't feel a lot of brotherhood for him. That's barely above mall security. I mean, come on, he cares about littering."

"He should care about littering! We live on a damn island. Everything that gets dropped here goes directly into the ocean! And maybe you don't see the dead sea life full of plastic that washes up on the beach, but we do."

"I meant that he threatened to ticket you for littering. That's not exactly real law enforcement."

"He was joking! If he'd wanted to ticket me, he would have done it already for having Coats off leash in a state park!"

"He can't ticket anyone for anything because he's under investigation for *murder*!" Greg yelled.

"Stop being a dick!" Tish yelled back. Coats began barking again, lining up with Tish against Greg.

"Stop barking!" yelled Greg, which had the opposite effect.

Tish took a deep breath and put a calming hand on the dog's head. Coats sputtered to a stop, but settled into a low growl of discontent.

"Well, I'm sorry that you feel that way about San Juan County police. I guess maybe I feel a little bit differently because he saved my life at least once."

"I'm glad he did," said Greg, through gritted teeth. "But they put him on administrative leave for a reason."

"Yeah, it's called procedure and you know it."

"They're looking at him really heavily. They would not do that if they didn't have reason. All I'm doing is suggesting that you be careful. I'm not really sure why that is such a problem."

"It's a problem because you're being a dick," said Tish. "Come on Coats."

"Where are you going?" demanded Greg.

"I'm jogging back to my car," said Tish.

"Tish, don't be ridiculous."

"I'm not being ridiculous. I came here to run. This is me running."

"Tish, get in the car."

Without turning around, she held up her middle finger and broke into a jog. She was parked at a lower lot and by taking the road she could cut the distance and time to her car significantly. A few seconds later she heard Greg's car start up and then saw him drive past her without stopping.

"Well," she said to Coats, slowing down in surprise. "I guess the break-up is now official." Coats let his opinion be known with a sneeze. "I'm surprised too," she agreed. "Also, I can't believe he was such a dick."

Tish spent the rest of the jog trying to assess how broken hearted she was.

A little? Shouldn't I be more upset? It's hard to feel anything but angry at him right this second. He didn't even give Nash a chance.

She turned the corner for the parking area and saw Greg parked next to her car, waiting for her.

"So," he said, as she approached, "it turns out that I may have been a dick. You and Tobias both like him. I shouldn't assume he's guilty."

"No," said Tish, "you shouldn't."

"I deal with a lot of scumbags," he said with a shrug. "I assume everyone's guilty. And you're probably right. I should probably care more about littering. Our planet is important or whatever."

Tish laughed. "Try not to sound like such a rabid environmentalist. You'll get mistaken for Green Peace."

"You don't know. I could have been protest kayaking last weekend," he said.

"Right. Of course. You're well known in the protest kayaking circles."

"The Masked Kayaker of Friday Harbor, that's me." Tish giggled. "Seriously," he said, ducking his head, in an *aw-shucks* maneuver that she suspected he knew looked adorable, "I'm sorry."

"You're going to be even more sorry when Granddad hits you up to misuse FBI resources," said Tish.

"He already did," said Greg, sneaking an arm around her waist and pulling her against him. "I may have been a little pre-disposed to be annoyed at Nash when I got here as a result."

"You really don't have to do whatever he wants," said Tish. She paused on her way to a kiss. "Also, I really am sweaty. This is not glowing. This is actual sweat. Just FYI."

"I got that," said Greg, kissing her anyway.

"You really can tell Granddad *no*," she said a little while later.

"Yeah, the problem with telling either of you *no* is that somehow I always end up being the jerk. Plus, he ends up being right a disturbing amount of the time."

"How often does he ask you for stuff?" asked Tish leaning back in his arms to look at him.

"He doesn't ask for stuff per se. He calls once or twice a year with what he calls *a thought*. I started out humoring him for my dad's sake, but after about the third time his random thought turned out to be a viable theory about an on-going case, I stopped being an ass and started listening. At this point, he's earned a few favors. I just hate feeling like I'm being backed into a corner by an octogenarian."

"Welcome to my life," said Tish with a laugh. "What did he ask you for anyway?"

"He wants me to get the autopsy report on Tyler," said Greg.

Tish's eyes widened. "Can you do that?"

"Would you be impressed if I could?"

"Yes! Granddad's been whining about that for days. Also, I'm starting to worry that we're not making enough progress. We ought to know more by now. Currently our top suspect is an event planner." Greg started to laugh. "I know, right? I mean, I'm sure she's capable of stabbing someone. She's got a history of it." Greg stopped laughing and looked thoughtful. "But it's nothing concrete and I wish we had something more to go on."

"You're so cute when you try to stop crime," he said.

"You think we can't solve this?" demanded Tish.

"That is not what I said!"

"No, it's fine. I'm worried about it too," said Tish deflating. "Nash is my friend and if we end up letting him go to prison and losing Claire because we couldn't figure out who killed Tyler I'm going to feel... I don't know what, but *black hole of despair* is a phrase that comes to mind. I don't know how I could ever face Claire again if I let that happen to her father."

"Hey," he said, hugging her more tightly, "we're not going to let that happen.

She kissed him again. "Thanks for saying *we*. I appreciate the team support."

The wind kicked up and Tish shivered. "We should go back to

the house before you freeze to death," said Greg. "Although, I am enjoying those tights."

"Granddad says they're entirely inappropriate to wear in public," said Tish looking down at the black tights with mesh strips in various places.

"He's right," said Greg, "But that's why I like them."

Tish chuckled. "Hey," she said, pulling out her car key from the waist pocket, and thinking of another item to add to Greg's to-do list. "Who do I talk to about looking into a sketch commune?"

"It's a comedy commune?" Greg looked highly confused.

"What?" Tish felt equally confused.

"You said sketch…"

"Oh," said Tish laughing and shaking her head. "No. I meant shady. Up to no good."

"Then it depends on what kind of shady it is," he replied.

"Tyler's sister is living at a commune that's somehow registered as a rehab facility. And number one, I don't think she can leave. And number two, there is no way that's a rehab facility. I know Tyler's record says that's where he went for his court ordered rehab, but I can't believe the court actually thought that was OK. And obviously, it didn't take—Tyler's liquor cabinet was fully stocked."

"Well, a facility isn't responsible for Tyler's long-term sobriety," said Greg, frowning. "But if it was court mandated they are required to have a certified program."

"Seems highly unlikely," said Tish.

"That actually is something I can look into without any trouble. What about Tyler's sister, though? Is she physically restrained?"

"No. It's just *Mars wouldn't like that* stuff."

"Mars?"

"The commune leader," said Tish making air quotes around *leader*.

"Don't hate on hippies," said Greg. "You'll start to sound like Tobias."

"I don't hate hippies," said Tish. "I hate users. This guy stunk like a grade *A* cult leader type. Seemed like he needed to be punched in the face."

"Funny how some people just need that," said Greg, his eyes twinkling.

"And it's amazing how rarely I'm allowed to do it," said Tish, grinning. "Anyway, meet you back at Granddad's?"

"Yeah," said Greg. "I told Tobias I was taking you out to dinner though, so you may want to change when you get home. Or maybe not. I'm open to suggestion."

CHAPTER 11

FRIDAY - NASH

The next morning Tish ate breakfast at the Orcas Hotel with Greg. It was a nineteen hundreds Victorian charmer of a hotel that overlooked the ferry dock and had hosted hundreds of weddings. It was also where Greg had rented a room. It was where she had stayed the night. And it was where she happened to see Deputies Ronny Pearson and Ray Fullbright coming off their night shift. Ronny's eyes had bulged a little bit when he'd seen her with Greg.

"What's the matter Ronny?" asked Tish, smiling at him as they entered the restaurant. "You look like a bug flew in your mouth."

"Uh," said Ronny, salsa dripping from the breakfast burrito in his hand and onto his uniform.

"Have you met my boyfriend, Greg Swensen?"

"Uh, no?" said Ronny, swiping at the salsa blob. "I thought…" He looked desperately from Greg to Tish. Greg smiled unhelpfully, enjoying Ronny's discomfort.

"Yeah…" said Tish. "Thinking isn't really your strong suit, is it Ronny? You kind of end up being wrong about people. A lot."

"That's not fair," said Ronny.

"Yes, it is," said Ray, shooting Ronny a dirty look. Then he looked up at Tish. "I hear you and Tobias are looking into Tyler Reich's death."

"There's no law against talking to people," said Tish with a shrug.

"Definitely not," said Ray.

"I don't think—" began Ronny, but there was a hard clunk under the table and Ronny winced.

"And I'm not saying that you should talk to the waitress at H2O, but you know, if you were looking for people to talk to, she might be interesting."

"Ray!" hissed Ronny.

"Go soak your head in a bucket, Ronny. Nash didn't do it," said Ray. "And you're an asshole for thinking he did."

"They're interfering in an ongoing investigation," said Ronny, snippily.

"I'm doing nothing of the kind. I'm having a nice conversation with Tish and her boyfriend, Greg. Anyone who says differently is a damn liar."

"Pleasant chit-chat about the weather," said Greg. "That's what I heard."

"Exactly," said Ray. Tish smiled at Ray. He was a forty-ish white guy with sandy brown hair and a wallflower personality. Up until now she had not considered that he might be an ally for Team Nash.

"Thanks Ray," said Tish. "I'll see you guys later."

Greg waited until they were out of earshot before speaking again. "I think I failed to take island life into account," he said.

"What do you mean?" asked Tish.

"Nash being a suspect. It's a big deal here, isn't it?"

"Yeah! Did you think it wasn't?"

"I got that it was a big deal to you. I just didn't get everyone else. In a big city, if a cop gets accused of something, it's a two-minute news story on a slow night. But here... Ray and Ronny aren't the only ones divided on this, are they?"

"No," said Tish. "We ate lunch with Nash yesterday, and it was pretty awful. Think about if everyone who'd known you for the last decade heard that you'd been accused of murder. And by the way, you'll be bumping into all of them next time you go to the grocery store. And now we get to the fun part, where you get to find out which ones think it's true."

Greg grimaced. "Tell Tobias I'll get the autopsy report for him."

"Thanks," said Tish.

She walked Greg down to his car as the ferry loaded, then she went down to wave as his car rolled across the ramp and onto the ferry. She was about to climb back up the steep embankment to the Orcas Hotel when she heard someone calling her name. She turned back and found she was being waved at by one of her grandfather's card playing cronies—a scraggly haired WSDOT employee with a beer gut and a cigar habit, named Barry.

"Hey Tish!" he yelled, panting a bit at having run the ten feet over to her. "Glad I caught you."

"Hey Barry, what's up?"

"You've got a shipment waiting in the next ferry load."

"OK?" Tish pulled up the mental list of things she was expecting to be delivered. Top of the list was the new dishwasher for Reginald's.

"But it's a big mother. And it's on one of them long trucks. I don't think it's going to make it up the grade." He jerked his head at the hill. "Or at least this driver won't. It's his first time making the run."

"Nooooo," wailed Tish. "I need that dishwasher."

"I can get him to leave it in the ferry office. If you grab a truck, you could hop on the next run and go collect it from Anacortes?" he suggested.

"Could you?"

"Yeah, no worries," said Barry.

"Thank you, Barry!"

"Heh. No problem. Just give me a sign next time Tobias gets a high hand in bridge and we'll call it even."

"Done," said Tish grinning. "See you next run!" She jogged up the hill to her car, fishing in her purse for her phone. Her grandfather did own a beat-up, rattle-trap truck, but it was currently full of her latest efforts to clean out the sheds and houses at both Reginald and Tobias's. She didn't think she had time to go home and unload. That meant she needed to borrow a truck. Which shouldn't be too much of a problem—half the island residents owned trucks. But most of them would be out using their trucks at mid-morning on a Friday.

She dialed Nash.

"What is it I'm I supposed to say? Nash residence?" he asked, picking up on the third ring.

Tish chuckled. "I caught Granddad saying *Yearly Residence* to his cell phone. It doesn't quite work when it's not attached to a house."

"True," he said, laughing. "What's up?"

"So… you're like home alone, moping, right?"

"Basically. Why?"

"And you have a truck?"

"Yes. Again, why?"

"So theoretically you could drive me over to Anacortes on the next ferry run and help me pick up the dishwasher for Reginald's?"

"Why won't they just deliver it?"

"Barry says the truck won't make it up the hill off the ferry. He's going to have the guy leave it at the ferry office. But I have to make it on the next run and go pick it up ASAP."

"Yeah OK. What time is it?" There was a blast of the ferry horn that silenced all conversation. "Never mind," said Nash, when he could talk again. "I'll see you in a little bit."

"Thanks!" said Tish.

There was a small silence on the other end of the phone. "Yeah, any time," he said.

Tish hung up and checked her watch and then dialed Sarah.

"Hey!" said Sarah picking up.

"Hey, when were you thinking about heading my direction?" asked Tish.

"I don't know. After lunch?"

"Well, what if you left like sooner?"

"What if I did?" asked Sarah.

"Well, if you did, then you could ride back on the ferry with

Nash and me. We're going over to Anacortes to pick up the dish-washer for Reginald's. And then I wouldn't have to make another trip out to the ferry dock to pick you up."

"You're coming over with Nash?" asked Sarah. "Hm. I could try to move up my leave time. But I've got some loose ends floating around here. Can you wait for me in Anacortes?"

"Probably? I don't know. I just told Nash about the dishwasher. I didn't tell him about my other plans."

"Plans, meaning multiple? What else have you got up your sleeve?"

"Depends on how much time I have," said Tish. "Give me a text when you're on the road."

"Will do!"

Tish hung up and dialed her grandfather.

"Yearly Residence," he said picking up.

"Granddad! Guess what? I talked to Ronny and Ray this morn-ing."

"Why?" he asked drily.

"Because I wanted to rub Greg in Ronny's face," said Tish.

"You know, it's not becoming to use a human being as an acces-sory," said Tobias.

"I am not using Greg as an accessory. He just happens to look extremely good on my arm. Anyway, there is clearly dissension in the ranks. Ray said we should talk to the waitress at the H2O and then he kicked Ronny under the table and called him an asshole. Oh, and also, Greg said he would work on the autopsy report."

"You seem to have had a very busy morning," said Tobias.

"Yes. I also talked to Barry and I have to go over to Anacortes and get the dishwasher for Reginald's."

"Truck won't make it up the hill?" asked Tobias, effortlessly fill-ing in the blanks on her story.

"Yeah."

"That's going to be a bit tough. We've got all that stuff in the back of the truck," he mused.

"I already called Nash," said Tish. "I figured I could use the extra muscles and he could use the distraction."

"You don't say," said Tobias. Which could mean nothing, or it could mean a great many things depending on Tobias's mood.

"And then, if we have lunch in Anacortes, I think that will give Sarah time to meet us up there and we can all drive back together."

"Ah," said Tobias. "That makes sense."

"But! I was thinking that while I was in Anacortes, I would go talk to the waitress. What do you think?"

"Hm," said Tobias. "Yes, but I don't think you should bring Nash with you. Could get him in trouble if Spring finds out."

"Oh, good point," said Tish. "OK, I'm sure Sarah can babysit him for a while. But what do you think I should ask the waitress."

"Well, if you can, figure out what the police asked her. I'm sure they would have asked if she had seen Nash, so maybe start there. Ask about Tyler's movements. Ask if anyone suspicious was lingering around. What exactly did Ray say?"

"He just said she would be interesting to talk to," replied Tish.

"Not a lot to work with," mused Tobias.

"I know! But I didn't think I could push it. He was already taking a big stand in front of Ronny."

"That is a big move for, Ray," agreed Tobias. "He's always been shy. Well, my advice, is to start with things that she might have seen and that the police might have asked. Try to sound official and if you can, try to sound like you already know the answers."

"That will be a bit difficult since I don't even know the questions."

"You're the actress," said Tobias. "So act."

"You're so encouraging," said Tish.

"Don't need to be encouraging for something I know you can do. Besides the worst that can happen is that they tell you to get out."

"Good point," said Tish. "OK, you're right. I got this."

"Hoo-rah," said Tobias. "As Reginald used to say. Give me a call when you're all headed back. I'll dig through the freezer and find some dinner for everyone."

"Mmm," said Tish. Her grandfather's cooking skills were famous.

More like infamous.

"There's still some casseroles in there," said Tobias, defensively. They had been the recipients of a freezer load of grief casseroles after Reginald's death.

"That's true," said Tish. "And we do need to finish those off. OK, I guess I'll see you later this evening."

"Sounds good," said Tobias. "Have fun."

Tish hung up wondering at her grandfather's idea of fun.

On the other hand, this is definitely more fun than youtube-ing How to Dry-Wall Videos.

Tish fished in the glovebox for one of the novels she kept on hand to pass the wait on ferries or to keep Tobias entertained and then stretched her legs over the parking brake and into the passenger seat. She was three chapters in when there was a knock on her window.

She jumped and then saw Nash grinning outside the car.

"They just found the body," she said, turning around in the seat and opening the door. "You scared the crap out of me!"

He laughed and crawled into the backseat. "I'm in lane two, so we should get on no problems, but we've got lots of time to kill. What's in the library?"

Realizing, that Nash wasn't planning on getting back out, Tish shut the door and opened the glovebox again. "Classic Dashiell Hammett with the *Maltese Falcon, She Rides Shotgun* by Jordan Harper and *The Right Side* by Spencer Quinn."

"Let me guess, Tobias picked them?"

"I do keep them mostly for his entertainment," Tish admitted.

But I still read all of them…

He leaned over the passenger seat and perused the book selections. "I hate it when they just put *praise for's* on the back cover," he complained. "I want to know what the book is about, not who else likes it."

Tish checked the book in question. "Yeah, I read that one already. It was good if you like your detectives gritty and your novels noir-ish."

He shrugged and settled back against the back door, propping his feet up on the opposite side. Tish chuckled.

"What?" he asked, looking up.

"You fit even worse than I do. We look like we're doing some sort of weird yoga."

"Car yoga. We should market it. We could have the latest fitness trend. Then later we'll branch out into airplane yoga."

"If I were still in LA, I would totally develop that," said Tish, seriously.

"I suppose we do look a bit goofy," he said looking over the front seat at her legs. I always forget that you're tall."

"How?" asked Tish, trying to contain a laugh.

"I don't know. You just seem normal sized to me. I don't notice until you're standing next to some of the midget people that populate this place."

"By *this place* you mean the rest of America?"

"Exactly." He scrutinized her face. "You look like you're having trouble with the idea."

"Yeah, kind of," said Tish. "When I was a kid, no one ever let me forget that I was tall. But then I moved to LA and I did some modeling and suddenly I was the shortest one in the room. It was always, *sigh, you're only five-eight?* I mean, really, I'm closer to five-nine, but I had to have two sets of headshots, one that fudged me at five-seven and one that fudged me at five-ten. It was like bouncing between a skinny and fat mirror. Feeling normal sized is not really a concept that I have a lot of experience with."

"Don't know what to tell you. You seem normal to me," he said with a shrug and cracked open the cover of his book.

But you were married to a five-foot-two pixie? I don't know what to think about that.

Sometime later they both looked up as a gust of wind hit the car with a splatter of rain from the overhanging trees. Tish checked the progress of the ferry across the water. She guessed they still had another twenty minutes before it even got close to docking. Then it would take time to unload. She looked back at Nash, who was staring in her general direction with a thoughtful expression on his face.

"Pondering the universe in all its infinite grandeur, or is my hair being weird?"

"I was wondering why you left LA," asked Nash, unbending his legs with a grimace of discomfort.

"I realized I wasn't going to make it as an actress," said Tish. She tried never to lie about her reasons for leaving.

"What are you talking about?" he asked draping himself over the back of the passenger seat. "I looked you up on IMDB. You had lots of credits. How were you not making it?"

"This is why I don't talk about it," she said with a sigh. "Everyone always, says, *but you had roles!*" He tilted his head with an inquisitive look, and for once Tish felt like breaking it down instead of simply smiling and changing the topic. "Sure, I had parts. And a lot of part time jobs. I was working, but I wasn't paying the rent with just acting. I went to LA when I was nineteen. But after six years, I wasn't new. I wasn't exciting. I was reliable and that was enough to get me roles, but it wasn't enough to get me farther. I reached a point where I realized if I was going to make the next level, I was going to have to do something drastic—boob job, new agent, kidnap a celebrity, something." Nash's face registered dislike at the mention of *boob job*. "After a while I realized that none of the drastic actions I was considering were guaranteed to get me where I wanted to go and I was at an age where I either needed to succeed or I needed to reconsider my career path. So I chose to take my toys and come home. But now that I'm home everyone acts like it was this grand, successful venture."

"You don't think it was?"

"I think if I had been successful, I'd still be there," said Tish.

He looked thoughtful. "You nicked the bullseye," he said.

"I don't know what that means," said Tish.

"Sometimes I go pick up Claire in the city and there's a shooting range between here and there. I stop and get some practice in. A couple of months back, I was running through some drills and I was feeling pretty confident because I'd been practicing up here, and I did a left handed, single draw. Then I pulled the paper forward and saw that I had just hit the edge of the black. And while I'm being annoyed at myself for sloppy shooting, I hear the guy in the next lane let out a big whoop. It was his first time shooting and he was really excited that he made it on the paper."

Tish made an amused noise, that wasn't quite a laugh.

"So, while we're all excited that you made it on the paper, you're pissed because you nicked the bullseye."

"Yeah," she said, nodding. "That sounds right. And whenever I try to explain it, people just tell me that I did such a good job. Which is infuriating."

"I can see that," he said nodding. "You don't need the compliments and none of us have the knowledge or skill to judge accurately."

"Yes!" Tish was startled to hear her problem articulated.

"Sorry," he said. Then he frowned. "Nineteen, really? I can't believe your parents let you go to LA at nineteen. That is the kind of thing that gives me nightmares."

Tish laughed. "Well, Dad died when I was a kid and Mom has never been particularly good at telling me *no*."

"No is something I can do," he said, looking reassured.

"Claire is going to have to leave home at some point," said Tish.

"No," he said firmly. "She's going to stay at home and be ten forever."

"College. It's a thing that's going to happen," she said cruelly. "There will be boys and possibly pot and poor clothing choices."

He covered his ears with his hands. "Ahhhh. Why? Why would you say such horrible things?" Tish giggled. "Seriously, it's not funny. Wait until you have kids and then you'll be trying to figure out how to dip them in carbonite. They grow so fast."

"I don't know about having kids," said Tish. "I'm not sure I'm that person."

"Why not?"

Tish shrugged. "I'm not really a stable individual, am I? Look how well my career choices are panning out. How am I supposed to voluntarily bring a kid into this mess?"

He laughed. "I know the feeling. It wasn't like Claire was planned on. But I promise it works out."

"I don't know," said Tish looking out the windshield at the approaching ferry. "Sometimes things happen, but that doesn't mean they happen for the best. Why put a kid through that?"

"What is that? A greeting card for the depressed? Like you're the worst mess a kid could ever have?" he asked, and Tish blushed. "Get over yourself," he said, smiling.

"You must have gone to the same encouragement school as Granddad," said Tish.

"The Tobias Yearly *Stop Yer Complaining and Get the Job Done School?* I took a few classes. Ferry's just about in. We should go get in my truck. We wouldn't want to hold up the ferry line." He looked at her side-long, distinctly not mentioning their first meeting.

"Hey, I had just gotten fired, evicted, and my cousin stole all my stuff! That wasn't a good day for me!"

He chuckled. "No, it clearly wasn't."

They were settled upstairs on the ferry each of them taking up one side of a six-foot booth, their legs stretched out along the hard benches, reading their respective novels when Tish's phone burbled.

"Ah!" exclaimed Tish, checking the message.

"Ah?" repeated Nash, looking up.

Tish immediately looked guilty. She knew because Nash immediately looked amused and suspicious.

"How do you feel about lunch in Anacortes?"

"I could eat. Why?"

"My friend Sarah is coming up this weekend to help work on Reginald's and she just left Seattle, so if we were to take some extra time…"

"She could ride back with us and you wouldn't have to make a second trip to the ferry dock?"

"Yes?" She smiled winningly.

"You could have included that in the original ask," he said.

"I called her after I called you."

"Of course, you did. It's like you've been spending too much time with Tobias."

"Are you saying that Granddad likes to ambush people with surprise requests to capitalize on their confusion and reduce the chances of their saying no?"

"Yes, that's exactly what I'm saying." Tish laughed, then he shrugged. "Yeah, sure. It's not like I have anywhere else to be."

"Can I ask you something?" asked Tish.

"Depends on what it is," he replied.

"That was a random conversational opener, not an actual question. I'm going to ask you the question no matter what you say."

"Then why not just ask the question?"

"Because you just objected to ambush questions. I thought you might like some warning."

"Ambush requests are different than ambush questions."

"Are they?" asked Tish, pondering that one.

"I have no idea. Now I'm just arguing to argue."

Tish threw her paper bookmark at him— it fluttered uselessly down to the middle of the table. He laughed. "What's the question?"

"Why Orcas? I've tried asking some other people and they give this look like I've asked the most insulting question ever."

"Well, sure, the implication is that they should be living some place, any place, else and they've got to be crazy to live here."

"No!" exclaimed Tish. "No, I'm really not saying that. I'm trying to figure out what makes the island what it is. Who are the people who live here and what makes them choose this place?"

"You want to figure out our motivation?" he asked his blue eyes twinkling. In the cold light of the winter sky they looked more gray than blue today.

"Well, yes," said Tish, refusing to blush.

"You're not going to find a lot of people willing to answer though. We're self-conscious about it. There's always the idea that we couldn't hack it on the mainland. Which, to be fair, some of us can't."

"But that isn't… There's nothing particularly special about the mainland."

"Except that you go visit it an awful lot."

"Yes, because I like big cities," said Tish. "Not all the time, but I like the energy. But it's just different, not better."

"Well, maybe we like the energy of islands."

"OK, but what is that? I like the cities because someone is always making noise, music is always playing somewhere, something is always happening."

"Hate that. To be able to turn off at the end of the day and hear nothing but wind, waves and wildlife, that's what we love."

"Yeah, I can hear the damn deer eating half the garden."

"Yes," he agreed, chuckling. "That's the wildlife I was referring to."

"Well, what about the ability to pop down to the grocery store at two A.M.?"

"What about the ability to know your grocer?"

"Consistent cell phone service."

"Stop staring at Facebook and go talk to someone. Besides the phone book and a land line work just fine."

"Movie theaters."

"Twelve-dollar popcorn."

"You know what I like?" asked Tish, switching tactics. "It's all the art. There's art everywhere on the island."

"I miss fast food," he said.

"But the island food is so good!"

"But so expensive."

"Yeah," agreed Tish. "But what about the music? So much live music."

"You can get that in the city. Anyway, whose side are you on?"

"No one's side. I'm trying to understand what makes the island tick. I'm not Granddad. I can't..."

He raised an eyebrow. "Keep secret files on all of us? Those have been an island legend for decades. Please, please, please tell me those are real."

Tish wavered. "OK, yes, but you can't tell anyone."

He grinned as if his face would split. "I knew it. I knew it!"

"He is going to be so mad at me," said Tish, instantly regretting her decision.

"I won't tell."

"Mmm," said Tish, now more worried than ever.

"What does he have on me?"

"Just the basics," said Tish. "Seriously, if you ever let Granddad know I told you, I'm so dead."

He grinned, unrepentantly. Then he turned, dropping his feet under the table, and dog eared the page of his novel. "You want to know why Orcas?"

"Yes," said Tish.

This is the longest amount of time I've been alone with him. Ever. It seems like it should feel weird. But it really doesn't.

"Nora and I were in college. I had just graduated, and she got pregnant. So we got married. And before you say we didn't have to and times have changed, no, we didn't and yes, they have. But we were planning on getting married anyway, so it seemed like the thing to do at the time. Anyway, I needed a job, and no one was hiring in my field."

"What was your field?" asked Tish.

"It's not in the file?"

"No," said Tish primly.

Although, yes, I totally looked.

"OK, then you have to promise not tell anyone or I'll blab about the files."

Tish crossed her heart and sat up straighter in the booth.

"Library sciences."

Tish covered her mouth with both hands to hide her smile. "You're a librarian?" she whispered, trying to contain the giggle that was threatening to burst forth.

"Yes," he said. "You're going to have a hard time holding this one in, aren't you?"

"No. No, I'm good. I can maintain. I just need a moment."

"Take all the time you need." He waited. "Should I go on? Want to go shout *he's a librarian* at the ocean?"

"Oh! No, I don't. But I do love that idea. However, please continue."

"Anyway, I looked around. A friend of my dad's suggested the police force and San Juan County was the first place that offered me a job. And once I got here I realized it was a pretty ideal place for kids. Crime's minimal and everyone looks out for each other. Also, everyone reads." He held up the novel he'd borrowed as proof. "I wasn't planning on building a career in law enforcement exactly, but it's a good job and a good place to be. I figured we could stick around until Claire got into high-school and then maybe I could go back to school and get a masters or something. I don't know. It seemed like a good plan. At least to everyone but Nora."

"Sorry," said Tish.

He shrugged. "If the last two years have taught me anything, it's that I have zero control of the universe."

"I hate that feeling," said Tish, sympathetically. "I don't like not being master of my own fate. I know it sounds stupid, but I really thought I'd have things more together by twenty-seven. It seems like at least one of my plans should have worked. Like, enough already. I get it—I can't control anything and the universe owes me nothing. Can we maybe not be quite so blatant about it? Lately, it just feels like someone's decided to hammer that lesson home with a mallet."

"Hey, could be worse. At least you're not being investigated for murder and no one has served a search warrant on your house."

"They searched your house?" Tish felt a squirmy horror at the idea of anyone pawing through every drawer and belonging.

"Yesterday. They didn't find anything," he said with a shrug. "There's nothing to find anyway, but usually it seems like they confiscate computers or something. They didn't even take that. Just made a mess of my house and left."

"Well, that's good then!"

"Sure," he said with a shrug. "Good."

"We're going to get you out of this," said Tish.

"You just said you can't control the universe," said Nash.

"The universe can go…." Tish paused as a small child ran by, trailed by a tired looking parent.

"Taken as read," said Nash. "Looks like we're about to dock. Let's go get a dishwasher."

CHAPTER 12

THE DISHWASHER

The dishwasher was right where Barry had said it would be. Nash loaded it into the back of the truck and then they drove to Nash's preferred burger spot. Thirty minutes later, Sarah walked in looking work fabulous and slightly out of place in the down-home restaurant.

"Great," said Tish, shoving a French fry into her mouth, and standing up to hug her. "Sarah meet Nash, Nash meet Sarah."

"Hi," said Nash standing up to shake her hand.

Because he's that guy.

Sarah looked Nash over with a measuring look but smiled.

"And now that you're here, can I borrow your car?"

"My car?" repeated Sarah, looking from Nash to Tish.

"I have another little errand to run while I'm in town," said Tish.

"Then wait until we finish lunch, and we'll all go together," said Nash reasonably.

"Yeeeeah," said Tish. "I don't want you to go. You should stay here with Sarah. Keys?" She held out her hand to Sarah.

"You're going to the H2O, aren't you?" demanded Nash.

"I may have gotten a tip from Ray this morning," said Tish, waggling her fingers at Sarah.

"No," said Nash. "You're not going down there."

"Yes," said Tish, taking the keys from Sarah's reluctant hand. "I am. Stop fussing. Besides, you agreed to this."

"I didn't agree to let you interfere in a police investigation."

"They've already talked to everyone," said Tish, grabbing another French fry. "How is it interfering?"

"I was wrong," said Nash. "The problem is not that you've been spending too much time with Tobias. The problem is that clearly interfering is genetic."

Sarah laughed and then stopped as they looked at her. "Sorry," she said. "You two were arguing. Please don't let me interrupt."

"Sit tight," said Tish, backing up. "I'll be back in a jiff." She bolted out of the restaurant before either of them could say anything else.

Tish arrived at the H2O and realized that she still had no clue about what to say. She also hadn't realized that they'd be closed. On impulse, she went around to the kitchen entrance. A young-ish guy was standing out by the dumpster smoking.

"Hi," said Tish, getting out of Sarah's silver Honda, and smiling warmly. The dishwasher ran an eye over her and decided that her stats rated a response.

"S'up," he said with a nod.

"I'm with Yearly Investigations," she said. "We're looking into the death of Tyler Reich. Is anyone in that was here last Sunday night?"

He nodded and took another drag on his cigarette. "Jacy and I were wondering who to talk to about that."

"What do you mean?" asked Tish.

"We told the cops about that woman, but they didn't want to hear it."

"Which woman? Brunette, curls, big tits?"

Private investigators say tits. Pretty sure.

He shook his head. "The redhead in the picture. The cops showed us a picture of some guy. It was a wedding photo. They wanted to know if we'd seen him. We hadn't. They kept pushing, but we really never saw the guy. But the wife in the photo. We saw her. Jacy told the cops, but it was like they just didn't want to hear it."

Oh, shit.

"Hold on." Tish texted Sarah. "OK," she said, turning back to the dishwasher. "What did the redhead do?"

"Nothing much. She asked Jacy about Tyler, but he'd just finished his last set and she didn't know where Tyler had gone. It was about eleven. I went out into the back hall and I nearly bumped into her—the redhead—with a giant bag of garbage. She asked me about Tyler, but I hadn't seen him since he came in pre-set for some water. Then the redhead left and I went outside to dump the garbage. And when I opened the dumpster, that's when I found the dude's body."

Tish's phone plinged and Tish opened up the snapshot of Nash. "Was this the guy in the photo the police showed you?"

"Yeah," said the dishwasher. "But like I told the cops, I've never seen him here before."

Tish nodded and scrutinized the dumpster. It was the standard double wide, flip top open metal container. But the opening was at least four feet off the ground. Tyler had been six feet tall and while admittedly skinny, the idea of tiny Nora Na…Harlow hefting him into the container seemed improbable.

"How did the redhead seem? Upset? Pissed? Weepy?"

"Hard to say," said the dishwasher. "Pissed, I guess. She showed up right before closing. Jacy said she didn't order anything. You really a private investigator?"

"No," said Tish. "I just play one on TV. Sorry if this is upsetting, but what did the body look like?"

"Like a bloody mess. I had two of the guys help me get him out because I thought he might be alive, but it was too late. He was stabbed like six times or something. His torso looked like a pin cushion. The cops went through the dumpster. I hear they found the knife, but I didn't see it."

"There was blood all over his chest? OK, but what about the rest of him?"

"What do you mean?"

"Well," said Tish, grabbing an imaginary knife, "you just stabbed someone six times. And now you want to put them in a dumpster."

She stabbed her invisible person. "You don't have a lot of time. It's a bar, it's about to close, so people will be milling about. You have to be quick. You open the dumpster." She flipped the lid. The dishwasher was watching her in fascination. "You toss the knife in. And then you grab the body. He's a big guy, so you grab around the chest. You hoist him up. But it's a body. It's floppy. There's a lot of man-handling. There should be blood on the rest of him."

And on the killer's clothes.

"There was a lot of blood," said the dishwasher. "But now that you mention it, I didn't see any hand prints or anything. But I wasn't really looking and it was dark."

"Fair enough," said Tish. "Did anyone else ask about Tyler that night?"

"Not that I know of," he said. "Jacy might know. But if she did, she didn't mention them to the cops."

"No problem," said Tish. "What time did you find the body?"

"Just after eleven. We were starting to close. The dead guy played his last song at 10:30, no one remembers seeing him after that."

Tish nodded as if that was what she had expected. Struck by a sudden thought she looked up the Doe Bay Blues Festival website on her phone and pulled up the photo of Clover. "How about her? Did you see her that night?"

He shook his head. "Come back after five and you can ask Jacy."

"Won't be tonight," said Tish, with a smile. "But I might have to. Thanks for your time." She held out the one business card she had from Tobias. "Can I get your name?"

"Boleslav," he said. "Boleslav Sokolov."

"Thanks, Boleslav," said Tish with another smile.

"Come back any time," he said with a grin. "You're a lot prettier than the cops."

"Yeah, well, Detective Spring doesn't know how to accessorize," said Tish, with a wink, and he grinned. "Thanks again for your help."

Tish got back in Sarah's car and dialed Tobias.

"Yearly Residence," said Tobias.

"Hey Granddad. I need help."

"What kind of help?" His voice became more clipped and urgent.

"Advice kind of help. We need to decide what to tell Nash."

"What do you mean?"

"I was just at the H2O and the dishwasher and the waitress did not see Nash that night, but Detective Spring used an old wedding photo of Nash and Nora as his ID photo, and both witnesses saw Nora Nash. Harlow. Whatever."

Tobias inhaled.

"Both the dishwasher and the waitress told Spring that they had seen Nora, but apparently he kind of blew them off. And that is annoying, but it's at least partially understandable since Tyler was stabbed six times in the chest and then thrown into a dumpster. I'm not saying Nora isn't in shape, but lifting him into the dumpster seems a bit much for her."

"And getting a knife through a rib cage isn't as easy as the movies make it look," said Tobias.

Do not ask him how he knows that. Do not ask him how he knows that.

"But that don't mean she didn't have help," he mused.

"But why would she?" asked Tish. "I would swear that at minimum she was genuinely fond of Tyler, if not actually in love with him."

"Maybe she found out he was lying to her and tricking her into giving up custody of Claire," said Tobias and Tish grimaced.

"That's actually pretty reasonable. I feel like Nash is going to freak out about this."

"Probably," agreed Tobias. "Like I said, I think he's always going to have a thing for her."

"OK, swell, good for them. I hope they reunite and ride off into the sunset. But meanwhile, I'm going to see him in about two minutes and he knows I was down there asking questions. What do

I say?"

"He's with Sarah, right? Just say that you want to wait until you get home, so you can talk with me at the same time. And kind of give the nod, like you don't want to blab in front of Sarah and the rest of the public."

"OK," said Tish nodding. "That plays. I can work with that."

"All right," said Tobias. "Good. Meanwhile, what do you think, chicken green bean or enchilada casserole?"

"Um, chicken green bean?"

"Sounds good. I'll get it out of the freezer. Good work today! Can't wait to hear all about it when you get home."

Easy for him to be all cheerful. He doesn't have to tell Nash that his wife maybe killed someone.

Tish worried about it for the remaining drive, and all the way into the restaurant, right up until she saw Sarah and Nash laughing like old friends in the booth, and Sarah finishing the rest of Tish's burger.

Clearly not that worried about me going off to a seedy bar to question disreputables. Which is totally unfair, because it looked like a fun place and Boleslav was really nice, but that is not the point.

"Hey!" said Sarah, looking up. "Columbo is back. How did it go?"

"Pretty good," said Tish. "We should probably line up for the ferry, yeah?"

"Yeah," agreed Nash, scrutinizing her. "But what does *pretty good* mean."

"It means I owe Ray a beer for giving me a solid tip," said Tish, grabbing the bill. "Come on, let's go."

"Did Ray really give you a tip?" he asked, standing up and following her toward the front of the restaurant.

"Yeah, and he called Ronny an asshole to his face," said Tish.

"Really?"

She glanced back over her shoulder and saw that he was smiling.

She wondered how awful Ronny had been the day Nash had been in for questioning.

"Really," she said.

"Good," he said, taking the bill out of her hand.

"Stop that," said Tish, reaching for the bill.

"Stop what?" he asked holding it over his head.

"You're going to look like the mean boy who pulls girls pigtails when I start jumping," she said.

"Please jump. Please," said Sarah. "But wait until I get my phone out so I can record it."

Nash laughed and lowered the bill to normal height. "I know all your money needs to go toward the kitchen. I can buy you a burger."

"No," said Tish. "I pay for my own burgers."

The waitress came to the register and looked at the trio quizzically. Sarah leaned in between Tish and Nash and put her credit card on the counter. "I'm just going to leave this here," said Sarah. The waitress shrugged and rang them up.

CHAPTER 13
DETECTIVE SPRING & TOBIAS

Tish and Sarah leaned against the dishwasher in Reginald's kitchen and panted.

"I'm not going to lie," said Sarah. "I was not at all convinced it was going to fit through the door."

"I measured it six times," said Tish, "if it didn't fit I was going to have a breakdown."

"It was the box," said Nash reaching in the fridge for a soda. "Once we took the box off it was fine."

Sarah looked around the kitchen and Tish watched the horror slowly dawn. "Holy crap, Tish. Why are there no walls?"

"Well, I had to upgrade the sink and once I did that it was discovered that the pipes were no longer up to code and were rusted through in at least one spot. But once I replaced those pipes it sprang a leak further along in the walls, which resulted in all the walls being ripped off and damage to the electrical. And then the electrical wasn't up to code anyway, so all of it had to be replaced. And I had to replace the floor of course, because I had to bump out onto the back porch to make room for all the industrial-sized appliances."

"How much did that cost?" she asked.

"Well, the Tim's did the floor and the bump out. That wasn't cheap. But Clarence, the plumber, showed me how to do the pipes and Frida, the electrician, showed me how to do the wiring, so it took longer, but it pretty much just cost me supplies."

"Is that legal?" Sarah looked concerned.

"Well, they have to come back and certify it and it still has to pass inspection, but yeah, it's legal."

"No wonder you haven't made any progress on the website," said Sarah.

"Sorry," said Tish, with a sigh. "I just can't seem to make it that far down the list."

"Maybe I can take a look at it," said Sarah. Tish shrugged uncomfortably. "What are we doing this weekend?"

"Um, dishwasher installation. Paint the bathroom. And then, figuring out dry wall."

"You're coming back tomorrow, right?" Sarah asked, turning to Nash.

"I have not been asked," said Nash.

"You're not going to be," said Sarah. "Tish Yearly does not ask for help. Help must be forced upon her."

"I ask for help," protested Tish.

I just don't like to owe people and I don't like to presume that people want in on my projects.

"I, on the other hand," continued Sarah, as if Tish hadn't said anything, "am fully comfortable asking for help. And I'm telling you now that we might be able to figure out painting and the dishwasher, but dry wall is not within the scope of our skills."

"I know how to do drywall," said Nash.

"YouTube is very helpful," said Tish.

I also don't like people thinking I can't figure things out for myself.

"Not that helpful," said Sarah. "And you've got to move this along. It's Christmas or bust, remember?"

"It hasn't escaped my mind," said Tish, sourly. "Do you really know how to make dry wall?" she asked Nash.

He nearly spit out a mouthful of pop. "It's hang dry wall or put up dry wall, but yes, I know how to do it. I did all the dry wall in my house."

"And those look like real walls!" exclaimed Tish.

"Thanks," he said. "That was the look I was going for."

"Well, that would really help a lot. Are you sure you don't mind?"

His eyes narrowed slightly as if trying to read her expression. "Yeah," he said. "I'm happy to help."

"Well, OK. That would be really great." She caught site of the clock on the microwave. "And now we should go back to Granddad's for chicken green bean casserole."

"Still not through the Reginald casseroles yet?" asked Nash, as they exited the house.

"Down to the last five I think," said Tish. "But any casserole is still way better than Granddad cooking."

"That's true," he agreed.

"Is he really that bad?" asked Sarah. "I mean, he's like 110. He must have figured out how to cook something edible at some point in his life."

Nash and Tish both paused. "It's edible," said Tish cautiously.

"It's just that until I had his food, I never realized how bad edible can be," said Nash.

"Now I sort of want him to cook for me," said Sarah. "It seems like an experience. Like bungee jumping off a bridge: you might puke, but it makes you appreciate your life more."

Tish laughed and Nash nodded. "That's surprisingly apt," he said.

They crammed into Nash's truck and wound down Reginald's drive-way, out on to the road and down the quarter mile to the turn-off to the Yearly house. Nash parked further up the semi-circle drive-way in the spot Tish thought of as guest parking and everyone climbed out again.

"Hey Granddad," said Tish, pulling off her shoes and tossing them into the shoe basket by the door. "We're home!"

From the living room, Coats barked and then abruptly stopped as he realized who was coming in. He trotted into the hall, swaying from the vigor of his wagging tail, which doubled in speed when he saw Nash.

"Hey there!" said Tobias, following Coats.

Nash kicked off his boots into the basket and knelt down to pet Coats.

"I'm going to run upstairs and change," said Sarah.

"OK, you know where the guest room is?" asked Tish.

"Yup. Back in a jiff, as the Yearly's say."

"Did you get the dishwasher in at Reginald's?" asked Tobias, leaning on his cane.

"Well, we got it into the house," said Tish. "I'll get it into place and hooked up tomorrow."

"Sounds good," said Tobias nodding. "I just put the casserole in, so we've got a bit of time."

"Great," said Nash. "We can talk about whatever Tish found out at the H2O and doesn't want to discuss in public."

Tish and Tobias shared a look.

"And she obviously already told you about it. You know, I wasn't worried before, but this," he gestured between the two of them, "is not helping."

"It's not bad exactly," said Tish.

"Exactly? What does that mean?"

Tish looked to Tobias for help.

"Let's go into the living room," said Tobias. "No point in talking about things in the hall."

Nash glared at Tish, and she smiled apologetically. He shook his head and followed Tobias. Outside the floor to ceiling wall of windows the sun was setting over the peek-a-boo view of the water through the trees. Tish walked the length of the room, flicking on the lights, leaving pools of warm yellow light in her wake. Tobias lowered himself into an armchair and Nash flopped into the rocking chair. Tish began to gather up the discarded newspaper from the Chesterfield. Coats sat down next to Tobias and began to noisily lick himself until Tobias tapped him on the head.

"OK," said Nash. "Just tell me. Did someone see me there or what?"

"No," said Tish firmly. "No one saw you. But there was some-one else there."

"Yeah, at least one other person—the killer."

Tish looked at Tobias again and began to nervously roll the newspaper into a tube. "So, Tyler finished his set at 10:30 and told people that he was going out for a smoke."

"That's about when I got there," said Nash. "I walked over from Matt's and I saw him in the alley."

"What happened next?" asked Tobias, leaning forward.

"I told him I wasn't going to pay. He told me not to be stupid. I told *him* not to be stupid, because if Nora ever found out, she'd…"

"Kill him?" supplied Tobias.

"Those were the words I used. Which now seems in decidedly poor taste, I admit. But anyway, we yelled a bit more and then I left."

Tobias nodded. "Well," he said, and Tish found that her hands were clamped around a tight roll of newspaper. In the hall, she could hear Sarah coming down the stairs, and Tish moved to intercept her, but as she stood up there was a crash as the exterior door slammed against the wall and Sarah screamed.

Nash bolted upright and Coats tore into the hall barking. There was yelling and the room filled with men. Only Tobias sat still in his chair.

"Emmett Nash," yelled Detective Spring over Coats' barking. "You're under arrest!"

Tish raised her hand with the newspaper, preparing to bring it down on Detective Spring.

"Tish!" yelled Nash and Tobias at the same time. Tish brought the paper to a halt within inches of Detective Spring's head.

Coats also stopped barking. He knew very well what rolled up newspapers meant. The room was silent as everyone watched Tish and Detective Spring.

"Hands behind your back," said Detective Spring to Nash, still eyeing the newspaper.

"He gets to put his shoes on," said Tish, not moving the newspaper away from the detective's face.

Detective Spring reluctantly pulled his eyes away from the newspaper to Nash's feet. "Um. Yeah, OK," he said.

"I'll get them," said Sarah from the back of the room.

"Nash," said Tobias. "Don't say a damn word until your lawyer gets there. Don't worry. I'll call 'em."

Nash nodded. Sarah returned with Nash's shoes, edging her way around the police officers to hand them over.

"Also, Detective Spring," said Tobias, "I assume you have a warrant."

"I do," said Detective Spring smugly, holding a piece of paper out to Tobias.

"Give it to Tish," said Tobias. "We'll be sending it to our lawyers to review."

"It's an arrest warrant, not a search warrant," said Detective Spring, gritting his teeth, but handing over a piece of paper. "I have the right to pursue my suspect to where I can reasonably expect to find him."

"Uh-huh. And I suppose denting my plaster and tracking mud all over the carpet is just par for the course?"

Tish saw some of the police officers look with embarrassment at their boots and then at the beige carpet.

"If you're harboring a murderer, then yes, it is," snapped the Detective.

"I didn't do it," yelled Nash.

"Don't say anything," said Tobias.

"Well, I'm saying that," said Nash, impatiently, finishing the laces on his boots and standing up. "I didn't kill Tyler."

"Detective Spring," said Tish, "last summer when Granddad and I told you who killed Reginald and you blew us off, Nash supported you and the police process. It's so nice to see that the time he spent giving you the benefit of the doubt is being appreciated."

"This is a matter of evidence," said Detective Spring, but he didn't look at Nash.

"No, it's a matter of pig-headed blindness," said Tobias.

One of the police officers stepped forward with hand-cuffs. "Cyrus," said Tobias, "I swear if you make him put those on, I will black ball you across the San Juan's. There won't be a single craft fair that will take your wife's beach wood candlesticks. Although, lord knows, I don't understand why they do it now."

Cyrus shifted nervously and looked at Detective Spring.

"You know," said Nash, "if you wanted to arrest me, you could have just called me up and asked me to turn myself in."

Detective Spring's shoulders sagged.

Bullseye. You know damn well he would have done it.

"Fine," Spring said bitterly. "Cyrus, go put him in the car."

The police began to file out and Tobias held out a hand to Tish to help him up. She levered him out of the chair and they followed the police into the hall.

"I'm sending you the bill for carpet cleaning!" Tish yelled as the door swung shut.

"Well," said Tobias, "this is going to put a bit of a crimp in dinner."

"What are we going to do?" demanded Tish.

"What I said we would do—call Nash's lawyer."

"Does Nash even have a lawyer?" said Sarah.

"Yes, he does. Woman named Laura Carmichael."

"I've heard of her," said Sarah. "And I've seen her on the news."

"When did Nash hire her?" asked Tish.

"He didn't. I retained her on Tuesday when we went into the city. I asked around and Ms. Carmichael is apparently as good as they get, so I figured I should get her ready to go. Detective Spring's an idiot after all, and they don't generally grow extra brain cells overnight."

"Oh," said Tish, blinking.

"Anyway, they'll take Nash over to Anacortes to book him, so that will give her and us plenty of time to meet them over there."

"OK," said Tish, feeling slightly dumbfounded.

"This is better than *Matlock*," said Sarah.

"Thanks," said Tobias, looking pleased. "That's mighty kind."

CHAPTER 14

PORT OF ANACORTES

Tish sat on the bench in the Anacortes police department lobby and watched Tobias talk to Laura Carmichael. Laura turned out to be a fifty-ish woman with sensible shoes, a quietly stylish haircut, and a pantsuit.

"I've never actually been in a police station before," said Sarah looking around. Tish looked at the interior. The interior was blonde wood and taupe paint with maroon accents. It went well with the outside that Tish thought looked a bit like a 1990s mall—all cement walls, clean lines, tasteful stonework and metal awnings and roof. It had *approved by a committee* written all over it.

Laura was listening to Tobias intently and nodding, then she spoke a few words and Tobias beckoned to Tish.

"Ms. Carmichael, this is my granddaughter Tish. She spoke with the staff at the H2O."

"You're absolutely certain that the staff told the police about Nora Nash?" Laura Carmichael didn't waste time on the pleasantries.

"Nora Harlow," said Tish. "She's returned to her maiden name. And yes, the dishwasher told me that he and the waitress had been wondering who to call. They thought their identification of Ms. Harlow was important and they felt they had been dismissed by the detective."

Ms. Carmichael smiled and Tish thought it was at her delivery. Calm professional spokesperson had been one of her most frequent roles. "Excellent," she said. "Well, the good news is that we've actually beat Detective Spring here. Which means that I have time to make some calls. With any luck I can have these charges dismissed before he's even booked."

Tish took a deep breath. "What does that mean? It won't stay on his record, will it?"

"No, if the charges are dismissed the arrest won't appear on his record."

Tish wanted to ask if Laura really thought she could accomplish that, but instead she nodded. Ms. Carmichael did not seem like someone who made errant promises.

"Also, I'll want to take a closer look at the warrant that was issued." Tish held out the piece of paper as if her arm were on a spring. Ms. Carmichael smiled again. "We may have a leg to stand on with illegal entry depending on how it was worded. We'll see."

"Good to hear," said Tobias. "See if we can bill them for the carpet cleaning."

"Suing for damages may be an option," said Ms. Carmichael. "But you won't be able to simply invoice." Tobias clicked his tongue in disappointment. Ms. Carmichael looked amused. "All right, well I'm going to go to work. Please settle in. This may take a few hours. Nothing moves quickly in these situations."

"Thank you," said Tish smiling.

"It's my job," said Ms. Carmichael, which Tish didn't find particularly reassuring.

"So, we just wait?" asked Sarah, who'd been loitering in the background and pretending not to eavesdrop.

"Nope," said Tobias. "I just wait. You two are going to do some investigating while you're here."

"Really?" Sarah jumped up and down a little.

"What are we doing, Granddad?"

"Well, like you said, Nora Nash dumping Tyler in the dumpster seems a bit improbable. But she could have had help. And Jane Augestine is still a viable suspect. She was on the brawny side and had enough rage to make it happen. Then there's Tyler's sister Mary. She looked stringy, but she was tall like Tyler. She probably could have got him in the dumpster if she tried."

"Mary seemed genuinely upset," objected Tish.

"Crazy people frequently do," said Tobias. "I want you to pop down to the Port of Anacortes and see if any boats out of Orcas parked at the marina that night. They have a bunch of guest slips. That's the most likely place to tie up. And the port will keep records."

"Well, yeah, but they're not going to want to show them to us," said Tish.

"You're pretty girls," said Tobias. "I bet you can get a lot for a smile. And if that doesn't work," he fished in his pocket and pulled out a small wad of bills, "cash usually does the trick."

Tish took the pile of money, noting that it was mostly fifties and hundreds.

Where did he get that? I swear he doesn't keep that much cash on hand.

"OK," said Tish. "Do you also have some more business cards?"

He nodded and pulled a small stack out of his other pocket.

"Thanks," said Tish, taking them.

"And if you've still got time," said Tobias, "pop over to the ferry dock and ask them about Clover and Mary. I've hit most of the rest of the crews, but I haven't hit the weekend shift yet."

"You bet," said Sarah, beaming and snatching a few business cards out of Tish's hand. "You can count on us!"

"Thought I could," said Tobias, his eyes twinkling.

"I'll call if we get anything," said Tish and he nodded.

"This is awesome!" chirped Sarah as they went outside.

"It's busy work," said Tish, sorting through the cash. "To keep me from bludgeoning Detective Spring."

"Don't care," said Sarah. "Which one do you want to be: Cagney or Lacey?" Sarah caught Tish's expression. "Yes, I know, this is a very serious situation. Nash is in pretty hot water. I get it. But Laura Carmichael is like the hottest of the hot shots and she seemed pretty confident she could get him un-arrested or whatever. And meanwhile, you and your grandpa are like Crockett and Tubbsing it all over the place with the speed boat ride over here."

"Amber's boyfriend does like to drive fast," admitted Tish.

"Uh, yeah, I got that," said Sarah. "I think my hair still hasn't recovered. I'm just saying this is awesome. When you said he wanted to start a detective agency I thought it was code for old dudes hanging at a coffee shop. I didn't think you meant actually solving mysteries! And actually solving mysteries is the awesomest thing *ever*. I will finally be Encyclopedia Brown."

"I always wanted to be *Magnum P.I.*," said Tish.

"The moustache needs work," said Sarah, "but you do both look good in short-shorts, and you *do* live on an island."

"I'm going to need to invest in Hawaiian shirts," said Tish.

"You're getting one for Christmas," said Sarah. "But I'm not investing in any Dobermen. Dobermanns? What's the plural of Dobermann? I'm not being Higgins is what I'm saying."

Tish laughed and then impulsively hugged her friend. "Thanks for hanging with me on this."

"Ride or die, bitch," said Sarah cheerfully. "Now let's go sleuth the crap out of some stuff. And for the record, I'm Lacey."

"Sure," said Tish. "I can never tell which one is which anyway."

They drove Sarah's Honda back to the marina. They had paid at the guard shack for a guest slip and had been given a passcode for the keypad on the gate to the marina.

"Shouldn't we talk to the guard?" asked Sarah, as Tish made her way through the gate and onto the dock.

"I want to go back and talk to Kyle first," said Tish.

"The speedster that drove us over here? Why?"

"I had an idea."

They made their way back to where they had docked the boat and found Kyle heading down the dock toward them. He had peeled off his layers of rain gear that he'd been wearing on the ride over and was down to a normal Washington level of hooded rain jacket and jeans.

"Hey Tish!" he said, looking surprised. "Already going back? I was just going to head over to a bar and wait for you guys."

"No, not leaving yet. I wanted to ask you some questions."

"It's just recreational," he said automatically.

Tish rolled her eyes. "Kyle, I know you buy in bulk, remember?"

"Right," he said, looking guilty.

"But toward that end, what do you know about Matt Jones?"

"Don't mess with him," said Kyle. "I buy for personal use and sell a bit on the side. Matt is high-volume and exports out of state. He doesn't even sell on the island because he doesn't want to attract attention."

Which is why you can sell as much as you do.

"Do you know how to get in touch with him?"

"Why?" asked Kyle looking worried.

"Granddad or I need a word with him and I hear he's out of state. No trouble, no cops. We just need a word. Could you pass the message on?"

"I can try," said Kyle. "But I can't guarantee anything."

"That's fine. OK, next question: we want to find out if anyone from Orcas docked here last Sunday. I'm willing to toss a little cash at someone, but I don't know who to approach."

"And you know how it is with bribes," said Sarah trying to look tough. "Approach the wrong person and it could piss someone off."

Kyle shrugged. "I don't know about that. I take every bribe I'm offered. Not that I get offered that many. But yeah, um, well, that info would be in the visitor log book up at the gate."

"Could someone get out or park a boat without someone knowing?" asked Sarah.

"Park a... No. Not really. There's only one entrance. You saw how it's set up. You need a pass code to get in. Even if you left without the guard at the gate seeing you, you'd still have to get back in and they change the code every week."

"OK, so last Sunday if someone from Orcas... rented a slip?"

Tish guessed at the terminology.

"Close enough," said Kyle, with a grin.

"Then it would be on file up at the guard hut. So how do we get a look at that?"

"Go up and ask," said Kyle, with a shrug. "That's the best I can tell you."

"All right," said Tish, with a shrug. "Let's go give it a try."

"OK," said Sarah, her eyes looking a little big. "We're really doing this."

They all trooped up to the guard shack and Tish knocked on the door. Inside the small office a thick-set woman in a private security uniform stood up and opened the door.

"Can I help you?" she asked, looking at the three of them skeptically.

"Hi," said Tish, holding out one of her grandfather's business cards, "I'm Tish Yearly. I'm with Yearly Investigations. We're looking into a crime that occurred in Anacortes last Sunday."

"K," said the woman, her eyebrow raising even higher.

"We were wondering if any boats out of Orcas rented a guest slip last Sunday."

"That information is confidential," she said, crossing her arms over her chest.

OK, time to nut up. Let's give this a whirl.

"Is it fifty dollars confidential or a hundred dollars confidential?" asked Tish.

"Hundred," said the woman, uncrossing her arms.

Tish had placed the hundreds in one pocket and the fifties in the other and she reached in and snapped out the bill. The woman looked reluctantly impressed. But she grabbed a yellow bill check marker off the desk and ran it over the hundred.

"Give me a minute," the guard said, when the mark turned to the amber of real money. She went to a computer and typed in a series of commands. Moments later the printer next to the desk spewed out a sheet of paper.

"This is all of the boats out of Orcas for the last week," she said. "Arrival date in the first column. Then leaving date, slip number, registered name, registered owner and number of occupants."

"Perfect," said Tish. "Thanks."

"Anytime," said the guard, tucking the hundred into her pocket.

"That was awesome," said Kyle, climbing into Sarah's Honda with them. "What are we doing next?"

"I screwed it up," said Tish, flipping on the overhead light and peering at the sheet. "I should have just offered fifty."

"Shut up," said Sarah. "You're always so self-critical. Kyle's right. You did awesome."

"Yeah, but I just paid a hundred bucks for five names. None of which I recognize."

"Let me see," said Kyle from the backseat, holding out a hand. Tish handed over the list. "This one is that old guy over in Olga."

"That describes fifty percent of Olga," said Tish.

"The one with the weird saw art in his yard," clarified Kyle.

"Oh, sure," said Sarah, rolling her eyes, "that guy."

"These two are fishing boats. They make this run all the time. This Craig Larson guy—*Doctor's Note*—no clue who he is, but he was here on Sunday at the right time. This one—the *Yada Yachta*—she's out of Deer Harbor, owned by a guy that does road crew stuff for the county."

"Mm," said Tish. "I was really hoping this would lead to something. But none of those sound like promising suspects."

"Well, it's possible that it was just a mugging gone wrong," said Sarah. "It doesn't have to have been someone on Orcas."

"It was personal," said Tish. "You don't stab someone six times unless you really want them dead."

"Don't see why you would stab them at all," said Kyle. "Why not shoot him?"

"Didn't have a gun?" suggested Sarah.

"Who doesn't have a gun?" asked Kyle.

"Well, I don't for starters," said Sarah.

"Yeah, but if you wanted to kill someone, wouldn't you go get one?"

Sarah looked flummoxed.

"Kyle's right," said Tish.

"That seems unlikely," said Sarah, instantly.

"No, think about it. If you wanted to kill someone could you find a gun?"

"Find, no. But I could probably go buy one. But I'd be worried that they would track it back to me."

"They don't have ballistics on every gun that's made. You just have to dispose of the gun once you've used it and report it as stolen. No one's ever going to find it if you dump it in the middle of the ocean. And you know, half the vacation homes on the island probably have a gun in them somewhere. Stabbing someone means that you either wanted to use a knife or you grabbed the first thing that came to hand. One is impulsive and the other is trying to send a message." Kyle looked impressed. Sarah looked perturbed. "The dishwasher at the H2O said they found a knife in the dumpster. Now that I'm thinking about it, I want to know more about the knife. Was it one from the restaurant? If it was, then it was definitely someone who was in the bar that night. If it wasn't, then it tells us something about the killer."

"So, we're going to the H2O?" Sarah asked clapping her hands together.

"I'm in," said Kyle.

"No," said Tish. "I can see the ferry's almost in. I want to ask the crew about Clover Augestine."

"She's my Sunday morning coming down," said Kyle.

"What does that mean?" asked Sarah.

"Every Sunday morning, I take her some weed," said Kyle. "For a while there I was worried because she got herself a pot plant, but I think she killed it and now we're back on like regular. Pretty sure she and some dude with a man bun get high and bone."

"Man bun, really?" Tish rolled her eyes.

"I don't know," said Kyle. "He seems OK. He had some super advice on how to prolong a high. He said he learned it in school."

"Yeah, well, I learned how to make a pumpkin hookah in school," said Sarah. "That doesn't make me a genius."

Kyle grinned. "Maybe not but it makes you fun at a Halloween party."

"It was pretty fun," admitted Sarah, "but that's not the point."

"Poor Clover," said Tish. "She has got to start picking better dudes."

"Poor Clover?" asked Sarah. "Isn't she the one you said tried to cut off her boyfriend's junk after she caught him getting a Lewinski from the doorman?"

"No!" exclaimed Kyle.

"Well, yes," said Tish. "But I can't say I blame her. Anyway, let's go talk to the ferry crew and then we'll hit the H2O and hope that Nash is out of the pokey by then."

"I can't believe I'm on Team Nash," said Kyle shaking his head.

"Don't be a jerk," said Tish. "You don't want to be on the Empire side."

"Yeah, Kyle," said Sarah, starting the car. "Don't be a stormtrooper."

"I'm not!" exclaimed Kyle. "I'm totally a Han Solo. I'm helping. Haven't I helped?"

"Yeah, you've helped," agreed Tish. "How about helping a little more? Between the three of us we can cover a lot more of the ferry crew."

"Yeah, all right," said Kyle. "But you're buying me a beer at the H2O."

"Done," said Tish.

The rain had kicked up by the time the ferry had come in and the crew wasn't particularly interested in talking to them, but on the third guy Tish heard Sarah yelling at her. She jogged across the dock, watching her footing on the slick wood.

"What's up?" asked Tish, approaching Sarah and a burly ferry worker.

"This guy just changed shifts, from the weekend," said Sarah. "He says he's seen Clover a lot."

"Yeah," said the man. "Every Sunday for the last three months. She leaves on the 7:20 and then comes back on the first ferry on Monday morning. I think she sleeps in her car. She's always first in line."

"Where the hell is she going?" asked Tish.

"Dunno," said the ferry worker, "but you all have to get off my boat. It's unsafe and you're not authorized personnel."

"Thanks," said Tish. "We're leaving."

She waved at Kyle and they all trooped back to the car.

"Well," said Sarah, "we've successfully proved that known knife-wielder and Tyler hater Clover Augestine was in Anacortes on Sunday. Now what?"

"Bar time?" asked Kyle hopefully.

"Yeah," said Tish. "I guess so. I can't think of what else to do."

The trip to the H2O was short and the interior was loud with patrons participating in a trivia night. Kyle, Sarah, and Tish sat at the bar of the H2O and dripped.

"It's weird how you don't feel that wet until you get somewhere dry," said Sarah.

"Yup," said Kyle, taking a long draft of beer. His phone jangled and he checked it. "Hey Tish, can you text Amber and tell her you're with me? She's flipping out and thinks I'm making shit up."

"It's that last dingus boyfriend of hers," said Tish. "She doesn't trust people anymore."

"I know. He cheated on her, yeah, yeah. Asshole or whatever. But why I gotta make up for it?"

"Just take a selfie," said Sarah.

Kyle complied and Tish and Sarah wedged themselves into frame. Moments later, he laughed at an incoming message. "She says we look like drowned rats."

"I definitely feel like a drowned mammal of some kind," said Sarah.

"Hey! Detective chick," said Boleslav, coming into the bar area with a dish tub.

"Hey Boleslav," said Tish.

"Thought you said you wouldn't be back tonight?"

"The situation evolved," said Tish.

"Into standing around in the rain?" he asked.

"Something like that," said Tish. "Is Jacy working tonight?"

"Yeah, I'll send her over. Give me a minute to run these back."

"You know, rain aside," said Kyle. "This is a pretty good Friday night—we bribed some people, ran around on a ferry boat, which they usually never let you do, and now we're at a bar. Maybe Amber's right. Maybe I do need to hang out with some non-potheads."

"One or two wouldn't hurt," said Sarah. "It always pays to keep your friend group varied. It expands your marketing pool if nothing else. In your line of work, I imagine you rely on word of mouth, so having a wider network of acquaintances would really only benefit you."

"That is such a good point," he said nodding.

"Sarah, stop offering marketing advice to the pot dealer," said Tish.

"Marketing applies to all businesses," said Sarah, sipping her margarita.

"You're a private investigator?"

Tish found herself being addressed by a perky looking black girl in an H2O t-shirt. "A very wet one at the moment," said Tish, holding out a business card, "but yes. You're Jacy?"

Jacy nodded, looking amused. "What can I help you with?

Boleslav said he told you a bunch of stuff this afternoon."

"I wanted to ask you about the redhead, the knife, and if you saw this woman here that night?" Tish held out the picture of Clover on her phone.

"Nope," said Jacy, shaking her head. "Never seen her before."

"Aside from the redhead, did anyone else ask about Tyler that night?"

"A bunch of people," said Jacy. "They all wanted to know when he was coming on, etc. He's played with us before. He has a pretty rabid fan base. The redhead stuck out though because she didn't look like a fan girl—she looked pissed."

"See?" said Sarah.

Tish made a shushing gesture. "Boleslav said the police recovered a knife. Did you get a chance to see it?"

"They showed it to me," Jacy said with a shrug. "They wanted to know if I'd seen it before. Or if Tyler had been carrying it."

"Was it a knife from here?" asked Tish and Jacy shook her head again.

"No, it was a pocket knife. I guess. It was kind of wicked looking."

"Like this kind?" asked Kyle, flicking out a knife. It had a four or five-inch blade that was partially serrated. It was exactly the kind of thing that three-fourths of the population of Orcas carried.

"Kyle! Seriously!" snapped Sarah.

"We do not bust out with weaponry in public," said Tish.

"Sorry," said Kyle. "Just trying to clarify."

Jacy chuckled. "Yeah, it was more like that. But it had a blue handle. Like, bright royal blue."

Shit. Shit. Shit. Shit.

"Oh," said Tish.

Hold it in. Hold it in.

"OK, well, thank you for your time," said Tish. "Um, we have to go now."

"We do?" asked Sarah. Kyle simply began gulping his beer.

"Yes," said Tish. "We do." She handed Jacy a fifty. "Keep the change. Come on," she said sliding off her barstool.

Sarah and Kyle followed her with twin expressions of confusion, but she refused to acknowledge their questions until they were back in the car.

"What just happened?" asked Sarah, starting the car.

"Was the knife thing a clue?"

"Yeah," said Tish. "Sort of."

"What do you mean?"

"I know why the cops have been looking at Nash so hard."

"OK, I'll play," said Kyle. "Why?"

"Because that's Nash's knife."

CHAPTER 15

ANACORTES POLICE DEPARTMENT

Tish took the stairs to the front door of the police department two at a time and pushed through the door while Kyle and Sara were still on the sidewalk.

Tobias was leaning on the front desk chatting up the officer at the front desk and drinking a cup of coffee. She made eye contact and he nodded slightly. It took another minute to disentangle himself from the conversation.

"What's up?" he asked, coming over. Sarah and Kyle arrived, panting slightly.

Tish leaned close to his good ear and spoke at what she hoped was a level that was audible to him, but not to anyone else. "Last summer, Nash had a pocket knife. It had a custom bright blue handle."

Tobias nodded.

"I'm pretty sure it's the murder weapon and I'm pretty sure Detective Spring would have seen him with it when they were working on Reginald's case."

Tobias nodded again. "Any idea when he stopped carrying it?" he asked. "Or why?"

"I think before Claire went back to school, but I'm not sure. And I'm not sure about why either. My impression is that he lost it."

"But not recently. It's been a few months?"

"Yes," said Tish, confidently.

Tobias itched his nose and sniffed thoughtfully. "OK. Can you figure out how to email or text or whatever all that to Ms. Carmichael if I have the information?"

"Yes," said Tish.

Tobias patted his pockets until he came up with a business card and handed it over to Tish. And Tish typed it into her phone as a text and then, just to be sure sent it in an email as well.

"How bad is this?" asked Sarah as Tish typed.

"I'm not sure that it is," said Tobias. "We'll have to wait and see. Meanwhile, I'm going to go cozy up to the desk sergeant some more. Let me know if you get a response."

Kyle looked around the police department nervously. "I'm not sure I want to wait here," he said.

"You can wait in the car," said Sarah, "but you can't light up."

"No point then," he said dropping down onto the bench.

Tish nervously switched hands on her phone.

"I don't get it," said Sarah. "So, we have one suspect we know was there. And as the ex, I'm pretty sure she could have, you know," she lowered her voice, "acquired the weapon. But we don't think she did it?"

"She's tiny," said Kyle. "I'm not sure she could lift a dead body."

"Exactly," said Tish, checking the phone again.

"OK," said Sarah, nodding. "But our other suspect, who we know is a bit on the stabby side, was definitely on the mainland last Sunday, and probably could have done it, didn't have access to the weapon."

"Sure she did," said Kyle. "I heard they were knocking boots."

"They only went on two and a half dates," objected Tish.

"Yeah," agreed Kyle, with a shrug. "So?"

"Oh my," said Sarah.

I will punch him in the face.

"OK," said Tish calmly, "then we have two viable suspects."

Her phone buzzed in her hand and Tish nearly dropped it.

THANKS. IT'S UNDER CONTROL.

"What does that mean?" asked Sarah, standing up to read over Tish's shoulder.

"I don't know," said Tish, taking a deep breath and letting it out slowly.

He has a right to date other people. He should date other people. I am not mad about that. That would be ridiculous.

Tobias ambled back over. "Everything A-OK?

But we talked about her and he didn't say they slept together.

"She says everything is under control," said Tish. "So, everything is fine." She added her calm spokesperson smile.

The door between the public and private areas of the police station slammed open and Detective Spring stomped through. He pulled up short when he saw Tish and Tobias.

"You!" he barked, pointing a finger at them. "This is your fault."

"Yes," said Tobias, grinning. "I'm quite sure it is."

"You think you're so much smarter than everyone?" he demanded, stalking forward.

"Not everyone," said Tobias. "Just you."

"If you think I won't arrest a seventy-five-year-old for obstruction and interfering in a police investigation, you've got another think coming."

"Seventy-eight," said Tobias. "And go ahead and give it a whirl. I've got nothing but time to make court appearances and a lawyer or six on speed dial."

Detective Spring literally growled in frustration and then he looked at Tish. "You get him under control or I'll arrest you too."

"That's ageism," said Tish. "He's not a pet. Also, I feel threatened."

"What?"

"Oh my God," said Tish, raising her voice and wavering it. "Are you threatening us?"

The front desk sergeant looked horrified and came out from behind the desk. Tobias sank down over his cane and tried to look more feeble. Behind him the door opened, and Nash and Laura Carmichael came through, escorted by another man.

"What did we ever do to you?" continued Tish. She added an extra throb at the end as if she was going to cry. "You stay away from my grandfather! What's wrong with you? He's an old man."

Detective Spring realized what she was doing and his face twisted in impotent fury. "I hate you," he said. "I hate both of you."

"OK, Detective Spring," said the desk sergeant. "Maybe we should, um, go somewhere else." He pulled the detective by the elbow. "We apologize profusely and of course, we have nothing but respect for you and your grandfather," he said, as he pushed the detective away. Tobias waved.

"Chief," said Laura Carmichael. "This clearly shows a pattern of harassment toward my client and his friends. The next time something like this occurs we will be filing lawsuits against your department and against Detective Spring personally.

"I assure you Ms. Carmichael," said the Chief, "that Detective Spring will be reprimanded. He does not speak for this department."

"First and last warning Chief," said Ms. Carmichael and swept out the door. The rest of the party followed hurriedly—trying not to ruin her exit.

"That was cute," said Ms. Carmichael, turning to Tish when they were all outside. "But don't push your luck. It won't play twice. And let's be perfectly clear," she surveyed the group, "they're not going to stop. The next time they come at us, they're going to be certain. If you're going to come up with additional evidence, you'd better do it soon. I'll be in touch." She nodded to both Tobias and Nash and walked away, heading for a BMW in the parking lot.

"Well," said Tobias, "I guess we have our marching orders."

"God," said Kyle, "I need a joint."

"Yeah," said Sarah. "I know what you mean."

Nash didn't say anything.

He's not even arguing. He should be arguing.

CHAPTER 16

SATURDAY - BACK ON ORCAS

Tish opened the door and stared at Nash in surprise. The previous night they had all barely spoken a word and Nash had looked too dejected to yell at.

"Are we not working on Reginald's today?" He looked like he had barely slept.

"No, we totally are," said Tish. "I just didn't expect you."

"Well, it's either this or stay home and get black out drunk. And these days it feels like I need an alibi all the time, so I thought staying home was probably a bad plan."

Tish restrained the impulse to hug him.

"Come on in. Sarah's not ready yet. Do you want some coffee?" He shook his head and eyed the shoe bin. "Don't worry about it," said Tish. "You can't screw up the carpet any more than they already did."

"I'll help clean that," he said heading for the living room.

"Don't worry about it," said Tish. "I'm pretty sure that a shop vac and maybe a steam clean and it will be fine. Mostly I was pissed because they didn't even think about it."

"They were doing their jobs," he said.

"Yeah, their job doesn't mean they have to be assholes."

He shrugged awkwardly. Tish began to look for the newspaper. She wanted to see if Nash's arrest had made the local paper. "You know," she said as she lifted up a cushion, "this would have been a lot easier if you'd told us the murder weapon was your knife."

"I didn't know it was my knife," he said. "They never even asked me about it. I lost that knife over the summer. I don't even know where."

I will not laugh derisively. I will not laugh derisively.

"Yeah," said Tish, "but you had a pretty good idea, didn't you?"

"What?"

She stared at him.

Just admit it!

He stared back.

"Clover Augestine's bedroom?" she suggested. He looked surprised, as if he really hadn't considered that's where he left it, but not surprised at the idea that he would sleep with Clover. "You could have mentioned that you slept with her when we were talking about her the first time."

"We were eating lunch with your grandfather. So, no, I could not have."

Oh, God, you really did.

"You should have told me." Tish went back to looking for the newspaper, if only because it allowed her to fling pillows around. She heard the front door open again, and assumed it was Tobias coming back in.

"Why would I do that?" he demanded, apparently oblivious to the door.

"It was crucial information!" snapped Tish.

"No, it really wasn't!"

"Tish, what are you looking for?" asked Tobias, walking into the room followed closely by Greg.

"The newspaper!" yelled Tish.

"Why?" demanded Tobias.

"So she can hit me with it!" yelled Nash and yanked open the sliding door out to the porch. He stomped outside, slammed the door shut and they all watched him walk along the porch and around the corner of the house.

"For two people who generally get along you spend a lot of time yelling at each other," said Tobias.

"Yes, well he's stubborn and I'm argumentative," said Tish.

"You sure it's not the other—you know what, never mind. Greg's here." Greg looked as if he was trying not to be smug about Nash stomping off.

"Yes," she said. "I can see that. Hi!" She kissed him and then stepped back, frowning at him. "Sweetie, you do know it's Saturday, right? I mean, you always look good in a suit, but... Saturday."

"This is actually my lunch break," he said.

"It's eight-thirty in the morning," said Tish.

"I hopped a ride with a guy who was going out to Friday Harbor. He dropped me off at the airstrip and I have to meet him back there in about," he checked his watch, "forty-five minutes."

"He was in a helicopter," said Tobias. "I went to pick him up. You were in the shower."

"Ah," said Tish. "Well, it's always nice to see you. Even if it is for forty-five minutes. Do you need breakfast for your lunch break? I was about to make waffles."

He grinned. "Love some."

They headed into the kitchen and Tish paused to yell up the stairs to Sarah that breakfast was commencing.

"What did you find out?" asked Tobias, settling in at the kitchen table. "I'm assuming you got something, otherwise, you would have just phoned."

"Autopsy report," said Greg dropping a stack of papers on the table in front of Tobias. Tish filled the waffle iron and closed the lid.

"Highlights?" she asked.

"Stabbed seven times with a four-and-a-half-inch blade. Wounds are consistent with the weapon recovered at the scene," said Greg.

Tobias and Tish both made a grunt of dissatisfaction and Tish checked the timer light on the waffle iron. Greg looked torn between amusement and annoyance. "One interesting item is that all of the stab wounds are angled upward," he added.

"What does that mean?" asked Tish.

"It means that the killer probably held the knife in one hand, low at one side and jabbed upward." Greg stood up to demonstrate on Tish. She was about to comment when the light flicked off on the iron. She paused to flip out the waffles and popped them onto a plate, putting it down on the table in front of Greg. She moved the butter closer to him and pulled the syrup out of the cupboard. It was a bottle of homemade blackberry syrup that she'd picked up in exchange for some of granddad's junk.

"The wounds were single strikes and clean," said Tobias, reading from the report. "No wiggling around or having to work for it," he clarified for Tish's sake.

"Got it," said Tish.

This sounds less and less like Nora Nash. Why can't it have been her?

"Interesting though," said Tobias. "There was marijuana residue in the wounds. What does that mean?"

I am a horrible person. Claire would be equally devastated if her mom killed someone.

"Most likely speculation was that the knife was used to cut pot."

"That's more proof Nash didn't do it, then," said Tobias. "He never touches the stuff. Unlike some people."

I swear twice in one year is not exactly a pot habit.

"We're looking for a pot user, then," said Tish, ignoring the jab about her pot use. "That only covers about half the island. Although, it does at least include Clover."

"What makes you say that?" asked Tobias looking up.

"Who's Clover?" asked Greg.

"Clover is the event coordinator for the Doe Bay Blues Festival. She hired Tyler to headline the second stage and he no-showed, which meant that she had to refund tickets and that cost her a bonus. She hated Tyler with a passion and she was on the mainland at the time of death and she buys pot off…someone local every Sunday."

Greg doesn't need to know about Kyle.

"And she went on a couple of dates with Nash earlier in the

summer," continued Tish. "She would have had access to the murder weapon. Not that I can prove that yet."

"Wait, what? The murder weapon belonged to Nash?" Greg paused with a forkful of waffle mid-way to his mouth.

"He lost it over the summer," said Tobias, as Tish set down a plateful of waffles in front of him.

"OK, yeah, but," Greg looked from Tobias to Tish and back, "shouldn't we at least consider that maybe…"

"Maybe what?" asked Tobias, slathering butter onto his waffles.

"Well, that maybe Nash killed the guy. I mean, Reich ran off with his wife, was trying to run off with his kid. There's a lot of people who wouldn't take too kindly to that."

"Except that he wasn't," said Tish. "Tyler had papers that would have given sole custody of Claire to Nash. Why kill Tyler if there was even half a chance of getting sole custody?"

"Why would Tyler have papers? They'd have to be signed by the ex-wife, not him."

"Tyler told Nash that he'd get Nora to sign over custody if Nash paid him ten thousand dollars," said Tish.

"Only Nash doesn't have that kind of cash," said Tobias.

"It's a bigger motive for Nora, if you think about it," said Tish. "If Nora found out that Tyler had been lying to her or had even gotten her to sign paperwork giving up Claire, she'd be plenty pissed. And Nash picked up Claire at her place multiple times over the summer. She could have had access to his knife at any time. And the fact that she was there that night makes her even more suspicious."

"That actually does make sense," said Greg, finishing his bite of waffle with a thoughtful expression.

"But there's still the dumpster," said Tobias.

"Dumpster?" asked Greg.

"Getting Tyler's body into the dumpster seems improbable for someone of Nora's size," said Tish, pouring another batch of waffles. "And Boleslav the dishwasher did not recall her being covered in blood, which she would have been if she'd lifted Tyler into the dumpster."

"OK," said Greg, "Here's a question. Where are these custody papers? They weren't on the body. I'm assuming the police searched Nash's house?"

"Yes," said Tish. "Last Thursday. They didn't take anything."

Greg drummed his fingers on the table. "They may not know about the custody agreement. Nora's lawyers wouldn't exactly volunteer information."

"There's no indication that Nora knows what Tyler was up to," said Tobias. "She thought Nash was keeping the kid while they moved and then bringing her down once they were settled."

"And she bought that? Nobody does that. Not with joint custody."

"I suspect," said Tish, "that she believed what she wanted to believe."

"Mm," said Tobias, waving his fork at Tish in agreement, with his mouth full of waffle.

"Well, either way you slice it, it seems like someone might want to drop a word in the ear of the investigating detective."

"I don't think that Detective Spring cares to have our opinions at this juncture," Tish said, gloomily. "Also, he is aware that Nora was there that night and he chose to ignore it."

It was Greg's turn to grunt in dissatisfaction.

"Well," said Tobias, "I imagine he'll be talking to her soon. He looked like he was going to get an earful from his boss. He'll probably talk to her just so he can prove he was right the first time in excluding her as a suspect."

"Doesn't matter," said Tish. "I'm pretty sure the dumpster discounts her. Spring should really be talking to Clover and I'm not even sure she's on his radar."

"Well," said Tobias, looking at his waffles as if they were a magic eight ball.

"Oh," said Greg, interrupting whatever answer the waffles might have given, "I did look into the rehab center, by the way."

"Yay, waffles!" said Sarah, coming in time to be handed a plate. Tish smothered a smile at her friend's striped overalls. "And Greg! Did I know Greg was going to be here?"

"Hey Sarah," said Greg, with a grin. Tish could see him also appreciating Sarah's idea of work clothes. "No, I'm doing the proverbial drop-by unannounced."

"He flew in on a helicopter," said Tish.

"Well, la-di-dah," said Sarah. "So fancy."

"Now what about the commune?" asked Tobias.

"It's fully licensed by the state. Has about twenty or thirty patients a year. Mostly funded by Medicaid."

"That don't make sense," said Tobias. "Mary Sunshine said they only took patients in the summer."

Greg shrugged. "Don't know what to tell you. On paper they look fine. The director is fully certified as a Chemical Dependency Specialist. Which isn't top of the heap, but it's a decent certification. All their Medicaid paperwork is up to date. Nothing suspicious."

"Medicaid paperwork?" asked Tish. "What's Medicaid got to do with it?"

"Most court mandated rehab is usually paid through a combination of insurance and Medicaid," said Greg. "Which is why it's important to have a director who can navigate all the paperwork."

"They're probably familiar because they're a commune," said Tobias sourly.

"What?" asked Sarah. Tish felt equally lost.

"No one who lives on a commune is doing real work," said Tobias. "It's all very well to say alternative lifestyle, like they're out there surviving off the land, but the truth is that most of them are on disability of some kind. The tax payers are paying for their alternative lifestyle choices."

"Then we should pay them some more," said Tish. "That place

looked terrible."

"No, we should cut them off and make them get real jobs. Stop being a socialist!"

"Stop being a Paul Ryan!"

"Is it just me, or does that twerp look like Eddie Munster?" asked Tobias.

"He really does," agreed Tish.

Sarah choked on one of her waffles and Greg was quietly laughing into his coffee cup.

"Who is the director of the commune?" asked Tobias, ignoring their amusement.

Greg pulled a notebook out of his pocket and checked the name. "Some guy named Craig Larson."

"Why does that sound familiar?" asked Tish, pouring out another batch of waffles.

Sarah made a meep of excitement around a mouthful of waffle. She grabbed Tobias's coffee and took a gulp. "*Doctor's Note!*"

"What?" asked Greg.

"Last night! We…" Sarah paused to look at Tish and then back at Greg, "happened to see a list of boats that were in Anacortes last Sunday night. One of them was owned by Craig Larson."

"Happened to see?" repeated Greg. "You know what? I don't want to know."

"That brings us back to Mary Sunshine," said Tobias. "I don't know what her motivation would be for wanting her brother dead, but if the commune has a boat then she could have gone across, stabbed him and gone back."

"How'd she get Nash's knife?" asked Greg.

"Also, who the hell is Craig Larson?" asked Tish.

"I don't know," said Greg, checking his watch. "But it sounds like I should run both him and Clover through the system when I get back to the office." He stood up. "I should get back to the airstrip."

"Let me get my keys," said Tobias.

"I'll drive you back," said Tish, just as the waffle iron light flicked off.

"No," he said, "you stay—eat your own waffles." He waited until Tobias was out of the room before kissing her more fully than they had previously.

Tish smiled as she put her waffles onto a plate and then poured another batch for Nash.

"How do you end up with all the cutest boys?" asked Sarah as the front door swung shut.

"I hang out with more than engineers and architects," said Tish, sitting down at the table.

"There are some cute engineers and architects," objected Sarah.

"None of whom you'll date because you won't date people from work. And that just leaves the Amazon hipster freaks."

"I really can't date them," said Sarah. "They all have personality deficiency disorder. What do we do next?"

Tish's phone burbled with a text. She read it and read it again.

"Well, first we take apology waffles over to Nash up at Reginald's. And then I have to go shopping for everything on the list he just sent me because apparently getting in a fight does not necessarily mean that he stops doing work for me."

Sarah laughed. "Was that the yelling a little bit ago? Well, you're still trying to solve Tyler's murder. Getting in a fight didn't change that."

"Well, that's different," said Tish. "That's mostly Granddad. And besides that's not exactly hard labor. Meanwhile, who wants to help build a kitchen for a business they have nothing to do with?"

"Friends might," suggested Sarah.

"Well, yes," said Tish, "but you're invested and you have previously stated that you are guided by the Ride or Die principle. I have had plenty of friends who wouldn't help with this kind of thing."

"I would suggest that you have not," said Sarah.

"What? What's that supposed to mean?"

"I mean, that having listened to your tales of California, I am not convinced that you had very many actual friends. You had a very large range of acquaintances who could be relied on about twelve percent of the time. It has made you incredibly self-reliant, but also secretly worried every time I help you with something that I'm not really going to do it or that I expect something in return."

Tish stared at Sarah.

"I don't like it when you're insightful," she said at last.

"Well, OK, but you might want to consider my point when it comes to Nash. He doesn't understand why you won't behave like a normal trusting human being."

Because I'm not a normal trusting human being?

CHAPTER 17
APOLOGY WAFFLES

Tish put the plate of waffles into the room first and only put her head around the edge of the door when she heard Nash laugh.

"They're apology waffles," said Tish, as he took the plate out of her hands. "You were right. You can't really mention sex in front of Granddad. I'm just pissed that we were ambushed with the knife."

"I'm not any happier about it," he said, cutting into the waffles with the provided fork, leaning against the counter. He was wearing a tool belt like he actually owned it and a grubby pair of Carhartt's. "It also never occurred to me that I lost it at Clover's. Although, now that you've brought it up, that is the right time frame. On the other hand, it could have been anywhere. It had a loose belt clip that I'd been meaning to replace. When it disappeared, I figured it would turn up somewhere along one of my usual routes." He looked around suddenly, as if missing something. "Where's Sarah?"

"She couldn't get ready fast enough," lied Tish. "I'm going to pick her up on the way out to Eastsound so I can get your list of supplies."

Actually, she said she thought apology waffles were best delivered alone, but you don't need to know that.

"What about Greg?" he asked.

Was that sarcastic voice?

"He had to go back to work. Besides, he couldn't possibly help—he would get his suit dirty."

"I wasn't going to comment," said Nash. Then he pointed to the counter. "I found your binder." Tish felt herself begin to pink up. It was possible that she had gone overboard on the project organization, but it made her feel more in control. "You've done a really good job," he said looking around the kitchen.

"Yeah," said Tish, seeing each unfinished project and flaw. "I hope I can get it done by Christmas."

"What happens at Christmas?"

"I have to sign up for all the wedding expos in December. And they are not cheap—I have the registration money reserved to sign up. But every time I turn around the kitchen costs more money. It's possible that I'll need the reserve to finish the kitchen. If I sign up with an unfinished kitchen, then maybe I could book someone. On the other hand, if I don't have a catering ready venue, then there's kind of no point in booking anyone. So basically, if I don't have a finished kitchen by the time I have to sign up for the expos, then I'm going to have to go get a real job."

"Ask Tobias for the money."

"No!" snapped Tish. Then took a deep breath. "No," she said more calmly. "He's already given me a bunch of cash, free rent, and free run of the property. I can't ask him for more."

He took another bite of waffle, looking at her thoughtfully. "Sarah's right," he said. "You really can't ask people for help."

"I can," she said. "I just don't like owing people."

"You know this is one of the reasons for living on Orcas," he said, "is if I call up my neighbor, he comes over and helps. He doesn't think I owe him later."

"Yes, he does," said Tish. "You're right. It is very Orcas to come over and help. But the expectation is that at some point in the future they will need help and you'll be there. But I can't guarantee that I will be here, can I? And I won't take advantage of people. What if I have to get a job and leave the island then what will people think about Granddad?"

Nash burst out laughing. "You're an idiot. I mean, you're very smart, but you're being an idiot."

"Hey! I will take my waffles back!"

He moved the plate further away from her and shoveled more waffle in his face. "I thought it was obvious, since you were hanging out with me," he said around a mouthful of food.

"Clearly," said Tish and he grinned.

"Tish, do you think no one notices the fact that Tobias can stand up straight for the first time in five years?"

"I made him get a new cane."

"Or that you can walk through his front hallway without turning sideways. Or the cubic ton of crap you've removed from his house."

"That was all the stuff from the hallway," said Tish.

"Even if we didn't like you, we still like Tobias. And we would pitch in simply based on the fact that he is weathering Reginald's death pretty well because of you."

"He manages on his own," said Tish.

"Yes, he was managing on his own. But he's managing better with you around. And he's got more than a few chips in the bank that could be cashed in. No one is going to think badly of either of you if you asked for help."

"You think?" asked Tish.

"Yes. I do."

"Sarah says I should let friends do things."

"She's very smart," he said.

She looked around the kitchen. "Is there someone particular I should be cashing in?"

"Nah," he said. "You've done all the hard stuff already."

She glared at him. "Then what are you giving me crap for?"

"Because if the business takes off you're going to need to expand your septic," he said, a smile hovering on his face. "I'm trying to make a point for the future."

"That assumes I'm even going to make it that far," said Tish gloomily.

"You're going to make it." He said it with such confidence that Tish found herself actually believing him.

"Really? Please don't joke around or be nice—it will only give me false hope. Do you really think I can make it?"

"Yes," said Nash. "We'll get the dry wall up and the dishwasher in and then that just leaves you the backsplash around the sink, right?"

"Well, in here yes. There's a bunch of painting and stuff to do. But in order to open, the kitchen is what needs to happen."

"Well, you've got enough on hand to get me started. If you and Sarah grab the stuff on the list I sent, then we should be able to get a good chunk of it done this weekend. As long as I don't go to prison, you'll be in business."

"I should talk to Clover again," said Tish.

"You should not," he said.

"You want me to keep you out of prison, but you never want me to actually investigate."

"That's because I don't want you to die," he said.

"I'm not going to die. None of these women are batshit crazy like Steve Winslow. And, now that I've had to deal with Steve Winslow, I have learned that when investigating I should not turn my back on a suspect. So, problem solved."

"Unless they stab you from the front like they did Tyler."

"You just have to argue about everything, don't you?"

"Only when I'm right."

"I'm going now. I hope the waffles make you gassy."

He was still laughing when she shut the door.

So he slept with Clover, so what? God knows I wouldn't want anyone knowing about half the people I've slept with. The sad part is I really think she might be the killer and I still like her better than Nora.

CHAPTER 18
NORA & SUNSHINE

Tish jogged the short quarter mile home and popped into the house.

"Ready to go?" she yelled, grabbing the truck keys off the hook in the hall.

"Yup," said Sarah, coming out of the kitchen. "How'd the waffles go?"

"Fine," said Tish. "He says you're very smart."

"I'm effing brilliant," said Sarah pulling on her jacket. "What does he think I'm smart about?"

"Oh, the asking for help and relying on friends thing."

"Oh, that. Yeah, see, I'm not the crazy one."

"Keep saying it, maybe someday I'll believe it."

Sarah laughed. "So, everything's square? You two are cool?"

"Yeah, of course."

"Uh-huh. He's a hard to stay mad at kind of guy?"

"Well, he is when he's putting up dry wall in my kitchen," said Tish. "Anyway, he's going to get started while we grab the stuff on the list he sent this morning. Then we'll head back and get started on actual work."

"Sounds great," said Sarah. "My skills totally extend to shopping."

They trundled along the main arterial of the island, windshield wipers creaking, Tish studiously obeying the speed limit.

"The island isn't that big," said Sarah. "How come it takes forever to get anywhere?"

"Two reasons," said Tish. "One, wherever you're going isn't

going anywhere, so why rush? Two, Ronny Pearson is a sociopath who feels no guilt about ticketing anything that moves faster than a tortoise."

Sarah chuckled. "OK, but doesn't the island time mentality ever bother you?"

"I'm already living on old person time. Island time is actually quite speedy by comparison. No, you want to know what really bothers me about Orcas? And I blame you for this, by the way."

"Blame me for what? How am I responsible for anything here?"

"You're the one who trained me to notice this crap."

"What crap? What are we talking about?"

"There are two towns on this island. Well, there's one town and like three spots where buildings flock together. But specifically, there's Eastsound, all one word, which we're heading into now. And then there's West Sound, two words."

Sarah burst out laughing.

"Seriously," continued Tish over Sarah's laughter, "what the hell? Did no one think before putting those down on paper? Meanwhile, I spent a ton of summers here as a kid and I never noticed. I spend like a year working for you and suddenly it bothers me *every* time I see a map of the place."

"Parity and consistency matter," said Sarah, still chuckling.

Tish slowed down further as they dropped down the hill, past the pie shop and the old gas station location and into Eastsound proper. Eastsound was constructed on two main streets running parallel to each other and most of the businesses in town could be found somewhere within the few blocks that made up the village.

"Isn't that the hardware store?" asked Sarah as they passed a sign clearly stating that hardware could be found inside.

"We do not go to that hardware store," said Tish. "We go to Island Hardware."

"Why not?"

"Reasons," said Tish.

"That's it? Just *reasons*?" Sarah was laughing.

"I can add some jazz hands, if you want," said Tish. She took her hands off the wheel. "Reasons," she said, waving her hands in her best Bob Fosse style, which made Sarah laugh harder. "Trust me, it's some island feud that you don't want to know about. But the Yearlys have picked a side and we're on the side of Island Hardware."

"Gotcha. Hey, on the way back can we stop and find me some sort of fancy coffee drink? I tried some of your Granddad's coffee, but I don't think there was enough creamer to make me OK with that. I can't hang with the big boys."

"Little too much coffee in your coffee?"

"We needs more chocolate, precious," whined Sarah. "Needs it."

"Hang tough, Sméagol. I got you."

Tish stood in the breezeway next to her cart and stared at the list on her phone. Sarah was looking at cute décor items inside.

"Hey Tish," said Jeffery, the owner coming out of the lumber section. "You got the electrical approved?" he asked surveying her pile of drywall. "Tackling the walls?"

"Yup, but I can't find joint tape?"

Jeffery grimaced. "Sorry, we just sold out. We've got a shipment coming in on Monday though."

"OK," said Tish. "Thanks."

Jeffery jogged off in response to a call from the main building and Tish dialed Nash.

"Jeffery's out of joint tape," she said when he picked up. "He says he won't have some until Monday.

"Try the other hardware store," he said. "They usually have some."

"Are you trying to get me in trouble?" she demanded, lowering her voice. "I can't go in *there*!"

"I can't make walls without it," said Nash. "It's up to you. Flout island society, be a rebel, get some walls or... you know, wait until Monday to do things the approved way."

"Granddad's patio is on the damn Island Hardware website! If I go to," she looked around and whispered the next part, "the other place, I will be recognized, and Granddad will hear about it!"

"What's he going to do? Kick you out?" Nash was laughing at her, she could tell.

"No, but Jeffery will be so sad, and Granddad will be brutally sarcastic for the next two weeks."

"Yearly sarcasm—it is withering," he agreed. "You going to do it or what?"

Tish flailed her arms in frustration even though she knew he couldn't see her. She saw Sarah coming out of the main building with an ice cream from the case next to the cash register. "OK, fine," she said. "I will handle it. But if you ever rat me out, you are dead, dead do you hear me?"

"Wouldn't dream of it," he said, laughter bubbling beneath the surface of his voice.

"Who are we murdering?" asked Sarah. "And calories don't count on an island, do they?"

"No, of course not," said Tish. "And we might possibly be burying Nash in the back garden later. Depends. How do you feel about an undercover mission?"

"More detective work?" asked Sarah looking excited.

"Home improvement," said Tish. "I'll explain once we're in the car."

Tish parked on Main Street, well down from the hardware store. "OK, so if anyone asks, you're replacing a water damaged wall in your aunt's vacation home over by Deer Harbor."

"Why would anyone ask?" replied Sarah.

"Everyone asks," said Tish. "They're interested. It's called getting to know your neighbors or some crap. Plus, your construction outfit is the cutest thing I've ever seen, so I bet you get hit on about five times between the door and the joint tape."

"You don't like my overalls?"

"You're one pocket watch away from being the most adorable train engineer ever. You need a little cap."

"I thought it might be a bit much," said Sarah. "I didn't bring it. I can't believe I'm getting crap about my outfit from you, of all people. You spent the entire time we were working together complaining that Washington underdressed for every occasion."

"That is totally true," said Tish. "And I'm not giving you crap. I really think you look adorable. I'll just be sad later when you get dirty."

"No, you won't," said Sarah with a laugh. "You'll enjoy it."

"Only because I'm jealous of your overalls. All right, are you ready?"

"It's joint tape," said Sarah, hopping out of the truck. "Pretty sure I got this."

"Oh wait," said Tish. "What kind of coffee do you want? I'll grab it for you while you get the joint tape."

"Half-caf grande mocha latte," said Sarah.

"No two half-pumps of anything?" asked Tish, her eyes twinkling.

"No, thank you," said Sarah. "I'm trying to cut back on my asshole orders."

Tish grinned. "All right, synchronize watches. Meet you back here in twenty."

"Check," said Sarah saluting.

Tish headed in the other direction from the hardware store, enjoying the few minutes of dry weather. She really didn't mind the rain, but the monotony of western Washington's unchanging winters made her long for sunny, if usually drought-stricken California.

She had just made it to the door of the bookstore, a ramshackle old house with its labyrinth of bookcases and fully functioning coffee bar, when she saw Nora Harlow across the street outside the Yoga Elegance. Tish froze.

Do I say hi? I can't say hi. I have her husband at home in my kitchen.

Tish ducked into the bookstore and stared out the window trying to figure out her next move.

"Hey Tish," said Cokie Matthews, the owner of the bookstore. "What can I help you with today? More crime and mayhem for Tobias? I've got some good ones in. *A Brutal Bunch of Heartbroken Saps* by Nick Kolakowski and *Gun Monkeys* by Victor Gischler ought to be right up his alley.

"I'll take *Gun Monkeys* and a grande half-caf mocha latte," said Tish still staring out the window.

"Branching out in the coffee department? You usually like a tea."

"It's for my friend. Sunshine?" Tish gaped out the window as Sunshine Reich appeared, walking down the narrow space between buildings and out to Nora Harlow.

"No, still looks pretty gray," said Cokie, looking up.

Nora and Sunshine seemed to say a stiff hello, embracing, but coldly Tish thought.

Allies, but not friends.

"Did you want some tea, while I'm at it?" asked Cokie behind her.

"Yeah, sure," said Tish.

Across the street Nora and Sunshine's conversation was quickly becoming heated. Sunshine began to walk away, but Nora grabbed her by the arm, yanking the taller woman back. Sunshine knocked Nora's hand away, but it was clear, even under the ridiculous hat, that Sunshine was intimidated by the smaller woman.

"Cokie," said Tish, "I'll be right back."

Tish exited the bookstore and jogged across the street.

"Sunshine," called Tish, as she got closer. "Are you OK?"

Sunshine looked up and blinked tear-filled eyes at Tish. "I'm fine," she said.

"This is none of your business, babysitter," hissed Nora.

"Maybe it should be," said Tish. "Sunshine, do you need some help? You said Tyler wanted you to leave the commune. Do you need some help leaving? I will help you."

Why did I go there? Shouldn't I focus on Nora? It just felt like I should focus on what Tyler wanted.

"If that's what you want to do," said Nora, "then you need to sign the papers."

"I…" Sunshine opened and closed her mouth a few times. There was a blart of a car farting out a backfire from up the street and they all turned to see a ratty VW van turn onto Main Street. "I have to go," gasped Sunshine. "I'm supposed to be getting groceries."

Sunshine ran down the space between the businesses and out onto Prune Alley leaving Tish and Nora staring at each other.

"What are you trying to get Sunshine to do?" demanded Tish.

"None of your damn business," said Nora, turning away.

"What papers are you trying to get her to sign?" Nora kept walking. "It's a small island Nora, and Sunshine likes me better than you. You know I'll find out."

Nora turned back, her expression furious.

"It's a documentary about Tyler's life, OK? We need to strike while his death is still in the news. And she's the next of kin. I want her to give me the right to shop it."

That is so LA. She really does belong there.

"At some point they're going to want to talk to Claire and Nash, and he's never going to go for that," said Tish.

"Who cares what he wants?" screamed Nora and raised her hand to slap at Tish. Tish caught her hand and they both stared at it wondering what Tish would do next.

Uh… Just go with your first instinct. It's always 'yes and' then elaborate. What's her yes?

"It might be better to go for a fictionalized biopic. You could leave Claire and Nash out of it and you wouldn't need Sunshine's permission."

Nora yanked her hand away and stepped back breathing heavily. "I hate you," she said and then turned and followed Sunshine through the alley.

Tish walked back across the street carefully checking for cars and went back to the bookstore.

"So, it's true, then," said Cokie holding open the door. "You and Tobias really are investigating Tyler Reich's death."

"That's the second time in two days that someone has said they hate me," said Tish sitting down at the café table by the barista stand and scrubbing her hands through her hair, dislodging her pony tail. "I'm not sure if I'm cut out for being a detective."

Can I go back to being an actress when people liked me?

"Dunno," said Cokie, setting a tea and Sarah's latte in front of her. "If you believe the detective novels, the more people you've got mad at you, the more progress you're making."

She stared up at Cokie's earnest face. "And we believe the books, do we?"

"I have to believe the books," said Cokie, with a small smile. "It's my job."

CHAPTER 19
CLOVER & KYLE

Tish went back to the truck toting her tea, Sarah's coffee, a bag with both the novels Cokie had recommended and a cookie that Cokie had tossed in for free on the basis that it would make her feel better. He was not entirely wrong.

She had just opened the door to the truck and settled the cups into the cup holder when a car screeched to a halt within inches of the truck's front bumper. Tish slammed the door angrily and looked around at the other car.

"You bitch!" screamed Clover out of the window.

Tish stared in disbelief at the enraged brunette.

Clover tried to exit her car but was yanked back by her seat belt. Twenty seconds of scrambling and cursing later, Clover finally bounced out of the car toting a baseball bat.

"Ah," said Tish, "we're going full Beyoncé."

"You bitch!" said Clover, pointing at Tish. "You sent the cops to talk to me!"

"Did they?"

Clover yelled in rage and hefted the bat over her head.

"Hit the truck and you're getting the bill," said Tish. "I know where you live and I have a lawyer."

"Everyone has a lawyer," snarled Clover.

"Seriously though, did the cops come and talk to you?"

"Shut up!" screamed Clover.

"Where's Nash's knife?" asked Tish.

Clover stared at her, seeming to flounder for words. Then she pointed the baseball bat at Tish. "If you ruin this for me I will dent more than your stupid truck!" Clover threw the bat back in her car and began to climb back in.

"Did you have his knife?" asked Tish, leaning into the window. "Just answer the question."

Clover flipped her the bird and floored the gas pedal coming within inches of Tish's leg.

Tish stood in the middle of the street and tried to figure out what to do next.

Sitting down would be nice. The knees are a bit wobbly. Really ought to get in the car before I have to sit down in the middle of the street.

"Oh my God," gasped Sarah, running up with a plastic shopping bag bouncing in her hand. "What the hell was that? Are you OK?"

"That was Clover Augestine," said Tish opening the passenger side door of the truck and getting in. "And she was my number one suspect."

"What do you mean was? She currently is top of my list! She nearly ran you over."

"I'm sure lots of people have wanted to run me over," said Tish leaning back against the headrest and closing her eyes.

"How are you not taking this seriously?" demanded Sarah.

"I'm taking it very seriously," said Tish. "The problem is that I just saw Nora arguing with Tyler's sister."

"Ooh," said Sarah. "Did we know they knew each other? And what were they arguing about?"

"Nora claimed she wanted Sunshine to sign over rights to Tyler's life story to her so she could shop a documentary about him."

"Cold blooded," said Sarah.

"Or a lie," said Tish, picking up her tea. Hot beverages really did make everything less urgent.

"Possibly. Should we report Clover to someone?" asked Sarah.

"The reason Clover was pissed was that the cops had been to talk to her and she blamed me. If it was Detective Spring he's probably going to say it was my own fault."

"More like his fault if he told her that you're the reason he came to see her," said Sarah disapprovingly. "I still think we should get it on record or something." Tish shrugged. "Seriously, how are you being this calm about nearly being run over?"

"I'm not calm," said Tish. "I'm sitting in the car so I don't fall over. You're probably going to have to drive home."

"No problem," agreed Sarah. She went around to the driver's side and climbed in. "OK," she said once inside, "slight problem." She waggled her feet at the out-of-reach pedals. Tish laughed and helped scoot the seat forward until Sarah could touch.

"Is this my coffee? Yay!" Sarah started the truck and took a large gulp of her drink. "Ahhhhhh. Chocolate coffee—the best kind of coffee."

Tish laughed again. Having Sarah around was amazingly beneficial for recovering from near death experiences.

"Well," said Sarah when they were on the road, "while you were nearly getting mowed down I was doing some sleuthing of my own."

"Really? Who screamed profanities at you?"

"No one."

"Well, then I'm not sure it was real sleuthing. All my detecting seems to end in people hating me and calling me names."

"Maybe you're the one doing it wrong," said Sarah. "Ever think about that?"

"Yes," said Tish. "Kind of a lot." Sarah snorted. "Anyway, who did you talk to?"

"Kyle. We had the most hilarious clandestine conversation between the bolts and pipes aisles. He followed me into the store, where as you predicted, I was hit on multiple times. Which was terrible for his plan of talking to me covertly."

"OK, but *why* was he trying to talk to you covertly?" asked Tish laughing.

"He said he couldn't be seen actively helping Team Nash. It was bad for his rep. Anyway, he said to tell you that he passed on your message to Matt Jones. But that he didn't know the guy would actually make contact."

"Is Matt back in the state though?" asked Tish.

"He didn't specify, come to think of it," said Sarah. "But the way Kyle was talking, I assumed so. Why do we want to talk to Matt Jones? Who, apparently, is a drug dealer of a much larger scale than Kyle, if I'm reading between the lines correctly."

"If Granddad and I can't figure out who actually killed Tyler then we're going to need Mr. Jones to provide Nash with an alibi."

"Police don't like drug dealers and courts aren't likely to believe them," said Sarah.

"I'm aware of that," said Tish. "But unless something happens soon, he may be what we have to work with."

"Basically, he's a contingency plan?"

"Pretty much," said Tish. "But don't mention it to Nash, OK? I don't want him thinking that I'm getting desperate."

Which I kind of am.

"Also, we probably shouldn't mention the whole nearly getting run over by Clover thing. He was kind of specific about preferring me not to die. It will only upset him."

"There's a general way of preferring someone not to die?" asked Sarah.

"Well, it generally goes without saying. Usually it's the wishing death on someone that requires speech. The assumed neutral state is preferring non-death for everyone."

"Except that he feels the need to state his alive preferences in regard to you."

"He seems to think I'm likely to get attacked or whatever. Some crazy tries to kill me one time and suddenly he thinks I'm making it a habit. It's ridiculous. He's way more likely to be shot at than me."

"Except that someone just tried to run you over!"

"See? If we say that, he'll just think he's right."

"And he's not right?"

"No! Clover wasn't really going to run me over. She didn't even hit the truck with her baseball bat."

"Wait, she had a baseball bat? I just saw the car part. We really should report this."

"No! She was just mad and trying to scare me. Which admittedly worked. But I'm not going to stay scared. If she acts this crazy for a mere conversation with the police, then she's way more likely to make a mistake and do something else stupid."

"Uh, sure. Like, come back later with a gun."

"You're over reacting. It's not that big of a deal. If she killed Tyler, I want her running around and doing stupid stuff so we can catch her. Granddad will agree with me."

"Because you're both crazy?"

"We're not crazy," said Tish.

I hope.

Tish and Sarah returned to Reginald's and began to unload.

"Joint tape," said Tish triumphantly, hoisting Sarah's haul from *the other place* as they walked into the kitchen.

"I knew you could do it," said Nash without looking up from the sheet of drywall he was cutting. For once, Tish didn't take a moment to check out his butt. Instead she was staring at the back wall of the kitchen where the new bump out section now had a dry wall over it.

"Where do you want this stuff?" asked Sarah coming in with another bag. "The rest of the drywall is in the truck covered in plastic." She looked from Tish to the wall. "Tish, are you getting teary eyed over a wall?"

Nash looked up, clearly startled.

"No," said Tish sniffing. "No, there's just a lot of dust in here, right now."

"Tishkins," said Nash, putting an arm around her shoulders, "don't cry over drywall. You'll break character."

"Shut up," said Tish, shoving the bag at him. "Take your stupid joint tape."

He laughed and took the bag over to the counter.

"Tishkins?" repeated Sarah.

"Haven't you heard Tobias call her that?" he asked.

"No. How have I missed this? That is priceless."

"Oh, like you two don't have weird nicknames from your families," said Tish, feeling defensive, and wiping at her eyes.

"I like it," said Nash. "It makes you sound like a Russian kitten."

"That makes no sense," said Tish, but feeling rather pleased with that interpretation.

"My cousins all call me Sare-sare," said Sarah. "And my mom calls me Jelly Baby. So, you know, Russian kitten is probably fine."

"Jelly Baby?" asked Tish.

"Apparently I was very plump as a baby."

"With the fatty little leg rolls?" asked Nash, grinning. "I loved that stage."

He really does love babies. It's weird to see a guy openly acknowledging that. But he melts a little whenever he talks about Claire and babies and that is so sweet.

"Yes, personally, having seen the photos, I would have gone with Stay-Puft as a nickname, but to each their own."

"Are you the gatekeeper?" asked Tish immediately.

Ghostbusters, 1984, directed by Ivan Reitman who also directed Stripes and Kindergarten Cop.

"You realize that makes you Rick Moranis," said Sarah. "I mean, I'm fine with being Sigourney Weaver, I'm just pointing it out."

"No," said Nash, "I'd be Sigourney Weaver. We've already established that you're the Stay-Puft Marshmallow Man."

"Damn it," said Sarah, "Outsmarted by my own nickname."

Tish laughed. "Come on, you dorks. Let's get the drywall out of the truck before it rains."

By the time they stopped for lunch, the kitchen had dry wall in the entire bump out and along one wall where the refrigerator would go. Sarah was most of the way through painting the downstairs bathroom and Tish had finished recaulking the shower stall.

"Are we walking back over or driving?" asked Sarah, wiping her hands.

"Walking?" suggested Tish, looking speculatively at the still improbably dry sky.

"I want to take your truck," said Nash. "I think Tobias has a texture spray gun. I want to bring it back with us. Unless you got rid of it?"

"I doubt it," said Tish, tossing him the keys. "If it looked construction-y I kept it on the theory that I might want… oh, God, I'm turning into an islander."

"No, no," said Sarah, reassuringly. "It's different if you have an actual project that you're planning on doing. You haven't violated any of your professional organizer standards."

"Professional organizer?" repeated Nash, opening the truck door.

"One of my many LA jobs," said Tish.

He climbed in and immediately looked as if someone had jammed him into a shrink wrap package. "OK," he said, "I give, why is the seat this far forward?"

"I had to drive us home," said Sarah laughing. "Tish didn't want to after…" Sarah made a face at Tish as she realized the words that were coming out of her mouth.

"After what?" asked Nash calmly, climbing out of the truck.

"Clover yelled at me," said Tish. "It wasn't a big deal."

"I yell at you all the time," he said. "You never need someone to drive you home."

"Yeah, well," said Sarah, "you probably don't wave a baseball bat and try to run her over with a car."

Nash let the seat slide back with a loud ratcheting crash that made both Sarah and Tish jump.

"You had to open your big fat mouth," said Tish to Sarah.

"Sorry," said Sarah. "I guess this means I won't get promoted out of junior detective."

"What did I say?" demanded Nash. "I said, no dying!"

"I'm not dead! I'm fine!"

"Yeah, that's the Tish Yearly mantra. And it works right up until you pass out and end up in the hospital."

"One time," said Tish. "That was one time."

"One time too many!"

"You worry too much," said Tish.

"And you don't worry enough!"

"Come on, Sarah, we can walk home while Nash takes deep cleansing breaths."

"Walking is my punishment for spilling the beans, isn't it?" asked Sarah as a splatter of rain fell on them.

"Oh, good grief," said Nash. "Get in the truck. I'll take deep cleansing breaths out the window, which I'll have to roll down because your windshield wipers haven't been replaced in a decade."

"I keep meaning to do that," said Tish, climbing into the truck, "but I keep forgetting to check which kind we need before I actually get to a store."

"You can go on line and type in your make and model," said Sarah, wedging in next to Tish. "Also, I think there are universal blades. And you could order online. Jeez, you people have acres of leg. Seriously, I could pack luggage in all the floor space you've got going on right now."

"I believe you mean, that you finally have a normal amount of leg space," said Tish and Nash almost laughed.

They pulled up at the house, and Tish frowned to see that her grandfather's car was still gone.

"He did just say he was going to drop Greg at the airport, right?" she asked Sarah.

"That's what I thought he was going to do."

"He probably just stopped to catch up with George or Eleanor or something," said Nash.

"That's true," agreed Tish. "He usually does like to pop in on Eleanor if he goes through Eastsound. I'll call over there and see if we should save some lunch for him."

CHAPTER 20

OUTLOOK INN

Tish hung up the phone with a frown. "Eleanor hasn't seen him," said Tish.

"He's an adult," said Sarah, coming out of the kitchen. "Is it that big of a deal?"

"No?" She looked at Nash.

"He probably popped in somewhere to pick up today's gossip," said Nash.

"He'd better not be investigating without me," said Tish.

"Ah," said Sarah, "now I see what the problem is. You don't want to be junior detective either."

"Of course not," said Tish, flashing a smile. "All right, what are our lunch options?"

"We've got—" began Nash but cut off as his phone began to ring. His face made a peculiar pained expression as he looked at the number. "Sorry, I'm going to have to take this." He walked out to the living room and they could hear him pick up the call. His voice sounded annoyed. It was the tone Tish had heard him use a lot when she had first arrived on the island.

"What do we think?" whispered Sarah. "Ex-wife?"

Tish shrugged.

Probably. He always takes her calls.

"I thought there was some sort of macaroni," said Tish, opening the fridge. "I could do a Granddad special and fry it up in cakes with some hotdogs. It sounds disgusting, but it tastes ridiculously good. Except when Granddad makes it, of course. Then somehow it gets weirdly greasy and I think he puts hot sauce in it."

"Shh," said Sarah, "I'm trying to eavesdrop."

"And I'm trying to stop you," said Tish.

Sarah rolled her eyes. "OK, fine, macaroni cakes. Whatever."

Tish couldn't keep from looking out into the living room where Nash was pacing. He hung up the phone and Tish heard a muffled thump as Nash kicked a pillow and sent it flying across the living room. They both heard him go into the hall.

"I have to go," he said, picking up his boots and sitting down on the bench by the door to put them on. He stood up and seemed about to say something, then shook his head. "Sorry."

Both Sarah and Tish jumped slightly as he slammed the door shut behind him.

"You're right," said Sarah. "Using his words is not his strong point."

Tish was about to reply when the phone in the kitchen began to ring. Tish grabbed it and lifted the receiver. "Yearly Residence."

"Tish," said Tobias, "good, you're back. I think you should come out to Eastsound."

"OK," said Tish. "Why?"

"Detective Spring is about to question Nora over at the Outlook Inn. And I think it might be best if you showed up to take care of Claire while they're chatting."

"Uh," said Tish.

There's a lot to respond to in that statement. What to go with first?

"How do you know where Detective Spring is?"

"You are annoyingly perceptive when you choose to be," said Tobias. "We'll talk about it when you get here."

"Did you switch teams? Granddad!"

"No, don't be ridiculous. Now hurry up."

Tish glared in frustration at the phone as the line went dead.

"What was that about?" asked Sarah.

"Apparently we're going to Eastsound. Although," Tish stopped and scratched her nose, realizing half way through that it was the same gesture her grandfather used. "OK, is this bad? Granddad just told me that Nora is about to be questioned by Detective Spring."

"Good!" exclaimed Sarah.

"Yes. However, Granddad did not say to tell Nash. He told me to come take care of Claire. But I'm guessing that's why Nora called Nash."

"Makes sense," said Sarah with a shrug.

"Yes, but am I obligated to tell Nash that's what I'm doing? Is he going to be pissed because I'm invading on his marriage stuff?"

Sarah made a face. "He was on his motorcycle, right? So even if you called him, he wouldn't be able to pick up. And you don't know that's where he was going. He never even specified it was her."

"Excellent, defensible points," said Tish. "I mean, he won't believe me for a second, but I can work with that. OK, grab your coat. We can get lunch in town."

"Good, because I'm starving."

"Me too," agreed Tish. "Sorry. I don't know what's going on. Usually we manage to feed people better than this."

"I'm going to have to go update your Yelp review," said Sarah.

They climbed back into the truck and Tish ran the defroster to defog the window. Even if it wasn't raining, damp in Washington was a consistent problem, particularly this close to the ocean. Sarah poked at her phone in frustration as they left the driveway and pulled onto the road.

"Seriously? Why can't I check my email?"

"Dead zone," said Tish. "Not enough cell towers for coverage. Not to mention the hills and the serious amounts of water. There are dead zones all over the island. The only reliable phone is a land line."

"So put more cell towers in!" wailed Sarah.

"You would have to get an Orcasite to rent out their property and they tend to believe that cell towers give you cancer."

"It's worth it," said Sarah seriously and Tish laughed.

"I'm pretty sure you would not agree if you had cancer."

"Maybe," said Sarah. "Could I answer my email while I had cancer?"

"Such an addict," said Tish, shaking her head. Sarah laughed.

Tish pushed the truck above the speed limit, but managed to escape police notice, arriving at the white Victorian forty room hotel overlooking the water in what, for Orcas, was an exceedingly timely fashion. Unfortunately, Nash's white Ducati Monster with the distinct red frame was already parked in front.

"Well, theory confirmed anyway," said Sarah. "What do you want to do?"

"Find Granddad," said Tish. "He's the adult leadership in this party."

They climbed the front stairs and found Tobias waiting for them in a wicker armchair outside on the porch. "Everybody's inside," he said as they approached. "Pop in and get Claire."

"Will they want me to?" asked Tish nervously.

He nodded. "They were all being viciously polite to each other. If you take Claire, they can take the gloves off. But take your time— see if you can overhear anything. Otherwise I'll have to do my deaf routine and sneak inside."

"Granddad, you are deaf," said Tish.

"Only partially in one ear," he said. "Got my hearing aid in and I'm good to go."

"All right," said Tish. "Sarah, you wait here."

"Wasn't planning on anything else," said Sarah. "This is above my paygrade." Tobias grinned.

Tish squared her shoulders and went into the lobby. Nash, Nora and Detective Spring were standing in the lobby with plastic smiles plastered on their faces. Claire hung onto Nora's hand and watched the adults with a worried frown. She was the first to see Tish. The three adults looked equally annoyed at her presence. Nora particularly looked as though she were about to be ambushed.

"Tish!" Claire yelled, running at Tish and jumping on her. Tish caught her and swung her around to a piggyback position.

At least someone's happy to see me.

Now that she had met Nora, Tish could see Nora's features in Claire's face, but the dark hair and lanky frame was all from her father.

"Granddad called me," said Tish, smiling at the silent trio. No one responded. "I thought maybe Claire and I could go have lunch. Do you want to have lunch with my friend Sarah and me?" she asked Claire, looking up at the girl.

"Yes! Can I, Mom?" asked Claire, her blue eyes sparkling with excitement.

"No," said Nash, looking tired. "That really isn't—"

Nora looked startled at his response, and then turned to give Tish a smile. "That's fine," said Nora. "You'll stay in Eastsound?"

"Yeah, we'll probably just go over to Mijitas. Can we say, Mexican for the win?" she asked Claire.

"Mexican for the win!"

She caught Detective Spring almost smiling. It was one of the few unforced, natural smiles she'd seen from him. Nash had gone into grumpy deputy mode and Nora looked as if she was trying to figure out how much Tish had said about their earlier conversation.

"OK, do you need a jacket or anything?"

"No, I'm fine," said Claire.

"Jacket," said Nora, sternly, holding out a rain jacket. Tish angled Claire to take the jacket, and the girl took it with a graceless pouting gesture.

"We'll be back after lunch," said Tish. Nora nodded.

"And away my unicorn!" proclaimed Claire pointing to the door.

"No, I'm a Pegasus," said Tish. "We fly!" And they galloped to the door.

"What luck?" asked Tobias as they came out onto the porch.

Tish shook her head. "Claire, Sarah and I are going to Mijitas for lunch. Are you coming, or should we order you something?"

"Get me one of them burritos," said Tobias. "I'll be over in a little bit."

Tish nodded and then jerked her head at Sarah and began to walk up the street. "Hi, I'm Sarah." Sarah extended her hand to Claire who shook it as Tish walked.

"I'm Princess Claire and this is my Pegasus Patricia."

"Oh? Is it?" asked Sarah, grinning broadly at the use of Tish's full name. "Well, that is just so fantastic."

"Sarah is a dragon," said Tish.

"What kind of dragon am I?" asked Sarah. "Am I a wobbly Chinese dragon, or a ferocious fire breather who eats saints and princesses."

"You're the King of the Dragons," said Claire.

"Shouldn't I be the Queen because I'm a girl?"

"No, Queen is a different job. The King is in charge of things."

"Well, then you're right," said Sarah. "I'm definitely the King. Do I fly and breath fire?"

"Yes," said Claire. "And I'm your princess and we go on adventures together."

"With Pegasus Patricia? That sounds awesome."

"It is," said Claire confidently.

"Our current adventure is to get the King of the Dragons fed," said Tish. "She is very hungry and when the King of the Dragons gets hungry… whew, everybody better look out!"

Claire laughed. "We will feed her a flock of sheep in taco sauce."

"I could be OK with that," said Sarah.

They arrived at the one-story bungalow home that had been converted into a restaurant. In the summer getting a seat on the cool, brick patio with overhanging tree boughs required a half-hour wait. But in the middle of November, getting a seat at one of the inside tables was instantaneous.

They were seated and had put their orders in when Claire turned to Tish with a serious expression.

"Mom says Dad's in trouble because Tyler got killed. Is that true?"

Aw, crap. Uh… Going with simplified honest. Like that time she asked about kissing.

"Yes," said Tish. "Sort of. The police are confused. Nobody is quite sure what happened to Tyler and because he and your dad didn't get along, they want to blame him. Granddad and I are helping sort it out."

Claire looked relieved. "I didn't really like Tyler," she said. "He didn't like me either, so I figured that was OK." She glanced up to make sure this was acceptable.

"You don't have to like anyone," said Tish. "My dad always said that as long as I was polite, I could hate anyone I wanted."

Claire grinned, then the serious expression returned. "Mom wants me to be sad. But I'm kind of not. Is that bad? He wanted to move to California and buy catalogs. I didn't want to do that."

"Catalogs?" repeated Sarah. "What do you mean?"

Claire shrugged. "I heard him on the phone. He said at thirty dollars it was a steal and a once in a lifetime opportunity and it would make him a fortune because there was a movie coming out and he would have a whole catalog of backs. Is there really a whole catalog of backs?"

"I think you mean back catalog," said Tish. Claire shrugged. "Did he say whose back catalog it was?"

"Someone named Jimmy Blue? I'm not sure. I wasn't really paying attention."

"Did he really say it was thirty dollars?" Tish reached for her phone.

"He said thirty large."

"Ah," said Sarah. "Large actually means thousand."

"Really?" asked Claire looking interested. "That seems like a lot of money for a catalog."

"Depends on how important Jimmy Blue is," said Tish.

"Do you know who that is?" asked Sarah.

"Not a clue. Look him up for me."

"What are you doing?"

"I'm emailing some producers I know. If there is a movie coming out, they'll have heard something."

Sarah typed into her phone and then shrugged at the response. "He's a blues singer from the sixties. Sort of second tier, but played with everyone if this Wikipedia page is to be believed. Good looking guy, lots of talent, tragic death, yeah, I'd watch that."

Sarah flipped the phone around to show a picture of a handsome black guy in an early sixties suit.

"Says his widow lives in Seattle," said Tish, squinting at the text below the picture.

"I guess now we know what he wanted the money for," said Sarah.

"Is it important?" asked Claire.

"I don't know exactly," said Tish. "Did you hear Tyler make any other phone calls that seemed unusual?"

Claire shrugged.

They were part way through lunch when Tobias and Nash appeared in the doorway. Nash still looked pissed and Tobias looked like he was holding onto his patience.

"Oh good," said Tobias settling down. "Burritos are here."

"Hi Dad!"

"Hi, Claire-bear. Tish, can I talk to you outside?"

Tish looked at Tobias. His expression was both a warning and an apology. "Sure," said Tish sliding out of the booth. Claire was looking at them with big eyes.

"You can't keep doing this." said Nash as soon as the door closed.

"Doing what?" asked Tish, startled by the attack.

"I don't need rescuing. Stop trying to make everything better."

"I'm not," said Tish, taking a step back. "Granddad called. I thought Claire…"

"Claire is my problem."

"She isn't a problem!"

"You know what I mean," he said through clenched teeth.

I knew he'd be annoyed. I didn't think he'd be actually mad.

"I was just trying to help," said Tish.

"I do not need help with Claire," he said.

Tish found tears springing to her eyes. The door opened, and Claire leaned out. Tish automatically turned toward the yard, so Claire wouldn't see her face.

"Dad?" Claire sounded uncertain. "Should we order you lunch?"

"No," said Nash. "I'm going to eat at home. Tish is going to take you back to your mom after you're done."

"Tish?" asked Claire. Tish took a deep breath, blinked and cleared her throat.

"We're almost done, sweetie," she said, with a smile. "Just give us another minute or two."

"No," said Claire. Nash and Tish both stared at her. Claire licked her lips nervously. "I mean, don't fight. Adults only go in another room to fight. You're fighting, aren't you?"

"We're not fighting," said Nash.

"We're fighting," said Tish.

"Tish!" Nash's face flushed angrily.

"What? We are. Claire-bear, don't worry about it. You know your dad and I fight all the time." Claire half-nodded but didn't look entirely convinced. "And don't we always get over it?"

"Yes, but…" said Claire, looking at both of them.

Tish put on her most convincing smile. "Back inside with you. Otherwise the King of the Dragons might eat your quesadilla."

Claire grinned and ducked back inside, closing the door with a solid whack. Tish turned back to Nash. He was looking at her with an expression that could have been an emoji of frustration.

"I'm going home now," he said. "You'll take her back to Nora and you will not go on any more *condolence* visits." He made air quotes around *condolence*.

"OK," said Tish, sadly.

"Don't look at me like that. Claire is not your puppy that I'm taking away."

"No," agreed Tish.

He stomped down the porch stairs, muttering swear words under his breath.

That's better. If he's swearing, then he can't be all that mad. He's just frustrated with everything. He won't stick to this. If he looks back, then I've got him. Here we go. Look sad. Look sad.

Nash reached the gate and looked back. Then he slapped the fence angrily with an open palm and walked out of the yard. Tish went back inside and sat down.

"Everything OK?" asked Tobias, looking at her from under his scraggly, old-man eyebrows.

"Yup," said Tish cheerfully. "Everything's good. Nash is just going to go home and take a little break." Claire and Sarah exchanged looks. "He's had a rough few days," she said to Claire. "He's a little temperamental right now."

"Grumpy," said Claire.

"That too," agreed Tish. "He'll be better once the police arrest Tyler's killer."

"Oh, OK," said Claire with a shrug. "That would make Mom happy too."

"I bet," said Tish. "Show of hands, who wants to stop and get ice cream after lunch?" Everyone raised their hands. "The ayes have it. Ice cream here we come."

CHAPTER 21

DETECTIVE SPRING

Tish returned Claire to a warily polite Nora and went back out to the porch, where Sarah and Tobias were eating their ice creams and watching rain drip off the eaves.

"All right, Granddad," said Tish, dropping down into the chair next to him. "What is going on with you and Detective Spring?"

"What's going on with you and Nash?" he retorted. "He read me the riot act on the way over to the restaurant. Went on and on about asking for our help, not our interference in every corner of his life. And two minutes later, you're saying everything's fine. There's usually only one way a woman manages that."

Sarah half-laughed and then shoved more ice cream in her face. "Pretend I'm not here," she said.

"Nothing is going on!"

"I hope not," he said. "You'd be signing up for failure on that one. As soon as Nora decides she's done playing actress she'll snap her fingers and decide she's Mrs. Nash again."

"None of my business," said Tish, with a shrug.

"OK, but that does leave the question of how you got him to cool off," said Sarah.

"Oh, I didn't. He was still pissed, but I spend more time arguing with him than you two do. With him, there's every day mad and then there's actually mad."

"Well, I'd swear he was actually mad," said Tobias.

"Yes, but by the time he left he was down to every day mad. He'll think about it for a day or two and get over it. He's just stressed from all this nonsense. If we can figure out who killed Tyler, he'll forget all about it. But circling back to the top of the program, you avoided my question on Detective Spring."

Tobias sighed. "I had a good think about him. And as much as I like antagonizing him, and as much I find it the height of hilarity when you push his buttons, it ain't doing him, us, or Nash any good. If I learned anything in the CIA it was that I couldn't let pride get in the way of the objective. I called Detective Spring up bright and early this morning before Greg got here and had a little chat. Told him what we'd found out about Clover and Nora."

"And let me guess, he went and had a little chat of his own with Clover?" asked Sarah.

"Yeah, why?" asked Tobias, looking at Sarah in surprise.

"She threatened Tish with a baseball bat and tried to run her over, earlier this morning."

Tobias was silent for a long moment. "I can't say that I approve of that."

"Well, I wasn't a fan either," said Tish, but his expression did not clear up. "Anyway, I'm fine. Is Detective Spring really listening to us?"

His eyes narrowed, but he allowed the subject to be changed. "Somewhat. Appealing to him to be an adult seems to have worked."

"The problem with that technique," said Sarah, with a sigh, "is that you have to be an adult first."

"Well, at seventy-eight, I figure I can probably make the sacrifice. It's a bit of a stretch, but I can manage it every once in a while."

Sarah laughed. "I love hanging with the Yearlys! The two of you talk the most egregious nonsense."

"We do, don't we?" he agreed, his eyes twinkling. "It's the secret to our charm."

"No," said Tish. "He is not charming. He cut me out of the loop!"

"And I'm putting you back in," protested Tobias. "I meant to tell you this morning, but Greg came by and threw me off."

"Well, I guess if we're sharing information, I suppose I'll need to fill Detective Spring in on the rest of my day."

"Why? What happened besides Clover?"

"We found out why Tyler was blackmailing Nash," said Sarah. "Tyler wanted to spend thirty thousand to acquire the back catalog of a blues guy named Jimmy Blue."

"I always liked him," said Tobias nodding. "Reginald used to play his records quite a bit."

Sarah and Tish exchanged twin glances of frustration. "Well," said Tish, "the asking price was thirty thousand. He was asking Nash for ten. Where was he planning on getting the other twenty?"

"Good question," said Tobias nodding. "What did I say? I said it was about the money."

"I also found out that Nora knows Tyler's sister Sunshine."

"Mary," said Tobias automatically. "There's a name on her birth certificate and it ain't Sunshine."

"People can call themselves whatever they want," said Tish.

"No, they can't," said Tobias. "Otherwise I'd be known as Ace Commander, Duke of the Skies." Sarah choked on her ice cream. "You gotta work with what God gave you," he said, thumping her on the back.

"God doesn't have anything to do with it," said Tish. "Sometimes your idiot parents just have a moment and name you Patricia."

Tobias snorted. "And you're working with it," he said. "Completely fair."

"Oh my God," said Sarah, wiping tears out of her eyes. "You two are killing me."

"I can try and arrest them again," said Detective Spring, stepping out onto the porch. "I don't mind."

Was that a joke? Did he just make a joke? I'm not sure I'm comfortable with Detective Spring having normal human emotions.

"Ah, Detective," said Tobias. "We were just discussing Tish's very exciting morning."

"Thanks for taking the kid, by the way," he said settling himself on the porch railing. "Made my job a lot easier."

"Babysitting is my secret skill," said Tish.

"Uh-huh," he said. "What's this about an exciting morning?"

Tish glanced at Tobias. He nodded. With a shrug Tish filled him on her adventures with Nora, Clover and what they had learned from Claire.

"Do you want to file a complaint about Clover?" he asked when she was done.

"Not really," said Tish. "She didn't actually touch me or the truck."

"She physically threatened you. It's a serious matter."

"Told you," muttered Sarah.

"Yeah, but come on. With a two-mile restraining order in Seattle, if I get her banned here, she won't be able to work on the west side of the state!"

"There's always Tacoma," suggested Sarah.

"Don't be ridiculous," said Tish, rolling her eyes.

"Two-mile restraining order," repeated Detective Spring. "Who the hell has a two-mile restraining order? That's impossible. No one does that."

"It's what she said. She caught her ex getting a…" she glanced at Tobias, "extra special attention from the doorman, threatened him with a knife and got a two-mile restraining order out of it."

"No!" said Tobias grinning. "Ha!"

"That's what I said," said Sarah.

Detective Spring frowned. "I don't care if she took out his liver, nobody gets a two-mile restraining order. I'm looking into that." He jotted down a sentence in his notebook.

"What'd you find out from Nora?" asked Tobias. Detective Spring looked uncomfortable. "We're holding up our end of the deal. Next time I can tell Tish to keep her mouth shut."

Detective Spring sighed. "Nora admitted to being there that

night. Her lawyers sent her a copy of the custody papers that they had drawn up. She got pissed, got a neighbor to come over and watch the kid, and then went to the club. She couldn't find him, but did go into the backstage area, find his bag and his copy of the custody agreement with her signature on it. But she says she never signed, so Tyler must have forged it."

"So, she was there with motive and opportunity," said Sarah. "And we can assume that she's had access to Nash's knife."

"Yes," agreed Detective Spring, "but I'm still having trouble seeing how she got a dead body in the dumpster."

"With no blood on her," said Tish. They all looked at her. "Boleslav said he bumped into her on his way out to the dumpster. We know Tyler was already in the dumpster at that point. If Nora had managed to put him there, after stabbing him seven times from the front, then she would have been covered in blood. Something that Boleslav probably would have noticed."

"I hate it when you're right," said Tobias with a grunt.

"It's working for me," said the detective. "Also, how did you know he was stabbed seven times and from the front?"

"I'm psychic," said Tish.

"Uh-huh. Well, that brings us back to Clover. You really think she had the knife?"

"It's my best guess," said Tish.

"And she was on the mainland that night," said Sarah. "In fact, according to the ferry crew, she's been going to the mainland every Sunday for the last month."

"Who are you?" demanded Detective Spring, turning to Sarah impatiently.

"No one," said Sarah. "Pretend I'm not here."

"Junior junior detective Sarah Brooks," said Tish.

"Uh-huh." Spring made another note.

"I'm telling you it was a man," said Tobias. "Right now, my money is on Craig Larson."

"Who the hell is Craig Larson?" demanded Spring.

"Don't know yet," said Tobias. "But his boat was in Anacortes that night."

"Should I ask how you know that?"

Tish, Tobias and Sarah looked at each other. "No," said Tish.

"Right. You know, I used to think it was weird how much Nash argued with you and now I'm starting to see what the problem is."

"Told you I was argumentative," said Tish to Tobias.

"Still think you've got it backwards," said Tobias. "Anyway, Tyler did his rehab up at the Nanamuks Commune. That's Chinook for otter, by the way. I looked it up."

"Did you use the Google?" asked Sarah.

"Used the library like a normal person," said Tobias.

"Back to Craig Larson!" snapped Detective Spring.

"Craig Larson is supposed to be the program director for the rehab center. Where is he? Who is he? I never met the fellow."

"And you know everyone on the island, I suppose?" Detective Spring looked skeptical.

Tobias looked like he was thinking that one over. "Well, I haven't met everyone, but I got a pretty good tally of who all is here. And how is Mr. Larson affording a boat, when the damn commune looks like it's held together on a shoestring? And Tyler's sister is up there at the commune. We know he went and visited her that day."

"Yeah, but Sunshine just said he brought her veggie patties and told her to come to LA with him and Nora," objected Tish.

"Yeah, that's what she said, but people lie. I don't know what happened, but something did. I think something happened and I think Craig Larson sailed over and killed Tyler with Nash's knife."

"Women can kill people too," said Sarah. "Could have been Mary Sunshine."

"Yes," agreed Spring, "but statistically it's men. They're also more likely to be killed. But of the cases in the US where the offender is known, about ninety percent of them are male. The most likely murderer is a male friend or acquaintance, who uses a firearm."

"I would have thought it was family members," said Tish.

"Only about a quarter of murders are family members. You can see why I might think that someone who was male, an acquaintance, and owner of the murder weapon, was a viable suspect?"

"I get it," said Tish. "You're just wrong."

"Correct," said Tobias. "Nash didn't do it. It was Craig Larson."

Detective Spring rolled his eyes.

"Well, I can run Craig Larson, and now that I know Tyler visited the commune I can go talk to…"

"Mary," said Tobias.

"Sunshine," said Tish.

"But it's a paper-thin theory with no explanation on how the mysterious Mr. Larson ended up with Nash's knife or why he would want to kill Tyler in the first place."

"I got a theory on the why. Greg is looking into it for me," said Tobias.

"Who the hell is Greg?" demanded Detective Spring. "Aside from Tish's boyfriend."

Nicely remembered, Detective Spring. I only mentioned him once.

"He's an FBI agent," said Tish.

"Son of…" Detective Spring took a deep breath. "Why did I ever agree to this?"

"Because you know Nash didn't do it," said Tish. "And you know Granddad is smarter than everyone."

"No, it's because I know that you two are trouble and if I keep an eye on you I'm less likely to be ambushed. I will look into every piece of information you give me, but you two have to stop interfering with the investigation. That's the deal. I am running this."

"That's what we agreed to," said Tobias, looking unconcerned, but there was a twinkle in his eye that suggested agreements only existed as long as he wanted them to. Detective Spring pursed his lips and looked as though he were biting back more swear words.

"You wanted to know how the sausage gets made Detective," said Tobias. "You can't complain about the process now that you're in the factory."

"It's not a process!" snapped Detective Spring. "It's you and her and her and *Greg* talking bullshit at each other."

"No, that's pretty much the process," said Tish.

"You can't solve anything that way!"

"Sure I can," said Tobias. "Her and her and Greg do the legwork and then we hash it out. You have to admit that we told you a bunch of stuff you didn't know before."

"But none of it may be at all pertinent to the case!"

"We'll see," said Tobias. "You got to be willing to try new things, Detective. It keeps the mind sharp—staves off Alzheimer's."

"You're killing me," said Detective Spring.

"Well, I'm sure Nash will arrest us when you're gone," said Tish.

The Detective's eye twitched and Sarah smothered a laugh.

"I will talk to Clover again," he said, after exhaling a lungful of air. "And I will look into Craig Larson. But in the meantime, you two and the junior junior detective need to stay out of it."

Except I'm not sure we can at this point. But sure.

Tish put on the same reassuring smile she had used on Claire and nodded.

CHAPTER 22
THE NANAMUKS

"I don't know how you do it," said Sarah as they followed Tobias toward home.

"Do what?" asked Tish.

"How you can be so rude to authority figures. Doesn't it make you nervous to get all flippant and what not with a police detective?"

"Uh…" Tish tried to think about it. "No? I don't know. I guess if I thought about it ahead of time I might. But they're just people. I'm fit and relatively bright. I could be a police detective if I really wanted. Go through the academy, take some classes, pass some tests or whatever. And if I could do it, what's so special about him?"

Sarah was looking at her with the peculiar Sarah-type look that said she was keeping her thoughts to herself. "Is there any job that you didn't think you could do?"

"Astronaut. That looks hard and I kind of think I'd barf in zero-G. And I'm sure there's lots of other jobs I couldn't do."

"But astronaut is the only one you can think of?"

"Off the top of my head? Yeah."

"That doesn't strike you as possibly, maybe, a wee bit arrogant?"

Tish thought about that. "Not really. I've done a lot of jobs and what I've learned is that anyone, not just me, can do pretty much anything. And if you can't do it, you can certainly fake it for a limited amount of time."

"No, they can't! You can't show up one day and be an engineer! And I know I make it look easy, but someone couldn't show up and do my job either."

"No, of course not. You have years of experience and education. But my point is that while not everyone has the passion, money or time to pursue engineering, that's not to say that your average Taco Bell employee, given the right circumstances, couldn't do those jobs. People act like the non-college educated are somehow stupid. But we're not."

"I have never said you were stupid," said Sarah, firmly. "I wouldn't have made Carl hire you if I at all thought that."

"No, but there's this idea that's out there in the world. People think that human beings are somehow their jobs. Like that's all they'll ever be. And once you realize that really people are just people and that their authority is purely a function of their job, then what reason is there to be intimidated? And furthermore, once you figure out how to act like that job, why can't you have that power? That's all acting really is: trying to get other people to believe a certain set of circumstances that you've invented is reality. If I can get everyone to agree that I'm an architect for a day, then I'm an architect."

"No," protested Sarah. "No, you're not an architect."

"But if everyone believes it, then I'm an architect. Belief is reality."

"No, it's not. That's like saying that the people who believe that climate change is a fake are right. That is not reality. The reality is that the world is hotter, species are dying, and we're experiencing a global shift in weather."

"That's not the reality in Iowa," said Tish.

"No, it's the reality everywhere. We just have a bunch of people who don't like it in Iowa."

"How do you know that Iowa is reality? I mean, we all agree it exists, so it does, but how do you *know* it really exists? For all we know it's just a conspiracy of cartographers."

Sarah glared at her and then took out her phone and sent a text. Tish waited while she typed.

"I know that's a quote. I don't know where from, but I know it is. And I'm not having it, Tish Yearly."

"Not having what?"

There was a return text. "You think you can just go around spewing nonsense at people and we'll get so confused that we'll cave. But I know, it's from…" she looked at the phone, "*Rosencrantz and Guildenstern Are Dead* and I'll not be deterred. Iowa exists and you are not an architect. Reality is determined by observable fact."

"Did you use your *phone a friend* life-line?" asked Tish with a grin.

"Yes, I texted Nash. He's the only one who seems to track your bullshit."

"That's cheating!"

"No, it's not. I spend ninety percent of my life looking for ways to not argue with people. My job description is basically convincing people to do something of their own free will, and if I can, make them believe that it was their idea to begin with. Arguing is not what I do. I am not equipped to go toe-to-toe with a Yearly. I'm allowed to tag team."

"I can't believe you really texted him," said Tish.

"What? We are co-projecting on Reginald's. It's important to be able to contact your teammates."

Particularly the cute, single ones?

"Well, at least he texted back," said Tish.

"You said he'd get over it."

"Yes, but I couldn't be sure of the exact timeline. Responding to you is probably a good sign."

"Well, it probably helps that I was arguing against you. What's this?" They had turned the corner onto the driveway and found a VW microbus parked in front of the house.

Tish stared at the members of the commune arrayed on the porch. Sunshine and the other woman were both wearing rubber boots and long dresses, that were muddy and wet at the ends. The men were in a variety of kimono tops, parkas and stupid hats. "I think it's a sit in," said Tish.

"Do you think they all sleep together?"

"Sarah!"

"What? You know you were wondering."

"Well, I wasn't until you brought it up."

Tobias pulled his beat up 1980s Oldsmobile up to the house and began the process of getting out as Tish parked.

I think Granddad is faking it this time. I swear he's slow, but not that slow. Yes, he's hunching. It's the aged pensioner routine.

Sunshine looked as if she was trying not to sink through the porch floorboards in embarrassment. The others were looking truculent.

"If I'd known you were coming, I would have built a bigger porch," said Tobias.

"You so kindly visited our little home earlier this week," said Mars. "I thought we should return the favor."

Tish stared at Mars. Unlike Clover, who was easily pegged as a faux hippie, he had no tells to give himself away. He smelled like pot. He was wearing hemp pants and a homemade poncho and a necklace made—disgustingly—of what looked like human hair. They all had them.

That is so gross.

Mars stood up. Tish took a second look, searching for something that would justify her instinct that Mars was a human garbage fly. He was a little taller than Tish, and while lean, lacked the pinched quality of Sunshine.

Or the others. He's getting more than his share of the food.

"I also heard from Wind that you were harassing Sunshine today in Eastsound." He ignored Tobias and stepped closer to Tish, standing within her personal space. Not close enough to be looming, just enough to be uncomfortable.

No dirt under the fingernails. And seriously, Wind? Which one of you whack-jobs picked Wind as a name? No time to ponder that.

"I'm sorry Sunshine," said Tish, earnestly turning to address Sunshine directly and ignoring Mars.

Slower speech, nod while I talk. Be earnest.

"It really looked like Nora was bothering you. I just felt called to come to you. Sometimes I listen to my animal instincts too much, you know?" The taller man in back nodded as if what she was saying made complete sense. "I didn't mean to bug you. Like, I'm sure you can handle your own shit. But man, I just don't feel right about people telling Orcasites how to live."

"Mmm," said the other woman, a thirty-ish brunette with big hazel eyes, nodding. "Everyone has to be free to follow their own path." Meanwhile, Sunshine watched her with a tense, wary expression.

"Right?" agreed Tish, making eye contact with the brunette and smiling, then she turned the smile on Mars.

Your move, dickwad.

"Sunshine, you didn't tell me that Nora was bothering you," he said, still looking at Tish.

"I bumped into her on the street," said Sunshine uncomfortably. "She was going on about Tyler. She was upset."

"That's because she's a closed box. She's not open to the universe," said Mars, still staring at Tish. "You can't let yourself be distracted by her clouds of misunderstanding."

Subtle. Reinforce the us versus them mentality and underscore that Sunshine's feelings of loss are wrong.

"Did you want to come in?" asked Tobias, wavering his voice just a little. "We could make you dinner. We love getting to know our neighbors."

"We would love to hear more about your commune," purred Tish.

The rest of the commune looked interested, but Mars narrowed his eyes. "No thanks," he said. "We wouldn't want to put you out. But if you're really interested, please come visit us again."

He led his troop to the VW Microbus and Tish tried not to laugh as they piled in like a clown car.

"It's hard to look tough in a mini-van," said Tobias as they pulled away.

"That guy was a total creepster," said Sarah. "I mean, the car thing was funny, but I'm not laughing. Coming here was his way of saying that he knows where you live. That's a creepy college stalker move."

"Yes," agreed Tish.

"Everyone knows where we live," said Tobias, standing up straight and stretching his shoulders uncomfortably. "I'm in the phone book."

"Showing up with four other people is a threat," said Sarah and Tobias grunted his agreement.

"Well, if he comes back and I'm not around, remember that the pistol is in the remote caddy in the den," said Tobias.

"Thanks for telling me," said Sarah. "I wouldn't want to change the channel with a .38."

"It's a .45," said Tobias, "and I think about it every time I watch the news."

"And that's why we stick to *Matlock*," said Tish.

"Can we switch it up for Jessica Fletcher? Also, Tish, what the hell on the hippy-speak? That also creeped me out."

"I did a sci-fi movie once. It was about a time-travelling scientist who went back in time to form a cult of Satan worshipping hippies who would help keep Richard Nixon in power. It was a terrible movie, but I did end up doing a bunch of research on cults and love-child speech."

"Sadly, I would totally watch that," said Sarah.

"Did they do it?" asked Tobias.

"Do what?"

"Keep Richard Nixon in power?"

"Oh, no. They were foiled by the Voodoo Priestess of the Black Panthers and a time agent from the future. I played the cultist's head wife. The Voodoo Priestess and I ended up fighting in a circle of skulls."

"I'm so finding this movie," said Sarah.

"It was really bad," said Tish. "I'm making it sound more fun than it is. If they'd played it for laughs, it would have worked, but the director thought he was making a *statement*."

"About what?" asked Tobias going inside and sitting down on the bench to take off his shoes.

"I'm not entirely sure," said Tish. "But he was definitely stating it."

"What was the name of the movie?" asked Sarah walking in behind them, fingers already busy on her phone.

"Like I'm telling you," said Tish.

Sarah's phone pinged with an incoming text and she laughed at the message. "You know, I'm going to find it anyway," she said without looking up, responding to the text.

Why do I think she's texting Nash? I don't know why he can't text me. It wasn't like I pissed him off on purpose. Of course, I never try to piss him off on purpose—it just happens.

"That doesn't mean I need to help you," said Tish. She checked the clock in the kitchen and sighed. Today had not been nearly as productive as she'd hoped it would be.

"Are we going back over to Reginald's?" asked Sarah, proving that while she might be buried in her phone she was far from inattentive.

"Yeah," said Tish. "I still need to get the dishwasher hooked up and I need a second person to help move it around."

"That is what I'm here for," said Sarah. "We can do it."

"Could we do a nap instead?" asked Tish. Sarah laughed. "I know the feeling. This wasn't quite the stress-free weekend I was picturing."

"Don't wear yourselves out," said Tobias, putting on his house slippers. "I've got plenty of *Matlock* and *Murder She Wrote*, a couch and a spare Laz-E-Boy."

"Thanks Granddad," said Tish, impulsively kissing him on the cheek. "But we might as well try and get something done today."

"That's right. Can't spend all day detecting," agreed Sarah. "Back to the salt mines for us."

"Suit yourselves," said Tobias. "I'm heading for the Laz-E-Boy."

CHAPTER 23

SUNDAY - CLOVER

Tish checked her phone again and tried not to feel depressed.

"You said he'd take a couple of days to get over it," said Sarah, going past with an empty paint tub and a brush.

"I know he's not going to call me," said Tish.

"Then why do you keep looking at your phone?"

"Because I *want* him to call me. He made this crack yesterday about feeling like he needs an alibi at all times and I laughed it off, but now I'm not so sure."

Tish followed Sarah out to the porch and watched as she began to rinse off the brush. Tish watched sympathetically as Sarah tried to spray the brush from under the porch roof and avoid getting wet. It was a miserable day and Tish shivered in her sweatshirt, wishing she'd remembered to grab her jacket. On the far side of Reginald's pristine tennis club lawn, the inky black-green of the trees rose in a spiky line blocking any view of the road. It was easy to feel alone here.

"I thought the pressure was off since Detective Spring was looking at other suspects," said Sarah, checking the brush cleanliness.

"Really?" said Tish. "Because what I thought what he was doing was eliminating our suspects, so that he can say he's done his job and go back to focusing on Nash."

"Oh," said Sarah, going back to spraying. "That's not the same thing at all."

"No," said Tish, "it isn't. And I wouldn't mind quite so much, if Clover had at least admitted to having Nash's knife, but she hasn't." Sarah wrinkled her nose in dislike. "And all of that would be OK, except that Granddad totally went over my head!"

"What are you going to do about that?" asked Sarah. "Take away his Metamucil?"

"Refuse to change the up high light bulbs," said Tish and Sarah laughed. "I didn't say that out loud."

"And I didn't laugh," agreed Sarah.

"Anyway, I'll deal with Granddad when I get home, but Nash… I mean, it's perfectly reasonable to want me to butt out of his marriage."

"They are not married. You've got to stop listening to Tobias on this one. I don't know if he's just hung up on divorce or if he just doesn't want you to date Nash, but whatever it is, I really think he's wrong. Nash is not married to Nora and he doesn't want to be. He can't be mad at you for butting into something that doesn't exist."

"Well, his personal life then. Whatever. My point is that I don't mind him being mad, I just wish he'd be mad where I can see him."

"You could call him and tell him that," suggested Sarah.

"Oh, huge buckets of *no* to that. That would either make him think he won or would piss him off more."

"He won? What is this, team sports? Is someone keeping score?"

"Yes! And currently he's up on points because he won the last round."

"What was the last round?"

"Did you know that *Chitty Chitty Bang Bang* was not only based on a book, the book was written by Ian Fleming?"

"James Bond?" Sarah looked incredulous.

"Yeah."

"No, I did not know that."

"Neither did I! And he lorded it over me for weeks. There's no way I'm calling him just because he'd be better at moving a dishwasher."

"And because you're worried about him," observed Sarah. She looked at Tish's expression and raised an eyebrow. "What?"

"Well, I think the other part of why he's mad is that he doesn't want to be rescued. If I say I'm worried he'll think I don't think he can take care of himself. Which is not at all the case. He's a very capable individual, who currently happens to be in a worrisome situation." Tish stopped and waited for Sarah to speak. Instead, Sarah seemed to be thinking deeply. "You think we're crazy, don't you? You've got the look that says you're biting your tongue. I know it sounds silly to be caught up on pride with murder charges on the line, but sometimes pride is all you have. It's what keeps you sane, you know? I think he should be able to hang onto that."

"I guess I can understand that," said Sarah. "I just think that perhaps at some point, one of you is going to have to stop worrying about pride. But," she continued before Tish could interrupt, "I agree, we should not call him. We don't need him to move the stupid dishwasher."

It was two by the time the dishwasher was successfully connected and lodged in its cubby under the counter. Tish gave the dishwasher a final shove and glanced at the clock.

"Let's call it a day. We can go drink at the Orcas Hotel until your ferry comes in."

"I'm so into that plan," said Sarah. "Besides, I think I'm getting a hand cramp from reaching up with the brush. My arms are only meant for clicking mice. This lifting things above my head is a foreign concept. They're freaking out."

"I know, right? I think I spent the first three months on the island trying to stretch out computer posture and mouse arm. I have to say, that is one thing I don't miss about the mainland grind."

"Yes, your early retirement ass pisses me off too."

Tish grinned. "Mid-day runs for the win."

They tidied their mess and drove back to the Yearly house. "Granddad's still not home," said Tish. "This is starting to piss me off. Detective Spring decides to play nice and suddenly I'm chopped liver? This is so uncool."

"Maybe he found something and they're working on something that will help Nash," suggested Sarah.

"Then he should call me! I'm the T. Yearly on the business card. I deserve to be called."

"I thought he was the T?" asked Sarah laughing.

"Well, the phone number is mine, so I figured that makes it me," said Tish.

"Maybe he's feeling worried about getting you threatened yesterday morning?"

"Why would he be worried about that?" asked Tish dismissively.

"Gee, I don't know," said Sarah, sarcastically. "You did nearly get run over. Being worried would be totally normal."

"I don't want him to be normal. I want him to be Granddad. Normal people start talking to Detective Spring and disappear this morning and cut me out of the loop again. Normal people think that just because Steve Winslow went bonkers and tried to kill me that someone else might try the same thing. Which is not likely to happen at all because, despite recent commentary to the contrary, I am a very likable person!"

Sarah chuckled. "Sure, you are."

"It's not likely to happen again," said Tish. "Is my point."

"Mm," said Sarah.

Tish and Sarah sat at the bar of the Orcas Hotel and watched the ferry drift with deceptive slowness across the water toward the island. Sarah picked up her martini and was about to take a sip and her eyes got wide.

"There she is!"

"There who is?" asked Tish looking around the restaurant.

"The crazy lady who almost ran you over," said Sarah pointing out the window. Tish craned her head and saw Clover coming down the hill carrying a plastic wrapped sandwich. "It's Sunday!" exclaimed Sarah, smacking Tish in excitement.

"Ow! And yes?"

"The ferry guy said Clover always went over to the mainland on Sunday and came back Monday morning." They watched as Clover cut across the Orcas Hotel lawn toward the ferry line. "What was she driving earlier? Some sort of hatchback thing?"

"A green Subaru," said Tish.

"How do you remember these things?"

"Well, it was within inches of my face," said Tish.

"Right. That would probably do it." Sarah walked to the window, craning to see Clover as she left their view. "Wait here," she commanded then set her drink down and scuttled out the door. A few minutes later, she was back, brushing raindrops out of her hair.

"What was that about?" asked Tish.

"I'm going to follow her," said Sarah.

"What?"

"I walked on, which means I can beat her off the ferry. She doesn't know me. Once I get to Anacortes, all I have to do is get to my car and wait for her to get off the ferry. And then I'll follow her to wherever she's going."

"I don't know," said Tish. "You saw how angry she can get. I don't want to put you in any danger."

"I won't be in any danger. I'll be inside the car. And don't you want to know?"

"Yes," admitted Tish, "but I also don't want you to get in trouble. Maybe I should come with you."

"No, you have to stay here and make sure Detective Spring doesn't try and arrest Nash again. Plus, I think you're right. I think Tobias is up to something. You need to keep an eye on him."

"He's a trouble maker! People don't believe me!"

"Totally," agreed Sarah. "So, I'll follow Clover and then once I see where she's going, I'll call you with a report."

Tish shifted in her seat. "Yeah, OK, but I swear to God, that you had better not do anything crazy."

"How is it OK for you to do crazy things, but not me?"

"I've read almost all of Granddad's course material on being a private investigator. I'm practically trained."

Sarah literally laughed in her face. "You're so funny when you make crap up."

Tish grinned. "I have to try. You never know what kind of horse poop people will let you shovel. But let's put it this way, I don't have a cat who's depending on me to come home. And here on the island, I've got lots of back up I can call. Once you're in Seattle, I can't help if you get in trouble."

"You mean, I'll have to dial 911 like everyone else? I'm a big girl. I can take care of myself. Relax."

"I'm relaxed," said Tish. "Just be careful."

"Got it."

CHAPTER 24

TOBIAS & SUNSHINE

Tish watched nervously from the hotel as Sarah walked onto the ferry. She hoped she wasn't making a mistake by letting Sarah follow Clover. But she had the feeling that even an absolute ban on following Clover would not have prevented Sarah from doing it.

Now I know how Nash feels.

She settled back into her chair and debated the various benefits of finishing her drink and going home or just ordering dinner on her grandfather's credit card.

Probably ought to at least call him and invite him to come eat with me.

She dialed the house and let it ring until the message machine picked up. Frowning she checked her watch. The last thing he'd said this morning was that he was going out to do errands and might check in about the muddy spot. The fact that she hadn't heard from him told her that his excuse was a bunch of bullpucky.

I probably ought to just call Detective Spring.

On impulse, Tish dug in her purse, found the detective's card and dialed his number. Naturally, it went straight to voicemail. Tish waited for the beep.

"Peter," she said, using her best mom tone, "it's quite past Tobias's dinner time. So when you boys are done playing, I would very much appreciate it if you would send him home. Also, tell him that he's supposed to check in before playing detective without me."

She hung up the phone and waved for the bartender, a local favorite of her grandfather's, a prematurely balding thirty-something named Delbert.

"Hey Tish," he said wandering over. "Another drink?"

"And dinner," said Tish. "Granddad has wandered off without permission, so that means he's paying."

Delbert chuckled. "Has he ever asked for permission?"

"No, of course not. But he's supposed to take me along when he goes on adventures," said Tish.

"Ah, well, then of course he's paying," agreed Delbert. "Well, tonight we have—"

The kitchen door was flung open with so much force that it slammed into the wall and bounced off nearly hitting the man who had pushed it to begin with. He kicked the door again, took a firmer grip on the poodle under his arm and stormed through the bar. A cluster of people gathered in the kitchen doorway to watch him go. "And you can take the damn kohlrabi to hell with you!" yelled the man with the poodle and slammed the exterior door behind him.

There was silence in the bar. A young man stepped out of the kitchen, buttoning up the collar of his chef's uniform with the air of a sergeant taking a field promotion and command of the troops.

"Ladies and gentlemen, there will be a slight delay in dinner service. However, we will be with you shortly. Tonight's special will be a braised white fish with Lillet and brown butter glazed radishes with kohlrabi."

There was an audible sigh of relief from the kitchen and then a flurry of activity, that was quickly hidden from view as the kitchen door swung shut behind the young man.

"Right then," said Delbert. "So, that was the chef with the dog and it looks like Quest, our sous chef, will be taking the reins. You sticking around to see how this turns out?"

"Wouldn't miss it for the world," said Tish. "Bring me a Granddad special while you're at it."

"Bloody Mary extra tabasco it is," said Delbert.

Delbert had just set down the Bloody Mary when a man walked in and sat down at Tish's table. Tish stared at him in surprise. He was a dark haired thirty-something with a lean build, dressed in jeans, a well-worn cable knit sweater, and an REI jacket. His watch, however, was a Rolex Sea Dweller in Stainless Steel, which didn't sound that impressive.

Except that those retail for about thirteen thousand dollars.

"I'll take one of those, Delbert," he said without looking up at the bartender.

"It's got extra tabasco," said Delbert nervously.

"Sounds great," said the man.

"OK, Matt," said Delbert and walked back to the bar.

Tish took a sip and then crunched off a bite of the celery while staring at the man she could only presume was Matt Jones. He stared back.

CHAPTER 25
MATT JONES

Why do I always look like crap when I meet people that need to be impressed?

Delbert returned quickly with another Bloody Mary and set it down in front of Matt. "Should I bring a menu?" he asked.

"Ask Patricia," said Matt, "she called this meeting."

"You could stay," said Tish, "but it'll be a risk."

"You think so?" he said, his eyes were a hard dark brown.

"The chef just stormed out with his little dog under one arm and the sous chef has taken command of the kitchen. The inciting incident appears to have been some kohlrabi which is now on the menu with tonight's special. So, you know... Could go either way."

He's trying not to laugh. He's working really hard at it. Is it bad that I think a drug smuggler is kind of hot?

"And what did you order?" he asked.

"The special, of course."

"You like to live dangerously?" he asked.

"It keeps things interesting," said Tish.

"Put me down for one of the specials," Matt said looking up at Delbert, with a smile. The smile relaxed his face and made him look much less dangerous.

Delbert relaxed. "Got it," he said. "Tish, is this still on Tobias?"

"You bet," said Tish.

"In that case, we will need the dessert menu," said Matt.

It was Tish's turn to try not to laugh.

"I'll bring it with dinner," said Delbert. He looked at Tish and she got the feeling he was trying to beam a message to her brain.

"Thanks Delbert," she said, with no further conversational openings, Delbert went back to the bar. "It's Tish, by the way," she said to Matt. "My mother doesn't even call me Patricia and she picked the name."

"Matt Jones," he said, reaching across the table and offering a hand to shake. Tish dutifully shook it. "My condolences about Reginald," said Matt, leaning back in his chair. "He was a good man. He's missed on the island."

Tish had become used to these kinds of statements. She had known Reginald only a short time, but the assumption was that he and Tobias had been as close as family, so condolences had to be offered to any of the Yearlys.

"Granddad certainly misses having someone to make trouble with," she said.

"It's my impression that he's found a replacement," Matt said, with a flash of a smile.

"We'll see," she said.

"Meanwhile, I have also heard competing rumors that you're either going out with Nash or stepping out on an FBI agent with Nash. That's a lot of law enforcement for one girl to handle."

"Huh," said Tish. "My life always sounds more interesting through the rumor mill."

This time he did smile. "Mine too. So," he said, taking a sip of his Bloody Mary, "want to tell me why I'm here?" He put down the drink and then swallowed with a surprised and slightly strained look on his face. "He said extra tabasco. He didn't say half a bottle."

"It's a Tobias Yearly special. I'm pretty sure it's not just tabasco in there."

He took another cautious sip. "Are we sure it's not combustible?"

"Could be gunpowder for all I know," said Tish.

"I could see that." He took another sip, watching her over the top of the glass. She could tell he was curious, but she wasn't quite sure that she wanted to just blurt out what she wanted to ask in an open restaurant.

"What do you know about my grandfather?" asked Tish.

"I've heard he used to be a pilot and maybe some sort of spook."

Tish nodded. "Those are both true. He used to work for the CIA."

"Doing what?"

Tish shrugged. "He never specifies. He is also about a week away from becoming a licensed private investigator." Matt blinked and she could see a smile hovering around the corners of his mouth. "I know it sounds funny, but he gets… the shape of things. I'm not saying he's going to be chasing people across rooftops, but I think he can give Jessica Fletcher a run for her money."

"Fair enough. I take it you two are looking into matters for our mutual friend?" Tish nodded. "Then why are you talking to me?"

"Because we, I, promised our mutual friend that we would find Tyler Reich's killer and I want to know how big my safety net is if we can't find out who did it."

"You don't have one," he said, bluntly.

"So, you're saying that even if Nash was arrested, you wouldn't testify on his behalf?"

"I'm saying that even if I wanted to, which I don't, that I wouldn't do him any good. He went out. He came back. He got drunk and fell asleep. What does that get him? Nothing."

"You could testify that he went out and came back in the same clothes and those clothes were not covered in blood," said Tish, leaning forward and keeping her voice low.

"Quite true, but like I said, I wouldn't do him any good. The second a DA trots out my record, no one is going to believe a word out of my mouth. And besides, for all I know, he killed the guy." Tish raised an eyebrow and he had the decency to look embarrassed. "Yeah, OK, I know. He didn't. Here comes dinner." He nodded toward the kitchen and Tish watched as Quest came out followed by a waiter.

"Thank you for dining with us tonight," said Quest formally. "We appreciate the faith you place in this establishment."

"It's not the establishment," said Tish, as the waiter placed the plates. "I'm banking on you Quest." Quest managed to stand a few millimeters taller. "And I also think that Lillet and brown butter can make anything edible, up to and including, kohlrabi."

"It's locally sourced kohlrabi," said Quest, primly. "I believe the brief sauté will bring out the flavor and add a fresh texture to the meal."

"Me too," said Tish. "I'm excited about it."

Quest looked uncertain and Tish smiled her best *I think you're incredibly manly* smile. It had *a buy me a drink* success rate of nine out of ten. "I'm happy to cook anything for you," said Quest, which she was willing to bet was true. "If you're unhappy with the meal, just let me know."

"Thanks Quest," she said, smelling the fish. "You can go. We'll let you know if we need anything."

"OK," he said, blinking and then turned around and left.

"Why didn't you try that on me?" asked Matt, his expression warring between amused and genuine curiosity.

"Would it work?" asked Tish, looking him over.

Seems unlikely.

"For a short period of time," he said with a shrug.

"Let me guess—until about tomorrow morning?"

He grinned. "Yeah, about that long."

"No thanks," said Tish. "My bullpen is full."

He laughed, then cut into his fish. "Can I ask you something?" he said around a bite. "What makes you so sure that Nash, didn't do it?"

Tish frowned. "You know he didn't."

"Yeah, *I* know he didn't. But I've known the guy since college and I saw him that night. What makes *you* think he didn't?"

Tish sighed. "What do you know about Reginald's death?"

He shrugged. "Just what I read in the papers. Some hotel developer killed him?"

"Steve Winslow wanted to put in a resort hotel over at Olga. Of course, he had trouble getting water rights because Rosario will never give water to a competitor." Matt nodded in understanding. It was only off-islanders who couldn't wrap their heads around the fact that all of the islands' water was owned by a private company – the Rosario Hotel. "But Winslow believed that Reginald's property was sitting on a well that could feed his hotel."

"Is it?" asked Matt, looking up sharply.

"Don't be ridiculous," lied Tish. "And even if there was, it would be feeding all the wells in Olga. Tying it to a resort would dry out the town and everyone on that side of the island. It would be a disaster." Matt grunted his agreement. "But Winslow got it into his head that there really was a well and he kept after Reginald, and then he talked to Reggie Jr. And Reginald's son said he'd sell if and when Reginald moved back home with him."

Matt looked sour. "And let me guess, Winslow figured that if Reginald were dead and Reggie Jr. owned the property that it would be a sure sale?"

Tish nodded. "But Reginald was already dying of cancer and he'd had a lot of time to ponder what Reggie Jr. would do and what he wanted to do. So, he left the property to Granddad and all the contents of the house to Reggie Jr."

Matt chuckled.

"Then, Winslow decided that if he kidnapped me that he could get Granddad to sign the property over to him."

"That would never work," said Matt. "He'd either have to hang on to you or kill both of you to keep Tobias from contesting it."

"By that time, Winslow had rather," she put her hands together and then pushed them apart, "diverged ways with sanity. Anyway, I decided I didn't want to be kidnapped and got myself home. But

Winslow was already there, waiting for Granddad, and he decided to take the killing me option. Fortunately, Nash and Granddad came home just then, and Nash shot him."

"This is my point," said Matt. "Nash can kill people."

"And then he did first-aid and tried to save Winslow."

"Well, the police are supposed to do that," said Matt.

"You and I both know there's a world of difference between what's supposed to happen and what does."

He tapped his fork thoughtfully on the edge of the plate. "There aren't a lot of people who do what they're supposed to do."

"And even fewer who do it because it's the right thing to do," said Tish.

"He couldn't even bribe Tyler to get his own kid back," said Matt. "And I saw it in his face—he really, really wanted to. Which is why I'm surprised to hear that he spent all weekend on the island and no one can figure out how he could have gone over to Anacortes. I would have thought that he would have had a heart attack and passed out from trying to lie."

"What can I say? I'm a bad influence," said Tish.

Matt laughed and leaned back in his chair. "This is so unfair," he said. "Why can't I ever meet someone who's a bad influence on me?"

"You want to end up on the FBI's most wanted list?"

"Promise?" he asked, his eyes twinkling.

"My grandfather thinks I have a drug problem because I smoke pot twice a year," said Tish and Matt tried not to choke on another sip of his Bloody Mary. "I don't think you're compatible with my family."

"Fine," he said, with a sigh.

"My turn to ask you a question," said Tish. "You went to school with Nash. That means you knew Nora too, right? What..." Tish hesitated.

"What was he thinking?" asked Matt. "Yeah, I think he was thinking he was a shy guy who met a gorgeous girl who bothered to hang around with him."

"Not buying it," said Tish. "He's not shy. And also, he looks like, as one of his exes just described him, Mr. November in the Hunks of San Juan County Police Calendar."

Matt chuckled. "He's not shy now. But in college, yeah. He was quiet."

"Quiet, I'll buy. I mean, obviously he got over that."

"Did he?"

"He yells at me a lot, so yes. But that doesn't explain Nora."

"Nora, when she's not being a mega-bitch, can be charming and I think she actually loved Nash. I think she made it easier for Nash to fit in. You're right, he looks like Mr. November, but he's got his nose in a book half the time."

"He is kind of a dork," agreed Tish.

"And I don't think he really ever knew how to be Mr. November. Which is one reason I'll actually talk to him. But Nora was like his way to connect with that side of himself. Only, eventually, I think he realized he didn't really want to be on that side, and that he liked being Deputy Nash of Orcas Island, and then Nora got pissed that she didn't get to play dress up Ken doll anymore."

"I talked to her last week," said Tish. "She still thinks she can."

"If she could," said Matt, "she'd still be Mrs. Nash."

"Hm," said Tish. "My grandfather disagrees with you. He thinks she'll snap her fingers and he'll come running."

"Nash, as long as I've known him, has never gone running. Not even for Nora. I don't know your grandfather, but I think he's wrong on this one."

"We'll see," said Tish with a shrug. "Nora strikes me as someone who doesn't like to be single."

"She strikes me as someone who doesn't like to have a job," said Matt. "I say... three weeks before she whistles for Nash."

"I think she'll make it six," said Tish.

"Care to make it interesting?"

"In what way?"

"To be clear, I'm not betting on whether or not Nash says yes, only on whether or not she makes the offer. But if she does it before six weeks, then I win."

"What if we're both wrong and she doesn't try to get him back at all?"

"Then Nash will have a less stressful holiday season."

"OK, so what happens if I win?"

"I buy you dinner."

"What happens if you win?"

"I buy you dinner."

"I see where this is going."

"Do you?" he asked, grinning.

"Yes," said Tish, "to a very expensive restaurant."

He laughed, then he glanced at the kitchen doorway. "Quest is trying to see if you're enjoying the meal."

"So far, it's not bad," said Tish, eyeing Matt. "It's got a little more sauce than I expected and I'm not altogether sold on the flavor profile, but it's intriguing."

He chuckled. "I usually say that danger is my middle name. I mean, it's actually Cornelius, but who admits to that? But I could be talked into intriguing."

It was Tish's turn to laugh. "Are you sure?" she asked, suddenly turning serious. "Are you sure that you can't help him?"

"The only kind of help I could give him was the ten thousand I offered to loan him, and I'll donate that to the defense fund, but that's as far as I can go."

At least he's clear about his boundaries. And his intentions, come to think of it. Which is kind of refreshing. Granddad's right—playing it cool sucks for dating.

Tish nodded. "Thanks," she said. "But I think if we get to that stage, funding the defense will be the least of his problems."

Although…

"Maybe there is something you can help with though."

"Shoot," he said, eyeing her warily.

"Tyler was killed with a knife that had pot residue on it."

"And that's not proof enough that Nash didn't do it?"

"Detective Spring goes where the evidence leads, never mind hunches and friendships."

"Yeah, I've met him," said Matt. "That guy is a dick. What's your question?"

"How would pot residue get on a knife? I'm pretty enough that I usually don't have to buy my own." Matt coughed on a bite of kohlrabi.

"Damn it. Stop saying stuff like that when I'm trying to eat."

"You're an adult. I'm assuming you can manage mastication. But what I'm saying is that I don't know how much pot you would have to cut for residue to cling to a knife."

"You shouldn't need a knife at all. Unless you were trimming a pot plant. And even then, you should use pruning shears or scissors."

Tish frowned. "Thanks. It's weird. And that bugs me."

"Well, I guess that's why you're the PI," said Matt.

"I'm just the ex-actress who wants to run a wedding venue and not get a real job. Granddad's the PI."

"Right," said Matt.

Tish tapped her fork against the fish. "It's got to be Clover," she said. "She had access to the knife and Kyle said she owned a pot plant that she promptly killed."

"It's easy to over prune," said Matt, watching her in amusement.

"More likely to be improper watering," said Tish. "I may not know pot, but I know how to kill plants. My plant murder rate over the summer was quite high." She lifted the last bite of fish to her mouth and paused. "Man bun," she said.

"I know people hate them, but I think they look kind of cool," said Matt. "Not that I could pull it off."

"Kyle said Clover's Sunday afternoon was getting high with

some man bun that showed him how to prolong a high."

"So, you're looking for a man bun wearing pot aficionado who likes brunettes with big… eyes."

"Boobs," said Tish. "And yes. Unfortunately, last time I saw Clover she threatened me with a baseball bat. I don't think she's going to take too kindly to me asking about her love life."

Matt looked thoughtful. "I actually might be able to help with that."

Tish raised an eyebrow. "Close friends with Clover, are you?"

"No, I was raised here. Her neighbor is my fourth-grade school teacher. I might be able to find out what she's seen. Give me your number—I'll text you if I learn something."

Tish took out one of her grandfather's business cards and passed it across the table.

The rest of the meal passed in flirtatious banter and Matt snagged the bill as Delbert slid it onto the table. She had no doubt that this particular dinner was going to be grist for the island gossip mill by the time Granddad came down to breakfast.

Tish went out to her to car and checked her phone again—no messages from either her grandfather or Nash. She got as far as Eastsound before stopping at the drug store for some sundries and something to do. Regular weekend chores just weren't as exciting when she'd kicked off the weekend with an arrest and a speed boat ride across the Sound. On the way out of the drugstore, she glanced up and saw a black SUV trundling along Main Street in the steadily gathering dusk. And she blinked as she recognized her grandfather in the back seat. She waved frantically, but the SUV kept moving.

"What the hell?" she demanded of the empty parking lot. She jogged to her car, intending to follow the SUV, but as she reached the car her phone finally rang. She picked it up, expecting to hear her grandfather's voice.

"Hey," she said fumbling for her car keys.

"Tish?" whispered a strained voice, and Tish stopped moving.

"This is Sunshine. Mary. Reich."

"Sunshine?" Tish repeated, reaching for her keys again. There was something wrong in Sunshine's voice. "Are you OK?"

"No," said Sunshine. "No, I don't think I am. I don't think I have been for a long time. Tyler kept trying to tell me, but I didn't listen and now he's dead and it's my fault." Her voice cracked on a sob.

"Sunshine," said Tish. "It's not your fault. You didn't kill him."

I hope. I don't think you did. I hope you didn't.

"No," whispered Sunshine. "But I know who did. This is all my fault. It wouldn't have happened if I'd just left when Tyler asked me to. But I wasn't strong enough. This is my fault."

This conversation is going in circles. I'm getting nowhere.

"Are you strong enough to leave now, Sunshine? I will come get you. I will help you."

Maybe in person we can get to whatever you're babbling about.

"You'll come get me?" Sunshine's voice rose hopefully.

"Yes. I'm in Eastsound. I can be there in less than thirty minutes. I will come get you."

Sunshine was silent for a long moment. "OK," she gasped, as if the word were being squeezed out of her. "I'll do it. But please hurry. I think he knows I know."

"I will be there as soon as I can," said Tish, but the line was already dead. In frustration, she dialed her grandfather's cell phone again, but it went straight to voicemail.

"What do you want to bet he didn't even bring it with him," said Tish to her phone. She looked around at the parking lot. It was nearly five on a Sunday, no one was out. There appeared to be no help coming from any quarter.

Reluctantly, she dialed Nash.

"This is Nash. Leave a message after the beep."

"Hey," said Tish. "I know you're mad at me or whatever, but um… can you call me back? I just saw Granddad in a strange SUV and now he's not answering his phone. Which could mean that he just left his phone at home, but it's weird. And Sunshine Reich just called, and she says she wants help to leave the commune and she knows who killed Tyler and… well, I'm going to go get her. She sounded really scared. But, I don't know, I'd just feel better if someone knew where I was going." Tish sighed, realizing that she probably really did sound like a junior grade detective. "Yeah, OK, just call me back."

Slowly, she drove out to the commune. She felt like she ought to have a sneakier plan than simply driving up.

It could be a trap.

But she didn't think she could simply abandon Sunshine and not show up. Sunshine had sounded so frightened. And she would bet a stack of money on Sunshine not being that good of an actress.

It might not be a trap.

Tish strategized as she drove. She'd park closest to the exit. She'd get Sunshine and get out. She'd leave her purse in the car—just take the keys. And if anything looked remotely crazy, then she'd just leave. Tish got to the sign with the creepy otter and turned left. She bumped down the long private drive to the gravel lot and parked the car in the spot nearest to the road. On impulse, she turned the car around and backed into the spot, so that the car was pointed directly at the exit.

Her phone burped with an incoming text.

THIS IS MATT. MRS. HAYNIE SAID CLOVER'S BEEN "BOINKING CRAIG LARSON FROM OUT AT THE COMMUNE." HOPE THAT HELPS.

She texted a quick thanks and stared at the commune buildings in the rear-view mirror. Nothing was moving. Her phone rang and she jumped. Looking down she saw it was Sarah's number.

"Hey," she said picking up. "You're OK, right?"

"Yeah, I'm fine. I'm with Clover in a bar."

"What? I thought you were just following her!"

"I did and you're never going to believe what I found out."

"Probably not," said Tish. "What happened?"

"I followed her over to a house in Ravenna and she busts out this telephoto lens and camera and she starts creeping through the bushes, so I figure what the hell, now I've got to know. So, I drop in on her and tell her to spill the beans or I'm calling the cops."

"It's the ex," said Tish.

"Damn it. Stop guessing the punchline!"

"It's got to be the ex."

"Yes, but you'll never guess who he's getting it on with!"

"I have no clue," said Tish, still watching the compound in the rear view.

"The judge," said Sarah, savoring the words.

"What judge?"

"The judge who sentenced Clover to that two-mile restraining order."

"Whoa," said Tish, startled, but at the same time, suddenly scared.

"She's been trying for a month to catch them on camera, and we finally did it tonight. That's where she was the night of Tyler's murder. Which doesn't do us any good. But! I did get her to admit that she had Nash's knife. The problem is that she doesn't know where it went or when it went missing."

"Mars took it," said Tish.

"What?"

"Mars is Craig Larson. Clover was seeing Craig on Sunday's. I think he took it. Then I think he took the boat to Anacortes and killed Tyler. Probably because Tyler was trying to blackmail him for Medicaid fraud. The commune isn't a rehab center, and Tyler wasn't sober. They filed the paperwork, collected the money and I bet Tyler threatened to expose them."

"Oh," said Sarah, quietly. "That makes sense."

"Yeah, it does. Hey Sarah, can you do me a favor?"

"Sure. Can you call Granddad, Detective Spring and whoever else you can think of and tell them all of this and get them to go out to the commune?"

"Uh, sure. Why can't you call them?"

"Because I'm at the commune right now. I was supposed to pick up Sunshine and I don't see her anywhere."

"Shit," said Sarah. "Get out of there!"

"Not without Sunshine," said Tish, turning off the car.

"Tish, this is a bad plan," said Sarah. "Just leave!"

"I'll call you after I leave. Bye." Tish hung up and shoved the phone in her pocket. Mars might not know that she knew. Sunshine might just be hiding. It might not be a trap.

It's a trap.

CHAPTER 26
SUNSHINE'S BODY

Tish got out of the car and looked around the green landscape that was fast fading to shades of gray as the sun dipped behind the tree line. A harsh gust of wind tossed the trees surrounding the commune and making them sway with a sound like rushing water and Tish shivered in her sweatshirt. Around the perimeter of the open space some of the yurts leaked light through seams and cracks in the canvas, glowing through their impermanent walls. But the geodesic dome remained dark and, in the garden, the scarecrow swayed ominously on his cross.

I should have brought Nash. I would have if he'd picked up the phone.

Tish thought about yelling for Sunshine and then thought better of it. She approached the first yurt and peeled the door open an inch and peered through the crack. There was no one inside. The second was the same story. She pulled the third door open and angled herself to look inside.

The interior of the wood and canvas structure looked as if a hurricane had blown through. The back wall was shredded and splintered and a gaping hole looked out onto the quickly darkening woods. From her vantage point she could clearly see a bloody handprint on the canvas next to the hole.

I should leave. I should go now.

Heart pounding, she went around to the other side of the yurt.

There's no body. She might still be alive.

A path of light from the exposed interior showed staggering boot prints in the mud. She followed the path into the woods and, on the ground in front of her, saw Sunshine's ridiculous straw hat.

Time to call in the cavalry.

She fumbled for her phone and hit the speed dial for the Sheriff's station.

"San Juan County Sheriff's Department, this is Deputy Pearson," said Ray, his voice calm and reassuring.

"Ray, it's Tish." She kept her voice low, straining to listen for some hint of Sunshine above the sound of wind and trees.

"Hey Tish, what's up?" asked Ray cheerfully, but over his voice she heard the ratcheting sound of a shotgun being racked. On instinct, she dropped flat into the mud, just as the gun roared. The phone went bouncing out of her hand and the next blast destroyed the glowing phone. Tish rolled onto her back and began to crawl further into the underbrush. She could hear someone coming after her, but it was hard to pinpoint the exact direction in the gathering dark. She looked down at herself and realized that in the dark and now covered in mud she must be almost invisible.

"Get to the chopper," she whispered to herself.

Predator, 1987, starring Arnold Schwarzenegger.

"I know you're out here," a man yelled. "I know Sunshine called you." She finally recognized the voice of Mars. "I know she told you I killed Tyler, but I'm not going down for that. Come out and maybe we can make a deal."

Or maybe you'll just shoot me.

"I've got money," he yelled. He was drifting further away from her. "I just need a head start. Come out. We can work something out."

Tish began crawling in the opposite direction of the man, stopping whenever she heard him stop. She heard him crank the shotgun again and then a blast. She froze and then there was a thundering in the underbrush as two deer bounded by. Tish pushed herself to her feet and followed them, hoping their noise would cover hers. Sprinting, she ran after the deer hoping to put as much distance as possible between herself and Mars.

She came out into an opening, slipped on the mud, tripped over a rock and landed heavily on hard dirt. She tried to quiet her own panting and listen for Mars. It was lighter in the clearing and a few feet away she could see the outline of a shovel embedded in the ground. Next to the shovel was a bundle of canvas. Crawling forward, Tish tore it open.

Inside lay the body of Sunshine Reich, her eyes open and staring at nothing. Her pale skin was the lightest thing in Tish's field of vision and Tish found that she couldn't tear her eyes away. With a shaking hand she gently put the drop cloth back over Sunshine's face.

Move. I need to move.

Tish jumped as in the distance another blast of the shotgun split the air.

Move.

Tish stood up. She reached out and grabbed the shovel, hefting it one hand. It was an old shovel with a wooden handle and a metal scoop. The wood was rough in her hand and it hung in her hands with an efficient weight. She found the balance point on the shovel, shifting it nervously between her hands and tried to make a plan.

She had no phone and no idea where she was in relationship to the commune. She looked up at the sky. The ragged clouds allowed only sporadic glimpses of stars. From the vantage point in the center of the clearing she could see a trail entrance, but she knew once under the cover of the trees she would be virtually blind. But then, Mars would be too.

Tish counted over the people that had been called: Nash, the Sheriff's Station, Granddad. Sarah wouldn't let her down. Someone was sure to come.

Eventually.

Creeping forward onto the trail, Tish paused under an overhanging tree branch, trying to evaluate how long she could stay in one place. Could she afford to wait? How long before Mars circled back to this location?

I'll follow the trail. It must go back to the commune. If I can beat Mars back there, I've got a shot.

She couldn't hear anything, so she inched forward. Slowly, her eyes were becoming more adjusted to the dark. Against the black dark of the woods, she could see a ribbon of not-so-black that she thought must be the path. She moved as quickly as she dared, sliding her feet along the ground.

The minutes ticked past in nerve wracking slowness. Each foot forward seemed like it might be her last. After a seeming decade of darkness and a dozen frightening blunders into trees and bushes Tish saw a glimmer of light through the trees. She crept forward along the path, more sure-footed now.

She looked out onto the edge of the commune. Nothing moved but the scarecrow. She couldn't see her car behind the geodesic dome, but she knew it would be there. She felt convulsively in her pocket for her keys and breathed a sigh of relief. Crouching low, she jogged to the first yurt. She debated going from yurt to yurt or straight across the open space to her car. The only cover was a garden shed in the middle.

Tish waited, counting the seconds. At a minute of hearing nothing, she decided to risk the shorter distance. The sound of her own breathing was loud in her ears as she dashed to the garden shed. She winced as the shovel clanged off the corner of the shed and she pressed herself against the shadowed side of shed waiting for certain discovery.

More waiting. In the distance she thought she heard a motor, but it cut out.

Tish risked a look at the geodesic dome. Would the phone work? Should she go for it or for the car?

The car. Get the hell out of here.

Tish crept around the edge of the shed. She waited again, breathing as quietly as possible. Then she stepped out into the open.

Nothing. She took a few more steps. Nothing. She picked up the pace, hurrying now.

She was half-way to the dome when the door slammed open and three figures emerged. Tish froze.

Run. Damn it. Run. Don't freeze.

"You have to come with us," said the man in front.

"Mars is out there with a shotgun," said Tish.

"We know," said the second figure—a woman. "He's very upset."

"I'm leaving," said Tish. "You're welcome to come with me."

"Why would we leave?" asked the first man. "Mars needs us."

"Like he needed Sunshine?" asked Tish. "You know he killed her, right?"

"She was going to leave us," said the third man who was nothing more than a tall angular shadow against the dome wall. They were starting to spread out, attempting to surround Tish. "Wind and Moonbeam cried and prayed, but we had no choice in the end."

His voice was sad, but not overly concerned, as if he were discussing something unfortunate that had happened a long way away.

They're all crazy. They drank the Kool-Aid and it doesn't matter what I say, they're going to kill me.

Tish swung the shovel around in front of her, holding it with two hands like a kayak paddle. "I'm leaving," she said.

"Rain, is right. You can't leave," said the woman. "You'll ruin everything. You'll have to go with Sunshine."

"Sunshine is dead!" yelled Tish.

"Death is only the next stage," whispered the tall man.

As if that was the signal, the first man lunged at Tish, coming in from her left. She swung hard with the shovel and heard the satisfying pong as the metal end connected with something hard. The man grunted and crumpled to the ground, but Tish didn't have time to enjoy her victory. The tall man ran forward and grabbed her from behind, pinning her arms to her sides. The woman dove in, trying to grab the shovel. Tish kicked out, landing a foot square on her chest, sending the woman sprawling backwards onto the gravel path.

"Mars!" yelled the woman. "She's here!"

Shit. I'm going to die. Better think of something good Patricia. And do it now.

Tish shifted the shovel to vertical and swung it over her head, aiming for the man holding her arms. She felt it connect to something and he yelled and dropped her. Tish charged forward, running for the car, but the woman surged into her way, tackling her around the knees and Tish went down. She rolled to her back, kicking out with her feet, but the woman and her skirts were enveloping her legs like a wet blanket.

"Hold her down, Moonbeam," yelled the first man.

Tish hauled the shovel downward ramming the handle into Moonbeam. But she could see Wind and Rain quickly coming to Moonbeam's aid. Behind her she heard the crunch of running footsteps on the gravel path.

It's Mars and I'm going to die.

Tish kicked harder and rammed again with the shovel handle. Moonbeam yelled in pain and anger as the shovel handle struck against her shoulder. Wind and Rain were reaching for her, ignoring the runner on the path. But the runner leapt over Tish and cannoned into the two men. The runner scrambled to his feet and for a moment Tish saw him illuminated against the light from the yurts.

Nash.

Tish finally got a leg free and kicked Moonbeam in the face. Scrambling to her feet, Tish swung her shovel at Moonbeam, but the hippie scrambled out of the way.

In front of her, Nash punched Wind, or Rain, or whichever one it was, in the face and Tish watched the man collapse, unconscious. Moonbeam was running for the geodesic dome. The remaining man faced Nash and Tish uncertainly. It was the tall man, who Tish tentatively thought was Rain. Tish was panting, but took a firmer grip on her shovel.

"We're leaving," said Nash, backing up, without taking his eyes off Rain.

"You can't leave!" barked Rain in frustration. "Mars will be upset."

"No one leaves!" screamed Moonbeam, bursting from the geodesic dome, an enormous shotgun in her arms.

"Jesus!" exclaimed Tish and, with fear driven strength, swung the shovel like a baseball bat. The shovel connected with the shotgun, sending it flying even as Moonbeam pulled the trigger. The blast was like fireworks on a dark night, leaving trailing sparkles in Tish's vision. In one motion, Nash punched Rain, grabbed Tish and began to run down the path toward where the cars waited in the lot, illuminated in flashes by a single industrial light, swinging in the wind.

"Car!" gasped Tish, trying to pull him toward her car.

"Tires!" he said, pointing at her car. The tires were all flat. "My bike is on the road. We run for it. Get the hell out."

They had taken two steps toward the road when Mars came out from behind the VW Microbus.

"I hope you killed the rest of them," said Mars. "It would really save me a lot of trouble."

Nash dropped Tish's hand and stepped in front of her.

"It'll be a bit hard to steal their Medicaid benefits if they're dead," said Tish, stepping out from behind Nash. "That's what you're doing, isn't it? The commune members and all your rehab clients. You file paperwork for people who never go to rehab and collect the payments?"

"The best part is that the rehab patients actually pay me so that they don't have to come here. I get paid twice."

"Only Tyler threatened to expose you?" asked Nash. "How much did he want? Ten thousand?"

"Twenty. Just to keep his mouth shut. I think not. Although, honestly, I might have gone for it, except he said he was taking Sunshine with him. Sunshine gets the most disability money. I'm not letting her leave. Although, death won't be a problem. It won't stop the bennies from rolling in," he said grinning. "It just means I don't have to feed them."

"You'll just keep filing their benefits as usual?" asked Tish, stalling for time.

"Why not?" asked Mars, stepping forward. "Of course, I'll be filing it from Mexico, but with direct deposit, that won't really matter, will it? Now if the two of you would bunch together that would be real helpful like. I do hate to waste ammo."

Nash deliberately took a step away from her and Mars swung the shotgun in his direction. Tish swung the shovel into an upright position, readying it for an attack, and the shotgun swung back toward her. Nash took another step.

"Don't get cute," said Mars. "This isn't the movies. I can get both of you."

"You want to kill us?" Moonbeam's tremulous voice only underlined the steadiness with which she held the shotgun, aimed at Mars.

"Of course not *you*," said Mars automatically. "You're a part of my soul."

"That's what you said to Sunshine," said Moonbeam, her voice filled with a wavering panic.

"Put the gun down Moonbeam," said Mars, sounding less sure of himself. "You know I don't want any of you to sully your auras with weapons."

"Put yours down," whispered Moonbeam

Mars swung his gun toward Moonbeam. "Don't be ridiculous Moonbeam. You're letting these outsiders pollute your mind. You're better than this."

Tish began to back away, while Nash began to edge closer to Mars.

Damn it. I just want to get out of here. Why is he going toward the crazy person? I mean, yes, probably as soon as we run, they'll both shoot us, but that is no reason to fling yourself into danger.

"I'm the one you need to trust," said Mars.

Cult leader bullcrap! He can't even act. It's not even believable. I can be a better cult leader than you!

"Moonbeam," said Tish, taking a few steps in her direction. Mars and Moonbeam both swung her direction. "Sunshine told me that she thought of you as her true sister. She believed that you were destined to always be a part of each other's lives. She thought of you as a true example of the spirit."

"No, it was Sunshine," said Moonbeam, tears thick in her voice. "She was always the truest of us."

"She was going to leave us!" screamed Mars.

"That was your fault, Mars" said Tish, but without looking at him, continuing to walk toward Moonbeam. Nash was inching closer to Mars. "You killed her brother. You dirtied the aura of this sacred place. You brought violence and blood here. How was she supposed to stay?" Moonbeam was nodding. From the direction of the road, Tish thought she heard the sound of cars.

"Shut up!" yelled Mars.

"Mars," said Tish shaking her head. "You've lost the way. When did you stop believing? You're the one that drove Sunshine out. Turning the family against her. How could you do that?"

"Mars, how could you?" asked Moonbeam seriously, her shotgun dipping for the first time.

"Shut. Up." Mars took a step closer to Tish, shoving the shotgun out in front of him.

"Mars," said Tish, "I'm only speaking the truth. Sometimes the truth is painful."

"Yes," said Moonbeam nodding. "Yes, you've said that yourself, Mars. You need to listen. We need to listen."

"There can be no healing without listening," said Tish. "We're ready to heal," she said, putting one arm around Moonbeam's shoulders. "Are you?"

"I hate you so much," said Mars and for a moment his gun dropped, as if he was marveling at the depth of his own hatred. Nash tackled him, and Tish pulled Moonbeam onto the ground as the shotgun went off. Moonbeam was under her, struggling and seemed to be composed entirely of dress. There was a roar of motors and a spray of gravel as cars shot out of the tree line and into the parking area. Their headlights transfixing everyone on the scene.

Nash and Mars struggled over the shotgun and Tish watched, Nash kneed Mars in the gut, wrenched the shotgun away from him and hit the commune leader with the butt of the gun.

Moonbeam clutched at her, but whether from fear or anger Tish couldn't tell, but either way Tish couldn't stand upright. Finally, in frustration Tish, punched the other woman. She knew it wasn't a very good punch. Her only training had been aerobic kickboxing classes and a few hours with a stunt coordinator who walked her through a choreographed fight. But it did the trick. Moonbeam stopped struggling and lay on the ground staring upward as if catatonic.

Tish struggled to her feet, reaching for both her shovel and Moonbeam's shotgun. The door of the lead SUV popped open and Tobias climbed out.

The cavalry has arrived. Should we get an SUV? He got out of that one really fast.

"Granddad," began Tish, but Nash was moving, holding up the shotgun, putting himself back between her and Mars. She looked from Nash to her grandfather, who was now holding the beat-up pistol he kept in the remote caddy by his Laz-E-Boy in the den. "Don't do it, Craig," said Tobias.

What's he doing?

Tish looked around Nash and saw that Mars had his hand behind his back as if reaching for his back pocket.

More people were coming out of the cars. There was a lot of yelling. Tish really couldn't concentrate on what they were saying—it sounded like the barking of seals. She looked from Nash, whose face was grim, to Tobias whose expression was entirely calm. Tobias held the gun casually at his waist, but pointed at Mars, like a gangster from a black and white movie.

"This is your fault," said Mars, spitting out the words, staring at Nash. "Why couldn't you have killed Tyler. You should have killed Tyler. They should have arrested you."

"You killed Tyler," said Nash.

"And you," said Mars, staring at Tish, "you ruined everything."

"Don't do it Craig," said Tobias. "You can walk out of this."

"Damn you," said Mars. There was more yelling from the others. Tish locked eyes with Mars and she was surprised to see how much hatred there really was. Mars really wanted to kill her. In that moment, the entire world seemed quiet. She couldn't hear the yelling, the wind, or the trees. She knew they must still exist because the parking lot light was still swaying, throwing strange shadows over everything. She saw Mars move his arm and then the silence ended.

There was a sharp crack of a pistol and then the roar of the shotgun.

Then Nash was pushing her away.

"We're going over here now," he said. "No, don't look back."

"Moonbeam," said Tish. People were running at them and Tish flinched backward stepping into Nash.

"Give them the weapons," said Nash. He was handing over the shotgun he'd been holding. Tish held out hers as well. "The shovel too," he said.

Tish found that she was reluctant to give it up. Nash took it out of her hand and handed it over.

"Moonbeam," said Tish again. "She'll need help."

"They'll help her," said Nash. "We're going this way."

Tish found herself blocked and herded and although she wanted to fight it, at least they weren't trying to take Nash away, and at some point, it simply became easier to go where they wanted. And where they wanted ended up being the back of an ambulance. Tish sat on the gurney and let them shine lights in her eyes and take her pulse. There was also some attempt to scrub the mud off of the bits of her that were showing, but she suspected that only made her look worse because the policemen who came to ask her questions only stared at her and then backed away slowly and went to talk to Nash.

Tish tried to hear what they asked, but he was standing just far enough away that she couldn't quite make out their words.

"Hey Tishkins," said Tobias, appearing out of the dark. "How we doin'?"

"Hey Granddad. You tell me how we're doing. How much trouble are we in?"

"Not too much."

"What about Nash?"

"Oh, I think this'll actually get him out of trouble."

Tish breathed a sigh of relief. "Mars killed Sunshine," she said, remembering that she hadn't told anyone yet. "Her body is out in the woods."

Tobias nodded. "Moonshine, or whatever she's calling herself, said as much. They'll have to wait until morning to go retrieve the body."

"Sunshine was so scared," said Tish. "She just wanted to leave."

"She could have left at any time," said Tobias.

"It wasn't that simple for her," said Tish. "I wish I could have…" Tish didn't know how to say what she wanted.

I want Sunshine to be alive.

"Don't travel down that road," said Tobias. "There's no end to it. You did the best you could and Mars won't be hurting anyone else ever again."

"We've got to get better at this," said Tish. "We can't have people dying all the time. I knew Mars was a horrible person. I should have figured out what he was doing before he killed Sunshine."

"We're a work in progress," said Tobias. "We didn't have all the pieces to the puzzle."

"Well, I might have," sniffed Tish, "if you hadn't cut me out."

"You were working on Reginald's and that's important! And once Greg sent me the financials and a photo of Craig Larson, and I figured out what Mars was doing, then it was mostly just me sitting around waiting for Spring to get search warrants."

"You should have called me and told me what was going on!"

"I tried a couple of times," he huffed. "But I was in Friday Harbor and I think it was a dead zone because it went straight to your voicemail."

Tish deflated. "Yeah, that's what it did when I called you too." She was frustratingly all too familiar with most of the cell phone holes on the island.

"We're lucky that any of Sarah's calls got through. She and Clover must have been burning up the phone lines trying to get a message through."

"Is that how you turned up in the nick of time?"

"Partly. And partly we were just finally on our way out here. But your grandma always used to say that nick of time was my specialty," he said with a grin. "Anyway, I was going to call you once we got back here, but it didn't go through and then I figured Reginald's was important and I might as well let you keep working."

Tish eyed him skeptically. "You mean you wanted to keep me out of trouble."

"Yes," he agreed easily, flipping the argument like a judo master. "You're my granddaughter. I'm supposed to keep you out of harm's way, not throw you into it. It didn't occur to me that you'd throw yourself."

Tish sat up straighter, preparing to be annoyed, but Tobias continued on unperturbed. "Obviously, I should have circled back around once I hit the island and picked you up. But it also occurred to me that you've been working really hard on Reginald's, but I keep taking up your time. You've got goals and you shouldn't have to detour from yours just to make mine happen. Getting the kitchen done is important."

"Not as important as Sunshine or Nash," said Tish, swallowing the lump in her throat.

He looked sympathetic which was a bad sign.

If Granddad thinks I need sympathy, then I'm probably doing horribly.

"I got distracted by the dishwasher and walls. I shouldn't have gotten distracted. Did I tell you Nash put up drywall?"

"Yes, you seemed very happy about it."

"He said he can texture next week. I don't know what texture is, but he says it makes walls look like real walls."

"It's the bumps on the walls. It covers up all manner of construction sins," said Tobias nodding.

I am babbling. I know I'm babbling, but I can't seem to stop.

"Sounds great," said Tish, rallying. "But my point is, that I got distracted; we should have figured it out sooner."

"You can't spend every waking moment on a case," said Tobias. "Gotta leave room for *Matlock* and dishwashers. You tried to help her. You did your best."

"Seems like it's never good enough," said Tish.

Tobias reached out and seized her chin in one of his gnarled hands, lifting it so that she had to look him in the eye.

"Your best is a damn sight better than most of the population. If you couldn't do it, then it couldn't be done."

Tish smiled at him.

It's a total lie and I don't care. I love that he even maybe thinks that.

"Well, Miss Yearly," said Detective Spring, coming around the side of the ambulance, "you seem to have gotten yourself in some trouble again. Care to tell me about it?"

Tish glanced at Tobias. He smiled and shrugged.

"Sure," said Tish. "Can I go home afterwards? I'd like to not be muddy anymore."

"That seems entirely reasonable," said the detective. Tish squinted at him. He was suspiciously non-angry.

"You want to take out your notebook?" suggested Tish. "Usually you like to make notes."

The Detective held up his phone. "I'm going to record it. Save myself the hand cramp."

"Trying something new?" asked Tish.

"It's the only way to get different results," he said.

Holy cow. What exactly did Granddad say to him?

"Huh," said Tish. "Well, OK, then."

By the time she was finishing her story, Nash had finished his conversation and was sitting on the lower bumper of the ambulance, listening.

"You skipped a part," he said.

She stared at him blankly. "No, I didn't."

"Yes, you did. You skipped the part where we were staring down the barrel of two shotguns and you talked Moonbeam into changing sides."

"Yeah," said Tish uncomfortably. "Talking cultists into doing things isn't a real triumph and Moonbeam's not exactly working with a full deck." All three men were staring at her. "It's easy," she said. "I could be a cult leader if I wanted. Anyone could do it. It's acceptance, hope, fear and offering a simplified solution to life's complex problems, plus a strong delineation of us and them. And repeat the cycle."

There was more staring.

"You just have to use the right words."

"Well," said the detective clearing his throat, "I think we're all glad you've decided to pursue other life goals."

"Can I go home now?" asked Tish.

"No," said Tobias. "The tires are all flat on your car and I ain't done here yet."

"I can get someone to drive you home," said the detective.

"I can do it," said Nash standing up. "I've been told to vacate anyway to avoid the appearance of investigating my own case."

"Are you sure you don't mind?" asked Tish.

"Well, a bit," said Nash. "You're going to get my bike all muddy."

"Shut up," said Tish.

"I'll be home after a while," said Tobias.

"No rush," said Tish with a shrug. "I'm only going to be in the bathtub."

"There's a new rubber ducky in the upstairs laundry closet."

"Ooh! Ducky!" Tish caught Nash's expression. "You're just jealous."

"So true," said Nash. "This way."

They walked down the driveway, now illuminated by the headlights of a dozen police cars.

"The island doesn't have this many official vehicles," said Tish.

"Tobias got Spring to bring in extra. It's not every day you get to catch a million-dollar Medicaid fraud ring."

"Million dollars?" Tish looked up at him in surprise.

"Yeah. Then there's the murder. So, you know, it seemed important."

"He's scammed a million dollars and he wouldn't cough up twenty grand for Tyler? What an idiot."

"Yes," agreed Nash. His phone burbled, and he read the message with a frown. Then he dialed the number and waited for an answer. Whoever it was, was high-pitched, female, and upset.

Nora? Seriously, do you have to call now?

"Slow down," he said. "It's fine. I've got her." There was a tiny bleat of inquiry from the phone. "Yes. No. I'm taking her home. No, he's um…" he glanced at Tish, "dead."

There was a burst of panicked questioning.

"I swear she's fine. Here." He impatiently handed Tish the phone. "Tell Sarah you're fine."

"Shit! I was supposed to call her when I was leaving." She grabbed the phone. "Hi. I'm fine. I mean, covered in mud and I think I bruised the crap out of my knee, but I swear I'm fine."

"Tish Yearly, that was not OK! I thought I was having a panic attack. What the hell is wrong with you?"

"I wanted to rescue Sunshine," said Tish.

"Did you get her?"

Tish felt herself wavering on the point of tears.

"No," said Tish, gulping air. Nash put his arms around her and she leaned into him. "Um, no. Mars killed her." She mushed her face into his chest and concentrated on breathing.

"Oh," said Sarah. "Oh. I'm sorry."

"Me too," said Tish, taking a deep breath and inhaling the smell of Nash that was a mixture of his leather jacket, sweat, mud and underlying scent of mint that she knew from Claire was the all-natural wool dryer balls that he dried his clothes with. "Anyway, Nash came dashing to the rescue and Granddad showed up with Detective Spring and a bunch of police. So, they're taking care of things. And Nash is taking me home."

"Are you sure you're OK?" demanded Sarah.

"Oh, you know me," said Tish. "I'm always fine." She pushed away from Nash and wiped the tears off her face. "But I'm super muddy and I really want to go home, so can I call you tomorrow?"

"Yeah, of course, I'm just here with Clover. I think we're going to get really drunk."

"OK, sounds great. Don't let her talk you into slashing the ex's tires or blowing up the judge's house or anything."

"Heh. Don't worry. I'm not you. I'm not planning on taking unnecessary risks. I'll talk to you tomorrow. Try to get some rest."

"Yeah, thanks. Night."

"Night." She hung up the phone and handed the phone back to Nash.

"She's blowing up a judge's house?"

"God, I hope not," said Tish. "I can't take any more of my friends having legal troubles." She looked at his questioning expression. "I'll explain later. I promise. But right now, can we just go home?"

He nodded and pointed to the motorcycle that was only steps away. Nash's motorcycle generally looked as if it was never designed to carry a passenger, but she'd seen Claire ride on it, so she knew it was physically possible.

But my ass is a little wider than a ten-year-old's.

"Doubts?" he asked, handing her the spare helmet he kept for Claire.

"I was wondering how it is that when I get in trouble I always end up riding home on a two-wheeled death trap."

"Probably karma," he said, swinging his leg over the bike and starting the engine. "Get on. You'll like it."

Tish hesitated another second and then shrugged. "Just look out for cows in the road."

"I always do," he said, refusing to be thrown off by her non-sequitur.

Ten minutes later Tish had to admit that Nash was right. Riding with him was fun. But that might have had more to do with being able to snuggle up against him than with the riding itself.

Not that I'm going to tell him that.

But by the time they arrived at the Yearly residence Tish was thoroughly cold, wet, and starting to feel that perhaps she should have stayed in the ambulance and waited for Tobias.

She climbed off the bike feeling stiff. The bruises were starting to make themselves known now that the adrenaline was wearing off. She stared at her darkened house and felt the old dread that sometimes crept into her mind.

"Nash?" She stopped, turning the helmet over in her hands.

"Yes?"

"Will you come in and wait with me until Granddad gets home? Sometimes... The last time... I thought I was safe at home and then Steve Winslow... I know it's silly."

"It's not silly," said Nash, shutting off the bike.

"It is. He's dead. Mars is dead. I know there's nothing to worry about. But, I just..." She looked up at him embarrassed.

"Of course, I can stay," he said.

"You can put the bike in the garden shed," offered Tish. "So it'll at least it'll be dry."

"Thanks," he said, pushing the bike down the slope.

Coats was waiting for them in the hall by the time they got inside. Nash kicked off his boots into the shoe basket and knelt down to pet the dog.

"Nash, how did you know to come find me?"

"Ray called me. He was hoping I knew where you were. I had just listened to your message, so I did know. Ray said they had it under control, but I was already in Eastsound and I didn't think I should wait. And then on the way up I heard gunshots. I was worried if I kept the motor going I'd be shot. So, I parked the bike and approached on foot."

"Granddad said nick of time was his specialty, but I think he may have to fight you for the title," said Tish and Nash grinned. "OK, I'm going to take a shower. The TV's in the den. I'd warn you about the remote caddy, but Granddad's got his pistol with him."

"He keeps it in the remote caddy?" Nash looked torn between amusement and horror.

"He says it's conveniently located for emergency use," said Tish with a shrug.

"Has he always kept it there?"

"Oh no. When we were kids he used to lock it up. I remember Grandma yelling at him. Anyway, I'm sure there's leftovers in the fridge too." She glanced into the kitchen and caught sight of the clock. "Holy crap. Is that the right time? How is it only six? I feel like it should be midnight."

"Tell me about it," said Nash with a yawn. "I haven't exactly slept well since this thing started and while I appreciate the offer of food, I'm probably just going to turn on the TV and fall asleep."

"In that case, I recommend the fuzzy blanket over the afghan. My toes always get stuck in the holes of the afghan."

"Thanks for the tip," he said and went into the den.

She climbed the stairs with a smile. Having Nash around was ridiculously reassuring. She wasn't quite sure how he managed it. Was it being a parent? Was he naturally that way? Whatever it was, it was a relief to know that she only had to yell to have him come running.

Smothering a yawn herself, she headed into the bathroom.

CHAPTER 27

LAST CALL

Tish was staring at the toaster when the front door swung open with a bang. Tish jumped and stared in panic at Tobias.

"Hey!" he said cheerfully, toting his pistol into the den. He returned and then seemed to realize her startled state. "You OK?"

"Yeah," said Tish, shaking her head. "Yeah, I was just really zoned out on the toaster and you surprised me." The toast popped, and she started again. "I wasn't expecting you." She picked up the toast, dropped it on a plate and began to butter it.

Don't look at the shoe basket.

"George and I are going down to Olga and tie one on. Want to come?"

"Oh, no thanks," said Tish, taking her plate to the kitchen table.

"Don't you want to celebrate?" he asked.

Tish laughed. "I was planning on celebrating tomorrow. It was kind of a long day. I was looking forward to TV and reading crap articles on my phone."

"Are those jammies?" he asked squinting at her shorts and sweatshirt.

"Yes?" said Tish.

"Young people today," said Tobias, shaking his head.

"What's wrong with my shorts?" asked Tish.

Keep him looking over here. Don't look at the shoe basket.

"Nothing. I meant young people today don't know how to have a good time. Sure you won't come along?"

"Yeah, I'm sure. You guys have fun."

"Nash went back to his place? Maybe I should call him."

"He said something about sleeping for a week," said Tish. "I don't think he's been sleeping too well with everything that's been going on."

"I can understand that," said Tobias, nodding sympathetically. "Well, all right. If you're sure. I guess it will just be George and me closing the place down."

"Have fun," said Tish again, wishing she had a drink. The toast was like sand in her mouth.

"Will do. Don't just eat toast for dinner."

"I've got left overs in the fridge," said Tish.

"OK. Night!" he called as he closed the front door. Tish waited until she heard his car tires crunch on the gravel of the driveway and then she bolted from her seat. Grabbing Nash's boots out of the shoe basket, she sprinted up the stairs. He twisted to see the door as he jammed one leg into his pants and fell over. Tish dropped his boots and went to help him up.

"Tobias cannot know about this," Nash said when he was finally upright, pants still unzipped.

"Claire can't know about this," said Tish, as he scrambled to find the rest of his clothes.

"In the ranks of who can't know, it's Tobias and then Claire," he said, waving a sock.

"No, it's Claire then Granddad," said Tish.

"Tobias keeps a gun in the remote caddy!" argued Nash, gesturing emphatically with his shirt.

"But at least with Granddad you don't have to explain what sex is!" yelled Tish.

He paused clearly thinking that one over. "OK, yeah, fair point. Claire then Tobias."

There was another pause and Tish stared up at him, not really sure where to take the conversation from here.

"So he left?" asked Nash.

"He went down to the Olga Bar to celebrate with George," she said, reaching out and crooking a finger through one of his belt loops, tugging him closer. "He said they were going to close it down."

Nash nodded thoughtfully. "They close at eleven," he observed, sliding a hand around her waist.

Tish looked over at the clock on her bedside table and bit her lip. "And it is only eight now."

"That leaves a lot of time," he whispered in her ear.

TISH & TOBIAS ARE BACK.
BUT THIS TIME THEY'RE SWIMMING IN...

An UNFAMILIAR SEA

CHAPTER 1

FRIDAY - TISH YEARLY THE LIFE COACH

Twenty-eight-year-old Tish Yearly carried folding chairs across the lawn toward the gazebo in the glorious June sunshine and rehearsed the words she was going to say to her boyfriend.

"I'm pregnant."

Tish's thoughts and her feet came to a stumbling halt. "What?" Tish stared at twenty-two year old Penelope Drue, who was clasping and unclasping her hands in front of her chest. Penelope looked like she needed more than a one-word question, but Tish needed more than a two-word announcement. "Congratulations?" Tish tried.

When Tish had had set about opening her own wedding venue on Orcas Island, she had been prepared for inclement weather, she had been prepared for irate brides, she had even been prepared for the inconvenience of bribing the local Sheriff's deputies with food to keep them from ticketing her guests, but she had not been prepared to play den mother to employees that were barely younger than she was.

"I'm not trying to ditch out." Petite, purple-haired Penelope looked tearful. "I'll carry the chairs, but I don't think I should lift the dancefloor sections."

Tish had not been planning on asking Penelope to lift dancefloor sections. "OK," said Tish. "Uh… that's fine?"

"They say that, right? That pregnant women shouldn't lift heavy things?"

"I think so," said Tish. Penelope had big hazel eyes and a tawny complexion that always looked slightly sun-kissed and strangely natural with her purple hair. Currently, those eyes were set to maximum hugeness and Tish wondered if she could mimic that puppy effect with any sort of effectivity or if someone had to be twenty-two to pull it off.

"Bowen asked me to carry dancefloor sections," clarified Penelope. "But I can't! But I really need this job!"

"OK," said Tish. She had loaded three chairs onto each of her arms, and her left was starting to go numb below the elbow. "Just tell Bowen I put you on chair detail."

"I'll only be like four or five months along by the time wedding season is over, so it won't be a big deal. No one even has to know."

"OK," agreed Tish. She didn't know what else to say. Her experience with pregnant people was limited. *OK* seemed to be working so far—Tish decided to stick with it.

"Actually, I haven't actually told anyone else yet, so can maybe you not...?"

"OK," said Tish.

"But I just thought I should tell you because I didn't want you to freak out that I'm not a hard worker or that I'm being difficult and fire me."

"I won't fire you," said Tish. She didn't add that she was pretty sure that firing pregnant girls was not only illegal, but probably also a sure-fire way of going to hell.

"Oh, thank the goddess!" Penelope had been raised in a commune on Shaw island and therefore had some unique views on spirituality.

"You just found out then?" asked Tish, trying to do the math.

"Yeah. It's kind of an accident."

How is it only kind of an accident?

"Some of the coolest people are oops babies," said Tish reassuringly, since Penelope looked like she needed reassuring.

"You don't have to plan everything."

Penelope laughed. "I plan almost nothing. That's usually what I have Azalea for."

Azalea was Penelope's best friend and the OCD yin to Penelope's wild child yang. Tish had hired the pair of them and so far they were both operating above her expectations. Although, the pregnancy thing was a bit of hiccup that she hadn't included even on her top secret list of potential Orcas-wackiness.

"I guess I won't be able to have Azalea help me with this," continued Penelope, looking sad. "I also guess I won't be doing anymore drinking for a while. That's fine. Like I need beer calories anyway. I am nervous," she said with a nakedly honest expression that hit Tish right in the hug button, not that she could do anything about it with her arms full of chairs. "But the weird thing is, I think I've got this. I know what I'm supposed to do. And it's not going to be easy, but at least I'm not confused."

"Well," said Tish, "that makes one of us."

"Thanks for being understanding," said Penelope.

"No problem," said Tish. "Uh, but maybe you can carry one of these chairs though?" she asked, holding out her left arm.

"Oh! Sure!" Penelope took two of the chairs and Tish sighed in relief.

"It's really cool?"

"That's good," said Tish. "I'm glad you're happy. Babies seem nice."

Theoretically. For other people.

"No, that was a question. Is it really cool with you?"

"Oh. Uh…" Among the other things that Tish didn't think she had prepared for properly in her business plan was the idea that she would have any say or sway over the life of another human being. She wasn't the boss. As a former actress, she was ready to be a star. Maybe. But never the boss. She was at one with the proletariat. She loved the idea of contributing jobs to the Orcas Island economy, but she didn't think she was supposed to be able to devastate the hopes and dreams of another person. "Yes," said Tish. "It's fine. We can make it work."

Penelope's shoulders dropped as if a weight had slid off. "Thanks," she said, tears sparkling in her eyes. "This wasn't supposed to happen. I'm excited about it. But it's complicated and—"

"Tish!" yelled someone from driveway. "Tish, we've got a five-alarm emergency!"

"Is that Terry the florist?" asked Penelope.

"Yes," said Tish, looking down at her arms full of chairs. "Uh..."

"Just leave them there," said Penelope. "I'll take care of them."

"Thanks," said Tish, setting the chairs down on the grass with a clack as the wooden seats banged together. "I'll be back in a minute."

These last two days leading up to her very first wedding ever had been full of Tish telling people she'd be back. Unlike the Terminator, that wasn't remotely true.

Terminator, 1984, starring Arnold Schwarzenegger in a roll that was originally slated for O.J. Simpson.

She felt like she was being pulled in a million different directions at once. She was trying not to place too much importance on this one event. She had six more weddings booked over the next two months. But this was the first one and she couldn't help feeling that if it didn't go right, then *none* of them would go right. She'd been having constant naked-on-stage dreams for the last week. It was the worst case of opening night jitters she'd ever had. Only this wasn't a play and she couldn't slink home and drown her sorrows in red wine if the reviews came back poor. Orcas Island was now her home and if she screwed this up everyone on the entire island was going to know.

Tish walked up the rise to the driveway and gravel parking area in front of the house. Terry's bulbous, dark-blue Subaru was parked awkwardly in the middle of the drive as if she had seen Tish and promptly stopped the car where it was. Terry was standing at the edge of the drive watching her approach.

"Hey Terry," said Tish, swiping a chunk of her blonde bangs behind her ear. She really needed a haircut, but she winced at the idea of going to an on-island stylist. And then she felt pained and uppity for wanting to go off-island and then she didn't do either. "What's the emergency?"

"The flowers didn't make it on the ferry and now my flower guy is threatening to charge double-hourly for the wait time to get on the next ferry. I can't pay that. And if they make me pay that, I'm going to have to pass it on to you."

"So our emergency is that you want to charge me more money?" asked Tish and Terry froze seeming to think over the situation.

"I don't want to Tish, but I can't pay that amount of overage or I'll lose money." Terry was a constantly frazzled, forty-something brunette in her second year of business as the island's florist. Like many of the island's residents she was used to a level of informality that Tish found strange in a business person.

"This is why we have contracts," said Tish. "It's not like your address has changed. It's not your fault if your vendor didn't accurately account for the ferry time. Call them back up and tell them that they will not be charging you anything and that threats to change prices at the last minute are unacceptable and illegal."

"Well, what do I say if they say they're still going charge me no matter what I say?"

"You say that you'll discuss it later but you can't talk about it right now. Because the most important thing is that they deliver the damn flowers. You can refuse to pay afterwards and get Sam to send them some sort of strongly worded lawyer note."

"Oh," said Terry. "I don't know… I just I can't… That's so confrontational."

Tish didn't know what to do with that. "Uh… OK, so don't say anything."

"What?"

"Well, how are they threatening you? Did they call or email?"

"They left a voicemail."

"Well, just don't call them back," said Tish.

"Oh," said Terry. "I guess I could do that."

"Right. They can threaten your voicemail all they want. Just don't pick up the phone. As long as they deliver the flowers they can say whatever they want."

Tish had long ago mastered the art of aggressive non-response. She didn't understand people who thought the phone had to be answered.

"Right," said Terry, perking up. "Right. I can *not* answer the phone."

"The phone is not the boss of you! You are the captain of your own ship. You are the florist of your fate!"

"What?" Terry looked confused.

"Never mind," said Tish. "The point is that you are in charge."

"Thanks Tish!" exclaimed Terry. "You're so good at this stuff."

"Tish!" someone yelled from the house.

"OK, gotta go. Keep me posted on the flower situation."

"Of course," said Terry, "I've actually started on the boutonnieres already. I ran into a situation with the Baby's Breath, but..." Tish backed away as Terry continued to talk. She didn't think she'd ever actually concluded a conversation with Terry. She just slid out from under it and sidled away.

"Hey Tish," said Azalea, when she reached the front porch of the craftsman bungalow that was the home of Yearly Events. Azalea was Penelope's best friend and probably already knew about the pregnancy thing, but Tish had promised not to say anything, so she didn't immediately ask about it like she wanted to.

"Hey Zales, what's up?" asked Tish, looking up the few feet to the auburn haired waitress on the porch.

"I've done an initial count on the silverware. I think we're solid, but I'm worried about plates. We look short. I don't want to unbox everything, but if we're short tomorrow..." Azalea had a sharp pointed chin and a heart-shaped face defined by her widow's peak and dark wing-like eyebrows. At the moment those eyebrows were starting to V distressingly upward in worry.

Tish nodded. Somehow, despite being raised on the island, Azalea had mastered the mainland sense of urgency. She understood that it mattered when things happened and that *it will all work out* was not a realistic philosophy in the face of an Amazon-employee bride.

"OK, we'll grab a couple of box cutters and we'll just do a quick manual count. You're right we don't want to find this out tomorrow. If we're short, I've already talked to Quest down at the Orcas Hotel and he says we can borrow up to fifty plates."

Azalea nodded, looking relieved. "That would cover us." Her nod bounced one of her curls loose from her ponytail.

"I don't like the idea of not matching though," said Tish, as Azalea quickly undid the rubber band and swept all of her hair back into the proper form. Azalea always looked tidy. "So let's get counting."

An hour later Tish found herself on the porch and couldn't remember what she was supposed to be doing. Her phone burped up an incoming text and she looked at it with a nervous flutter in her stomach.

You coming?

Tish left the porch and walked down the meandering trail that took her to the wooded area of the property and lead to a ramshackle barn. It was her goal to be able to do fall and winter weddings in the barn, but that was a whole level of renovation that she couldn't afford. Maybe if she made it past her first year of business she might consider it. Once out of view of the workers on the lawn she jogged to the barn and swung open the door. She had barely crossed the threshold when a pair of strong hands grabbed her around the waist and pushed her up against the wall.

"Hi," she said, throwing her arms around Emmett Nash's neck and kissing him. Dating Nash had never been in her plans, but kissing Nash was always on her top ten list. He made her toes curl and today was no exception

"Hi," he said, pulling back smiling down at her with those blue eyes that made her melt.

Sheriff's Deputy Emmett Nash was tall, gorgeous, stubborn, well-read, and utterly delectable. He was also the divorced father of the absolutely adorable ten-year-old Claire who knew nothing about her father's relationship with Tish—Claire's preferred babysitter.

"I was starting to think you weren't coming," he said.

"And I'm starting to think that I'm the life coach for half of my employees."

"Oh God," he said, looking horrified.

"I am an excellent life coach!"

"Tish, baby, you live with your grandfather, and routinely find dead bodies."

"Twice is not routinely. And I don't think living with Grandad should count against me. It's for Grandad's own good."

"One more and the coroner has threatened to get you a punch card. And then there's the commitment phobia and the fact that you won't introduce your boyfriend to your grandfather."

"You already know Grandad! I don't have to introduce you!" He gave her a look. "I want to tell him about us." She knew it didn't sound authentic.

"Then why haven't you?"

"Because…" This was where the rehearsal would have come in handy. She should have her answer down pat already. She'd known this was coming. And she really did have a plan. She just wasn't sure everyone else would agree to her plan.

"Tish, I like afternoon delight as much the next guy—"

"After… Who *are* you?"

"A child of the oldies station. But I'm kind of over having to sneak around to spend the night with my girlfriend."

Tish's phone rang and she pulled it out to check if it was an emergency.

San Juan County Justice Department.

"I want to tell him, but every time I think I'm going to, he brings up how happy he is that I'm not dating anyone who's divorced."

"This is starting to feel pointed," he said. "Are you sure Tobias doesn't know already and he's just messing with us?"

"Always a possibility," she said, picking up the call. "Ronny, I swear to God, I have all the permits. The cars are allowed to park there. If you ticket them, I will sue. Not just the department, but you personally."

Nash rolled his eyes and made hurry up motions. Ronny was his least favorite co-worker.

Tish listened to the speaker on the other end of the line and felt an on-coming headache.

"Thanks," she said at last. "I'll be there as soon as I can."

She hung up the phone and looked at Nash.

"I'll talk to Ronny when I get back to work," he said. "But seriously, it's been months. I want to tell Tobias. And I want to tell Claire. And then we can stop sneaking around the damn island. It's ridiculous."

"I want that too," said Tish.

"So you'll go home and tell Tobias right now?" asked Nash, looking suspicious.

"I can't," said Tish. "I have to go bail him out of the Anacortes jail."

FIND OUT WHAT HAPPENS NEXT IN...

AN UNFAMILIAR SEA

LOVED IT?

Please consider leaving a rating on Amazon, Goodreads, or Bookbub. Reviews help authors gain advertising opportunities and new readers. Your positive reviews make a difference!

WANT MORE?

For a free e-story visit:
www.**bethanymaines**.com

ABOUT THE AUTHOR

Bethany Maines is the award-winning author of action adventure and fantasy tales that focus on women who know when to apply lipstick and when to apply a foot to someone's hind end. When she's not traveling to exotic lands, or kicking some serious butt with her black belt in karate, she can be found chasing after her daughter, or glued to the computer working on her next novel.

ALSO BY BETHANY MAINES

Made in United States
Orlando, FL
20 December 2022

27368601R00143